THE LIBERTY LAD

MAURICE LEITCH

QUARTET BOOKS   LONDON

Published by Quartet Books Limited 1974
27 Goodge Street, London W1P 1FD

First published in Great Britain by
MacGibbon & Kee Limited 1963

Copyright © Maurice Leitch 1963
ISBN 0 704 310872

Printed in Great Britain by
Hunt Barnard Printing Ltd, Aylesbury, Bucks.

You lads that are at liberty
Should keep it while you can,
Don't roam the streets by night and day,
Or break the laws of man.

WINTER

ONE

FIRST of all, a way to be tunnelled carefully through the blankets until the outside air and a triangular view of our chest of drawers and its mushroom knobs. Then, one arm, well covered with pyjama sleeve, down the tunnel and out into the cold on to the floor groping for the alarm. Up with the alarm (that hadn't alarmed) until, by squinting, I can just make out that it's – twenty past nine. *Twenty past nine!* And that's how the beginning of the best day of my week could have been ruined for me, for I was just about to fling off the bed-clothes and out on to the arctic wastes of our linoleum when it came to me. *Saturday*. Saturday? I lay as still as any wrapped old mummy, considering. . . .

Now you may think that this description of my waking on a February morning in this north-eastern part of Ireland has been a little overdone. I assure you it's totally accurate. Some of it may be due to my own lack of will-power certainly, but it is a *very* cold house we live in. All the houses in Kildargan, this mill village of ours, are the same. I blame the river running so close. And of course my brother's and my bedroom is right up under the slates. It isn't so bad *going* to bed because my mother lights the old Valor oil-stove with its artistically pierced top and sides and its little red glowing heart of a glass door for a few hours each night to heat the room up for us. Ever since I was any age I can remember watching its companionable wavering patterns projected on to the ceiling.

This room, I thought, now lazily lying, is the room you've spent most of your life in, do you know that, Frank boy? Say one-third of the day in sleep – three into twenty-four – that makes eight years. God! *Eight years*, spent solidly here in this brass bed, with the same awful old green wallpaper to meet your eyes when you open them; the same low billowing ceiling above; the same wormy old furniture around; the same mad lino below, and the air you breathe in, a compound of pine floor polish, moth-balls, paraffin oil fumes and the stale night smells of two grown men. Then I thought of the old woman and how much effort she puts into keeping it clean and respectable, and that made me ashamed of myself for thinking like that.

I decided to get up, so, putting my socks on carefully *under* the bed-clothes, I prepared myself for the shock of getting out of my warm nest. A jump and retreat was sealed off. Then, shivering, I began to hop rhythmically about on one leg trying to get into my grey gabardines. I was going to wear them over my pyjama trousers. Later on when I was more acclimatized I would be able to dress properly. I buckled my belt, straightened my socks, pulled on my old ladies' carpet slippers with their ridiculous red pom-poms, pressed my pyjama collar into place, looked in the cheval glass and tidied my hair with both hands in a backward brushing movement.

'*You're* up bright an' early this mornin'.'

Walter was sitting up in his bed watching me and grinning. He had on a normal buttoned-up, striped pyjama top for he doesn't feel the cold the way I do. One side of his face was inflamed – the side he had lain on – but the rest of it still had that crumpled look which disappears after you have been wakened about a couple of minutes.

'Yes,' I said.

'Oh, an' by the way . . .' he began.

'Yes?'

'There was a phone message for you last night. Mammy forgot about it. Wee Bertie Brownlees brought it up from Curry's.'

Curry's is the small grocer's at the end of our Row and has the only phone in the village, except for the old-fashioned, brass wind-up one at the Works. I wondered who the hell could be ringing me. Most of my friends know I hate to bother old sleekit Curry with his pokey wee shop and his old woman's gossip.

'It was Fanny – I mean, *Terry* Butler.' I smiled at his blunder.

'Oh? An' what does *he* want?'

'He wants you to come up and see him – before dinner-time.'

'Did he say what for?'

'No – just to come up to the house.' I laughed. Walter looked puzzled. 'What's the joke?' he said.

'Oh nothin' . . . you wouldn't understand.'

He wouldn't either, for he doesn't know old Terry like I do. My God, this was so typical of him. I could just see him in that brocade dressing-gown of his with the padded shoulders and black silk lapels, imperiously ringing up old man Curry and then calmly climbing up the stairs to bed again, to wait for me to dutifully turn up. And he could stay there for all *I* cared! . . . then I reconsidered. No, today it suited me to humour His Royal Bloody Majesty. I would take my time, and I would walk the mile or two to his house through the fields.

'Thanks, Walter,' I said.

'Don't mention it,' he returned cheekily and submerged into a big swollen lump under the chequered quilt that Granny had made as a girl.

*   *   *

Our stairs are completely enclosed and straight up and down – two brown grained doors at the top and two at the bottom – and there's a ten-watt bulb (an economical measure of my mother's) up near the ceiling where it does no good to any-one, and a stained oak hand-rail down the right side to break your fall, because you can never see where you're going.

I pushed open the door at the bottom. The kitchen was empty but at least, thank God, there was a good fire on. I stood in front of it and felt my backside begin to thaw pleasantly. The flames shone in the polished wood of the staircase wall opposite.

Whoever decorated these houses last had tongue and grooved boarding on the brain, *and* graining, believe me. They grained everything they could lay their hands on – doors, window-frames, skirting boards, mantelpiece – even the bloody clothes rack that swings on two ropes from the ceiling is covered with a rash of wriggling brown worms. Everything tarted up to look like something else . . .

I started to think about this because it was something that

11

had never struck me before – the motives, I mean, that make people do such things, when there was a knock at the door.

Grudgingly leaving the fire I went to open it and there was one of those Indian travellers with an old cardboard suitcase and a wide friendly grin. He was holding out a filthy little buff card to me with a lot of printed balls on it about him being a Wise Man and how he could bring me luck if I showed the good sense to listen to what he had to say.

'Iss the lidy of the house at home, young sir?'

'No.'

Slight pause to change tactics. 'Perhaps gentleman would like nice tie or pullover – plis? Cardigan?'

'Nothing today, thanks.' But he was on his knees pulling at the straps of the old case with long thin tea-coloured fingers, and you can't very well shut the door in someone's face if they're on their knees on your doorstep.

'Hankies, braces, socks, nice scarves, colourful ties and very nice Fair Isle pullovers.' I knew what *they* would be like – made in Hong Kong written all over them. He had on a greasy yellow turban and I wondered if he unwound it every night or did he just lift it off and hang it on the bed-post, bird's-nest fashion. His coat was one of those long, loose, grey gabardine efforts with patch pockets that went out about V.E. day, and from what I could see of his flapping pin-striped trousers they were strictly of the jumble sale variety too.

'Ah!' His white teeth showed triumphantly as the last strap fell away, and with a flourish he flung back the cracked lid. He delved luxuriously into the garish mass and came up with a hand-painted tie with a wriggling hula-girl playing a ukelele on its widest part.

'Nice tie, eh?'

I felt like saying, 'No, not nice tie – bloodee awful tie.' But then I thought, God, what a way to live. How they ever sell their cheap junk beats me, although some of them seem to do all right at it. You see the lucky ones sliding past in big cars with their sari-clad missuses beside them and the back windows full of wee brown heads. Every country town in the North here seems to have got one or two of them. In Annagh, where I teach, there's one with a shop on Irish Street. The son goes to our school.

'Gentleman work in office, yes? Very lucky gentleman, I can see. Yes, very luck-ee. Will have many children. Much money.' I was beginning to feel cold again and a bit tired of his old malarkey. Many children, indeed!

'I don't want *anything*,' I said, spelling it out for him. 'Nothing.'

'Braces?' His smile was beginning to tighten at the edges.

'No.'

The old scarf he was wearing parted and I saw of all things, an Ulster tie – tiny, boiled red hands on a blue background – the one you see on our fat red-faced Protestant businessmen who haven't got a grand enough old school tie to wear, or who haven't got one at all. I struggled to keep my face straight.

I waited until he had finished strapping up his old case and stood up. He was about my height and he had one of those Gurkha beards. Not a bad-looking chap either. I felt sorry for him and said, 'Try some of the other houses in the Row.'

He said, 'I have been to all the doors. No one at home or no want to buy. Good-bye, sir, and may you have luck.' Then he added something I didn't catch – in Hindu or something – which translated probably meant 'And up you too, Jack.'

I watched him trudging back up our red-brick Row towards the High Road, suitcase bumping rhythmically against his right leg as he walked. I could just hear myself on Monday, in front of the class, saying, 'I wonder has it ever struck you children just how lucky we are to be born in the British Isles? Have you ever thought what it's like for the poor people of India, for example, in that great oven of a sub-continent, boys and girls, where you would have to *fight* for a living if you were Indian children. Let me ask you a question. How many of you have ever *seen* an Indian?' Ach, balls ...

I went into the kitchen, up the stairs and into the bedroom; crossed to the wardrobe and put on my old corduroy jacket that I wear at the week-ends and my oldest pair of shoes. Then, with a muffler around my neck and my houndstooth cap on my head, I was ready for the road. Walter lay unmoving beneath the bed-clothes. I closed the door quietly behind me. After all, a big growing boy like him needed all the sleep he could get.

*   *   *

13

Kildargan isn't any different from any of the other mill villages which you see in this part of the North. They were all built about a hundred or so years ago and their sites chosen for hard-headed, money-making reasons when the linen bubble was at its fattest and most iridescent. For a start, they were placed as close to a river as possible; our Row have their privies on stilts out over the water, which is a good idea when there's a flood on but not so good in a July and August heat-wave. All the houses suffer from damp and there's a cold river mist which wraps itself lovingly around you as soon as you open the back door.

The Dargan slides along fast and rounded and the same colour as a gun-barrel too, in the straight, dangerous stretch behind the houses. Young Tommy Scullion from Number Seven was drowned there in the school summer holidays last year. Four miles further on the spate of water spearheads a way out into the big Lough, then loses thrust, merges into the buff, turgid waters and dies. It is twenty-eight miles in length, and there are derelict basalt-built mills on its banks and on the banks of its tributaries for most of that length. The black walls merely get blacker with age but the softer, less durable insides have rotted long ago. Each mill has its Row or rows or square of houses and these are still occupied, although any life centred around the Mill has long lost any meaning. They are ugly, depressing places to live in. There are about three mills left which are still in operation. Kildargan is one of them.

Some of the older people, like 'Dixie' Dean in Number Five, and my old friend Tom Snoddy one door up, talk about the days when the place hummed and seven hundred hands worked from early in the morning until late at night, six days a week. Now, my father – he's foreman in the Works – tells me there's only about forty left. And, as each month passes, the noise of the machines gets less and less, as one by one they change overnight from oily, rhythmic monsters to silent heaps of scrap. I can remember the time when you ate, slept and breathed against the low background rumble. Now you catch yourself listening to the quiet.

Our mill is going through what is known in the Trade as a 'recession'. I say *our* mill, but, frankly, I couldn't care less what happens to it. It never did the workers any good – it just gave them rheumatics through working in the steamy damp, stripped to their semmits and long drawers. The Spences who own it, and the houses, and at one time the workers too, from all I hear, got the profits, some of which should have been ploughed back but wasn't.

I was standing up on the grass verge of the High Road looking down on all this. The flat valley-bottom's narrow at that point – just enough room for the Mill buildings and the houses and not much else. The High Road is built on the first shelf above the river, and on the opposite shelf runs the railway and the main Belfast to Derry road. They converge on Annagh.

Away on the furthest, highest side of the valley rim facing me, Knockaddy Mountain, covered almost to its knob with regular afforestation, rose above the lesser, bluer Antrim hills.

Up there the roofs of the cottages are of bleeding, corrugated tin, and the people who live under them – large families packed into two – three, small, low, thick-walled, dark rooms – are as hard as the stones that break through the soil every time you strip off a sod. They haven't changed since their ancestors first arrived from Ayrshire and the other depressed Scottish shires three centuries ago, not to better themselves, as it turned out, but to mark time, strugglingly. Hill folk. The same as the other side of the valley too, behind me. In the valley, living *on* the valley, people of the same stock, but not so elemental – farmers with Land-Rovers and a new bright red or blue Fordson Major every other year. And then *us*, neither one or the other – the industrials ...

It was twenty past ten by my watch now, and the smoke from the Row's chimneys was rising straight and true into the light, cold air. There was still a wisp too of mist clinging to the river. An occasional car or lorry slipped past on the road behind me. Most of the cars were going up in the direction of Belfast – young country couples and families intent on getting the town's shopping done before the big shops closed. It looked like a grand day ahead, crisp and clean, the best kind of tail-end of February day.

15

TWO

INSTEAD of a hedge on the other side of the road there's a thick, shoulder-high wall in grey stone. I now heaved myself up on to its flat dry top, swung my legs until I was lying full-length along it and then dropped down on to the other side. Behind the wall it looks like a different landscape, acres of parkland with single oaks and sheep grazing in straggles. No hedges, no barbed wire, no fences – just smooth shoulders of cropped grass spreading out lavishly from the base of the wall. Its successive owners – a monastic order, various gentry, a retired colonel and now the Government with their school for handicapped children, where the big house used to stand – have all preserved its extravagant expanse in this valley of small mean fields and their land-hungry owners.

I hunkered down with my back against the pimply stone and had a quick look around, although I knew the 'Trespassers Prosecuted' notices didn't mean a thing. Just sheep industriously moving from one square yard of grazing to the next. No people. A person would have looked and felt conspicuous in that space. There was too much of it for the poor creatures up at the school. You can't play or go for walks in such bareness. I had a sudden mental picture of all those kids being turned loose on it, and them running aimlessly around, jabbering and dribbling and jerking their arms in the air, lost for something to touch and cling to.

I began to cross, making for the far hedge and the small plantation behind it. Once through that I would cross another road and then two field-lengths further on would bring me to Terry's house. The nearest sheep raised curious, narrow black heads and then dropped them again to nibble at the iced grass. Half-way across, I began to put an inch to my step and to look back compulsively over my shoulder at the wall and from right to left. You have to be born on a farm to feel really at ease with fields and trees and hedges. They're too raw and undiluted an experience for the townsman or even the villager like me.

16

I crawled through a hole in the hedge into the brittle dryness of the plantation. It seemed so much smaller than I had remembered it. I remembered that this was one of those quiet private places where sexual initiation took place after school. Small sly Molly Patton and big Bessie Murdock, whose crop of pubic hair awed us, and who laughed scornfully at our puny erections. After they had gone home giggling we compared cocks and held long worried discussions about the right way 'to do it'. And that time when First Kildargan Scout Troop week-end camped in this clearing (yes, this must be the very one) and caterpillar fingers crept under the khaki blankets and met no resistance in bed after bed. We must have been all teetering at that age. I couldn't think of one who hadn't succumbed. But old Terry was the only one who hadn't grown out of it.

I tramped round a thickly growing cluster of young ash plants. Hares had nibbled a pale sock on each one of them and I wondered if they would die before maturity.

At last I left the trees and came out on to the grass verge of Storey's Lane, a narrow, loose-surfaced track which drops sharply down to the High Road below. You never see much traffic on it except bread-vans or tractors and I was just stepping out to cross when there was a sudden loud bicycle-bell ring and a cry of 'Hey!' I jumped back on to the grass and Francie Moore the postman swept past grinning.

'Do you want to get knocked down, young Glass?' he called out without turning his head.

I couldn't think of a thing to shout back, I was so shaken, and his laughter died away unanswered as he disappeared over the brow. 'Silly wee *cunt*!' I said after him, angry at the panicky way I had jumped back out of his path. But I had recovered by the time I got in sight of the Butler's place.

It really is a delightful house; the sort of place I'd like to see myself spending 'the twilight of my days', as our man from the Prudential puts it. It's of warm faded red-brick with bulging windows on either side of a white door with a Georgian fan-light, and the roof's old greyish weathered slate. It even has this gorgeous creeper that goes every shade of red you've ever seen from August onwards. Terry's old fella wants to cut it down but he hasn't a hope – not with Terry and the mother against the idea. I hoped that I wouldn't run

2   17

into old man Butler because he's such a pathetic old bugger, with his clothes that she picks for him and his wee jobs around the house that are delegated the same way. He's a retired bank manager in his late sixties and if he ever had any authority behind that glass door in the bank with his name on it, then he lost it all when it closed behind him for the last time. I was slipping quietly round the side of the house when a voice came out of the privet hedge that keeps the wild fields around at bay.

'Hello, Frank, are you looking for Terry?' It was old Butler.

He put his head up over the hedge and smiled at me wearily. 'Oh hello there, Mr. Butler. Are you givin' it a bit of a trim?'

He looked at me and said quickly, 'Yes, you could say that. You'd be surprised how untidy it gets even when there's no growth. The odd wee clip here and there takes the bad look off it.' He gave a silly, useless, little snip with the shears and I felt concerned for him. I knew that the old doll wouldn't let him lift a trowel in the garden, let alone hedge-clippers, for she has a man in once a week. For a moment I thought he might have been going in for a quiet spot of rebellion but the shifty look he kept throwing at the house told me differently. I thought he was going to faint when a loud feminine voice suddenly cracked out, *'Crawford, are you there?'* and Mrs. Butler appeared at the front door. She saw the pair of us and her face went rubbery with the strain of changing her hard expression for her husband to a welcoming one for me. 'Oh, it's *you*, Frank. I didn't see you come up the drive.'

'No, Mrs. Butler,' I said. 'I came across the fields at the back. It's a lovely morning.'

'Yes, isn't it?' She smiled politely but her eyes were on her husband. She must have *smelt* that he was doing wrong.

'Crawford, dear—' she began. He came to attention, quivering like a well-trained gun-dog. 'That top shelf in the larder. It's slipped off the supports again. Do you think you could—' She smiled at him with an attempt at fondness that failed miserably.

'Right, dear,' he said, coming out from behind the hedge. He had enough gumption to leave the shears behind, I'll say

18

that for him. She waited until the poor old duffer got his foot on the front step, and then in a quiet voice, that just carried and no more, she cooed, 'Shoes, dear.'

Obediently, he fell on his knees, this time like a work-weary camel and began to unlace his muddy brogues. I saw his socks, those thick, grey, hand-knitted ones that old men wear, and, I don't know why, but it was the socks that made me want to cry. Good God, I thought, what did he *do* to her? She waited until he tip-toed inside on stockinged feet. Then she turned and faced me with the charm on full.

'Come and see my nice new rustic arch I'm having made.'

It sounded like an invitation to something much less innocent, and I must admit I wouldn't have minded, if it had been about ten years before her change of life. I could just imagine what she was like at her peak, one of those big women with big breasts and thin legs, whose busts get bigger and whose legs get thinner as they age. Now, she had her bosom and rump reasonably in control. Still, there were signs of the struggle showing through her thin paisley patterned frock. But she still *cared*, which was something I appreciated, and her blue rinse was one of the best I had seen.

She suddenly locked my arm between hers and her body and said, 'I'm so glad you and Terry get on so well together. He doesn't make many friends, you know.' Her perfume hit me and I was conscious of how scruffy I must have looked – unshaven, scarf crossed at the throat, duncher pulled down over my eyes *and* I hadn't washed yet.

It didn't seem to bother her any because she pressed me closer, if that were possible, and I got a whiff of her minty toothpaste. 'Tell me, Frank,' she began innocently, and I knew what was coming.

No, no, no, Mrs. Butler, I don't know any of Terry's girl-friends (God forgive me) I don't know where he goes to in Belfast on Saturday nights, I wasn't with him in London on his holidays last summer or even those week-ends to Dun Laoghaire either, and I haven't a clue who he writes all those long letters to ... I let it all roll over me, conserving my energies with the shortest answers I could give until she had to give up as she always does.

By this time I had seen her rustic arch and her vine in the hot-house and her latest batch of cacti in little brown pots and the site for the new sundial *and* her best Japanese cherry which she was worried about. We walked slowly back to the house, crunching over the raked gravel, and her arm never relaxed its hold on mine. Once she caught me looking at her eye-lids which she'd shadowed in moist blue and she must have thought I disapproved.

'I suppose you don't like women wearing make-up. Most young men of your age don't, you know.' She cocked her head to one side and her eyes sparkled.

'No, I – uh – quite like it. It all depends on how it's put on – I mean—'

She said, 'Oh?' and her grip on my elbow slackened.

'I like *yours*,' which was the truth. She showed restraint, which was rare in any of the women of her age I knew.

'Frank Glass, I feel sorry for the poor girls when you're about,' she laughed, giving me another conspiratorial squeeze with her elbow, and I felt foolish. I wondered what Terry would have thought if he'd seen us now from an upstairs window. A right pair of eejits we must have looked and no mistake – her, laughing up into my face like a silly young thing on the arm of her beau, and me, far from feeling like one, in my tramps' ball outfit, and the thing that worried me most – I hadn't even had time to brush my teeth that morning. I tried to keep from breathing in her direction.

'Who *is* the girl-friend at the moment, anyway? Do I know her?'

Christ, I thought, *and we're not even near the front steps yet!*

I tried to keep my voice as flat as possible. 'There's no one.' But she's one of those people who, if they can't discover an implication, invent one. She decided that I had said, 'But who would want *me*?' or something stupidly similar.

'Oh, I'm *sure* there's plenty of girls would jump at a good-looking boy like you. Those big brown eyes.' Her gaze never wavered. Calmly, clinically, she watched me blush.

She had her head cocked to the side like some old-fashioned looking, blue-rinsed black-bird.

'Well?'

'Well what?' I said stupidly. *Had she asked me something?* She burst out laughing and her bosom shook, not loosely, but in a tight disciplined way. She had tiny freckles all over her

20

corrugated breast bones and a soft dark down on her upper lip.

'Mrs. Butler,' I said, changing the subject. 'Where's Terry?'

'I'll take you to him now,' she said, in such a way that I didn't know whether I had offended her or not, though why it should have worried me I just don't know.

'Do you know where his room is?' So he *was* in his bed, the lazy bugger.

We were standing in the red and black tiled hall with its ticking grandfather clock and smell of wax polish and the armful of walking-sticks in the brass bucket in the corner. There was a phone too, on a tiny marble-topped table. I shook my head. I'd only been upstairs once and that was to their bathroom.

'Well it's the room at the end of the passage. It faces you at the head of the stairs. You can't miss it.' And then she walked away, leaving me, turning off all that concentrated infra-red charm without a smile or even a glance from under those carefully plucked eyebrows. I felt like a child who has just begun to enjoy the attention of a roomful of adults when they suddenly switch away from him to talking among themselves.

The steak-thick turkey-red carpet muffled my feet as I climbed the stairs. The balusters were painted white and, mounting the wall on a stepped line parallel to the hand-rail, was a series of engravings in black frames. Once again the luxury of the house after the cosy discomfort of ours, struck home to me. It didn't matter if the worn old furniture was chipped or scratched in places, or that the tripod tables had pale water rings on their surfaces, it was all 'good', to use my mother's word; chosen carefully and unhurriedly over the years and polished respectfully by many hands. I wondered if I would ever live in a house like this. It didn't seem likely with *my* prospects. The married teachers I know live in estate houses or subsidy bungalows with emulsion painted walls in apricot or peach with one picture over the mantelpiece and spiky, splayed legs on their 'contemporary suites'. Not that I was contemplating marriage. It's a thing I don't think about much, but in my more lucid moments I realize that I *will* end up like that some day even if it's only to satisfy the law of averages.

21

'Come in,' called Terry's voice, and I turned the knob and pushed the door open. He was propped up in bed with one of those breakfast trays with the cut-down legs in front of him. Lifting it down on to the carpet, he flashed me a bright smile. 'And how's Master Bates, the village school-teacher today?'

'Get stuffed,' I told him cheerfully and he threw up his hands and giggled.

'O-o-o-oh lovely! Have we time for a quickie?' He was giving one of his famous female impersonations but I knew damn well he wouldn't have dreamed of fluttering his eye-lashes like that at anyone outside the four walls. The performance was exclusively for me because he knew that I knew about him and his little foibles.

He patted the white candlewick bedspread and I came and sat down beside him. My eyes travelled round the room admiringly because I knew he had done it up himself. He had given me a blow-by-blow account of it at the time and I knew all the background story to the wallpaper and the carpet and the curtains and the pains he had taken to get things just right. He gets his taste *and* his single-mindedness from his mother.

'Well, I hope it meets with your approval.' He was watching me, smiling, with his head to one side. Across in the corner near the window was an intriguing wooden contraption that I couldn't place. I got up from the bed and walked over to it. Standing about waist-high, it had a coat-hanger thing at the top and a flat press for trousers beneath, all on two supports. It was the only modern thing in the room, despite its oily mahogany sheen.

'What is it?' I said.

'I think they call it "A Gentleman's Gentleman" or something. I don't know.' There was a petulant note in his voice.

'Was it expensive?' I asked.

'How should *I* know?'

'Well, it's *yours*, isn't it?'

'It was a *present*!'

I said, 'Oh,' and wandered over to the other window to look abstractedly out over the smooth lawn and the top of the weeping willow and across the fields to where the gleam of

22

the Lough was interrupted rhythmically by a row of poplars at the water's edge. What a view to waken up to each morning. Lucky bastard.

From the bed, Terry said, 'You're only a bloody peasant at heart, do you know that?'

Turning, I said innocently, 'Why do you say that?' knowing full well what was biting him. He was mad that I hadn't given the room and its cool white and gold elegance its full due of respect.

'I might have known that your imagination wouldn't go any further than a – *fucking* clothes-horse.' He dropped back on to the pillows, his face red with vexation.

I had to laugh. A real big child he was at times, and, in a parody of humouring a petulant child, I cooed, 'Ach, the poor wee soul. Is our pettie-wettie crossy-wossy? Ah-a-a ... What about a kiss to make it better?' I puckered up my lips, leaned forward and he laughed in my face.

'You're a right bloody eejit, Glass, and no mistake,' he giggled, and to hide my pleasure I grabbed suddenly at his hand, ordering briskly, 'Now then, up out o' your stinkin' bed with you, you lazy big blirt. Come on – *out*!' and on the last word I hauled him on to the carpet.

He stretched, his pyjama jacket lifting, and I saw a thinning black line of hair running upwards to his navel. He's the hairiest bastard I've ever seen stripped. We swim sometimes in the summer at a small sandy bay down at the Lough and the kids, who also use the place, all stare when he changes into his trunks. Of course he just loves that, and once, I remember, he took everything off and chased them in the nude for about half a mile, laughing and yelling like a madman. No wonder they took to their heels. It was a horrible sight for even a grown man. That tall thin bony figure with legs like pipe shanks – a skinny, white, hairy, upright caterpillar at speed.

'Do you think it's going back?'

He was peering into the mirror on the dressing-table, one hand pressing back his hair-line.

'There's no doubt about it. You'll be as bald as a duck-egg in another five years or so, and you know as well as I do there's nothing as pathetic as a baldy fairy—'

He slung a hair-brush at me and I managed to catch it

close to my stomach. I rolled with it on top of the bed and watched him dabbing his after-shave on.

'Don't forget behind the ears,' I called. 'It must go on all the pulse spots.'

'I know where I'll put some on you.'

He was at his hair now proper, sleeking down his smooth, black, Valentino-type mat with twin pearl-handled brushes. You couldn't call him good-looking though because he's too thin and his teeth protrude slightly. Sometimes I tell him he's got an X-certificate look – lean and hungry with dark eyes and a sensual mouth – Count Dracula-ish. He never knows whether to feel flattered or not because he's so conscious of his weight; he just can't get it above his nine stone or so, which, you must admit, looks ridiculous on a six-footer. I'm about five-eleven myself and I weigh twelve and a half.

'Darling, do you mind if I strip in front of you?'

He was fluttering his eyelashes again, so playing him at his own game, I drawled, 'Not at all, sweetie, go right ahead and do that very thing.'

His pyjamas were in blue and he had his monogram on the breast pocket. He pulled off the jacket and stood in front of the wardrobe full-length mirror sadly surveying his over-defined rib-cage.

'You, too, can have a body like mine—'

'—if you're not careful,' he finished it for me. 'Ha bloody ha!' Then he pulled at his pyjama string and he was in his buff.

We looked at each other for the briefest possible moment and then our eyes slid away. In that one second our mood changed to seriousness and then back again to the old flippancy. I was being scrutinized with an almost painful intensity for my slightest reaction. I didn't like the feeling and I said heartily, 'Did no one ever explain to you the meaning of private parts?'

I remembered one hot, lazy, August afternoon on the sandy beach at the Lough. Boredom had sparked off a fit of horseplay on the spread rug and, after a few minutes sweaty tussle, we had both drawn back laughing, pointing mockingly at the bulges that had suddenly appeared in our trunks. And I suppose before that there must have been other times too when we fumbled innocently with each other. Just how *normal* was

24

our relationship anyway? Most people would jump to one conclusion, only, if they could overhear most of the conversations we have, for most people, I have discovered, although they don't talk about it, are terrified of even thinking of *that* subject. I don't know if I have the same sort of fear myself deep down, because old Terry and I, we've talked about it so much and he's told me so much about *his* side of things, that it's hard to imagine what a 'normal' reaction is like. So that makes *me* not 'normal' ... All this deep thought was beginning to give me a headache so I decided to pay attention instead to what the horny old goat was bubbling about, as he was putting in his cuff-links. I joined him in the middle of a question.

'—what's it mean. That's what I'd like to know. What's it all mean? After all, you've read all the books on the subject.'

'What's *what* mean?' I asked blankly.

'Jesus Christ, have you not been listening to me?'

I shook my head penitently.

'Well, briefly – though why I am going over it again I haven't a clue, because I told it so well the first time – it's this. Last Thursday night one of the women in your Row – Mrs. – aah – ach, you know her – you poked her daughter once—'

'*I beg your pardon.*'

'Look, I was there.'

'Maybe you were but—'

'The sandhills in Portrush? That Sunday School excursion? We took them up behind the dunes after we'd had our lemonade and buns ... remember?' I remembered all right. We must have been about fourteen at the time. 'Jean Totten.'

'That's the one.'

'I thought this was to do with her mother.'

He rolled his eyes in martyrdom. 'It involves the daughter *too*. I wonder would you bloody well listen. Can I go on?'

'Okay. Okay.'

He paused as he tucked his shirt in all round.

'Well, wee Mrs. Totten was out at her back when she saw somebody down at her washing at the end of the garden. So she crept down to investigate – must have a heart like a lion that one – and guess who it was?'

25

'How the hell would *I* know?'

'Tojo McBride.'

'What was he doing?'

Terry's eyes sparkled. He shook one of his suede shoes triumphantly.

'He was pinchin' young Jean's underwear off the line, that's what he was doing, the dirty old thing. He was caught red-handed with it up his coat – brassiere, panties – the lot. An' when his house was searched it was comin' down with it; not only underwear, but silk stockings and blouses and shoes and women's hats. It's all over the country – about it.'

'First *I've* heard of it,' I said.

He laughed. 'Sure you might as well be living in Buenos Aires for all the interest *you* take in what's happening about the place.'

He was right. Although he lives two miles away, and is what you might call middle class, Terry is more accepted by my neighbours than I am. *His* white-collar job – he works in the bank in Annagh – seems to be no barrier. He goes into all the houses hereabouts for a bit of crack and they tell him all their secrets. On the other hand, they think *I'm* stuck-up because I happen to be a *teacher*. I resent this, not because I'm all that interested in their dirty little bits of scandal, but because I feel I understand them better than *he* does, and after all, I'm supposed to be one of them.

'Christ, what a place that Kitchener Terrace is! Between Curry's message boy chuggin' his wire all day behind the biscuit tins, and old Snoddy feelin' wee girls, the place is full of perverts.'

He was tightly knotting his best tie, the one with the tiny crossed riding-crops all over it.

'God! Look who's talkin'!' I exploded. 'Just *listen* to who's talkin'!' He grinned. 'And anyway,' I went on angrily, 'that's a damned lie about old Tom. That bitch next door to him started that up. She wants his house – the poor old bugger.'

'Well, if I were you, I wouldn't let your Jennifer go in near him on her own ... But – *hey!* to get back to Tojo McBride – what about that?'

'A clear case of fetishism or erotic symbolism,' I said. 'If you'd read your Krafft-Ebing you'd know that.'

He stopped buttoning his tattersall checked waistcoat and

26

in an awed voice he murmured, 'Erotic symbolism. What a wonderful bloody name!' Then he became brisk and craving for details – anatomical if possible. 'Tell me—'

'No,' I interrupted firmly. 'Look it up for yourself.'

I thought of that poor bloody wretch, who had never got over his spell in the prisoner-of-war camp, slavering over his hoard of women's things. He lived on his own three doors down from Curry's huxter's shop. By day, he sat peering out from behind his old lace curtains. By night, he roamed about in a long dirty raincoat and folded down Wellingtons. And the local smart alecks found just the right nickname for him too, so that he would never forget his little yellow friends and that home from home in the Burmese jungle.

Terry came over and sat beside me on the bed, one hand out soothingly. He was all rigged out now in his country squire's outfit – tight cavalry twill trousers, checked shirt, sporty tie, yellow waistcoat, suede shoes and his 'good' waisted hacking jacket with one long vent.

'Ach, now, Frankie,' he pleaded with soulful dark eyes.

'Don't "Frankie" me. When anyone calls me Frankie it means one of two things – either, they want me to do them one hell of a favour, or else, they've lost or smashed somethin' belongin' to me.'

He looked hurt.

'Anyway, just what did you want me to come up here this morning for?' I looked at my wrist-watch. 'It's a quarter to twelve already, did you know that?'

He got up off the bed and moved across to the window. 'Frankie—' he began.

'So it *is* a favour,' I said, slapping my knee.

He jumped nervously. 'Well if you don't want to – there's nothing I can do about it, only I would have thought that for once you might have ...' And then into a long, smoothly flowing monologue that had nothing to do with my question but was guaranteed to increase my suspense. I waited until he began to falter.

'Well?' I said. 'Are you going to tell me?'

It turned out that he wanted me to go with him to an auction (furniture and miscellaneous effects) that afternoon in Annagh. He got the bargain bug from his old lady at an early age and he loves nothing better than to travel to every

27

Sale within miles. I had never been to one myself and I was curious. He said, 'I'll stand you lunch at The Imperial and we'll take our car. You can drive.'

I'd only seen their car once, an old wine-red Citröen, cherished to the point of idolatry, like everything else in the house. I knew old Butler loved the car but that wasn't why Terry wasn't allowed to drive it. Even Mrs. Butler's over-developed maternal instincts had to grapple with reason when it came to Terry's driving – if that was the word for it.

'You'll go?'

I nodded. It was as good a way of spending the afternoon as any.

We went down the stairs, Terry chattering about the day's outing. He really was excited when it came to auctions. It was almost a *creative* thing with him. The chairs, tables, pictures, mirrors and Victorian oil-lamps he bought became so much *his* that all their previous owners seemed never to have existed. Everything in the house he had picked up over the years – always 'for a song' (so *he* said) – became an extension of his own personality as soon as he had brought it home. My mother takes the same sort of innocent delight in what is hers, although her small treasures never come from auctions. She wouldn't have the nerve to raise her voice in a bid.

From the smoothly concave surface of the front step Terry left me to dart back inside again, yelling for his ma, and I was forced to chat to the old man about the sharpness of the night frost for the time of the year, and weather prospects in general. I felt something of the boredom his clients at the bank must have suffered when he had them at his mercy behind his closed door ... twenty minutes talking about the weather and still no mention of the friggin' overdraft ...

Terry came out fighting a rear-guard action with his mother who was burdened with a camel-hair overcoat, a heavy woollen scarf and what looked like a fur cap with earmuffs. 'I'm warm *enough*, I tell you. Why do you keep on fussin' all the time? Let me look after *myself*,' he was snarling, and she would mutely thrust another garment at him. He threw the car keys at the old fella. 'Get the car out,' he ordered and turned to beat off another determined attack. They kept it up until the long, low bonnet of the Citröen slid round the side of the house. He finally eluded her by dashing down the steps and into the front passenger's seat before the car had stopped. I went round to the other side and waited until the old man elaborately changed into neutral, put the hand-brake on and switched off.

'It's a wee bit hard to get into reverse,' he whispered to me and I could see he was relieved that Terry wasn't driving. He closed the door lovingly behind me, I switched on the ignition and pressed the starter. Nothing but a choking whirr. The old man's frightened face appeared at the window.

'The carburettor must be flooded,' he suggested nervously and Terry gave a loud *'Christ!'*. I kept pressing the button.

'Here, that's no good,' said Terry, 'talk about a bloody museum piece! It should be roped off with a plaque on it!'

I didn't want to run the battery down so I sat back and looked helplessly at Terry. After all it was *their* car. Terry looked at me and saw defeat in my eyes.

'A shove?' he suggested. I nodded and let off the hand-brake.

I wouldn't have believed it if I hadn't seen it with my own two eyes, but, I declare to God, he leaned across me and said politely to the old man who was still fretting at my elbow, 'Give us a push, there's a good man, Daddy.' I gave him a hard meaningful look and said, 'Get out and *help*, Terry. It will take *two*.'

The gravelled drive sloped gradually down to the road in a series of full-bodied curves so the car began to crunch along under its own momentum after a bit and Terry flung himself into the seat beside me. I put in the clutch, there was a shudder and she began to purr. It was going to be pleasant driving a car like this, I thought, after the austere functionalism of my own old wreck. There was even that new leather smell about the upholstery that still lingered by some miracle of care and attention. Beside me Terry sulkily mopped his face with his handkerchief that matched his tie. In the driving mirror I could see the two figures on the steps. They seemed to be united by a common anxious expression on their faces, until I realized that the old man's was directed at the car and her's on my front seat passenger. I wondered how she would react if she ever found out about Terry, because I couldn't imagine her knowing now. I looked at him sitting

29

beside me. Our eyes met and he said, 'It's enough to make you *fucking* well leave home, isn't it?' I looked ahead with a straight face and swung the Citröen out between the gate posts and on to the main road.

THREE

THE auction was in the 'better' end of the town in a big florid, pre-war villa with garden urns on the front steps and 'Drumcondra' on a faded black and gold, recessed plate above the fan-lighted door. We had parked the car at the end of a queue and then walked along the quiet private road until we came to the 'Sale Today' sign. And from the sprinkling of Jaguars, two or three Mercedes and Doctor McRory's duck-egg blue Aston-Martin, it looked as if the élite of the town had turned out in force.

The two rooms at the front were jammed, and through the open door we could see the over-spill in the carpeted hall. Heads turned as we came through the gate-pillars and I thanked God that I had at least had a wash and changed into my dark Donegal tweed jacket and my second best trousers before coming. I was also wearing a navy wool shirt and I was struck by the thought that someone in the crowd might derive a certain quiet amusement from the contrast between my own casual effect and Terry's studied Master of the Hunt ensemble.

'Have you any change?' asked Terry as we neared the steps. 'For a catalogue.'

I dug out half a dollar.

'Enough?'

'They're two bob each.'

'But *I'm* not going to buy anything.'

He looked at me reproachfully.

'You have to pay to get in – *peasant*!'

I handed him another half-a-crown. After all he was standing the tea at The Imperial. The lunch idea had been wiped because he said he didn't want to miss any of the early lots.

The man at the door with a sheaf of catalogues under the

arm of his white laundered coat tipped his cap and said, 'Good afternoon, Mr. Butler.' I recognized him as one of the town's characters – a slightly touched wee man who goes about muttering to himself and who combs the local golf-course for lost balls which he sells back to the club members at a shilling each. The kids in my class make his life a misery but I never interfere because he's the sort who would call out, *What the hell are ye lukin' at?* in ringing tones across a busy street if you happened to let your glance linger on him longer than he thought necessary.

I purposely kept my head averted and waited to one side while Terry got his change. Then, in a quiet voice, that barely travelled (Christ be praised!) Terry said, 'Is your rhubarb up, Jimmy?'

I looked quickly to see if anyone in the crush had heard. Terry looked as if butter wouldn't melt in his mouth, as he gazed benevolently at the wee man, whose expression slowly changed from suspicion to dawning recognition of the *double entendre*. His eyes began to gleam.

'You're the one, Mr. Butler!'

He slapped his thigh.

'You're the fly boy! Always takin' the han' outa poor oul' Jimmy.'

He began to go red in the face with the effort of keeping his laughter in. He left down the catalogues and began to rock silently backwards and forwards up and down all over the steps. I felt worried in case he went into a fit or something. Terry just stood there smiling faintly at his antics and I wanted to thump him one, for the heads were beginning to turn again. One old bitch in a fur coat was openly glaring. Then, well inside, someone loudly said, '*Ssssh!*' and all the heads turned in dissapproval. The auction had begun.

'Come on,' whispered Terry. 'Stick with me, brother,' and he began to edge his way adroitly into the crowd.

I followed him as best I could, admiring the way he would move at just the right moment into a space as someone swayed back mometarily or leaned closer to talk to a friend. Most of these people would have been horrified at the thought of being wedged tight in a big, rough, football crowd at Windsor Park on a Saturday afternoon at this time, yet here they were packed in even closer. I kept getting the unmistakable whiff of the middle classes, as, alternately, I pressed up against someone, and they pressed close to me — the face-powdery or moth-ball odour of fur coats and fleece-lined jackets and 'good' sensible heather-mixture tweeds, for the women far outnumbered the men. And some of them I wouldn't have minded staying pressed up against. There was one piece, I'd never seen before, in jodhpurs and a tight yellow sweater and a black head scarf who was smoking cigarettes in a long holder. I stared at her and played my game of willing her to look at me. It must have worked for her eyes slid smoothly towards me across the serried faces, halted momentarily (but perhaps they didn't) at my hot glance, and then passed on to the auctioneer.

'Five pounds ... five pounds ... five pounds ten. Any advance now for this fine Benares brass tray ... beautiful, ladies and gentlemen . . . exquisite workmanship. No, they don't make things like this nowadays. Six? Am I offered six? Thank you, Mrs. Wallace ... six-ten ... Six pounds ten ... everything has to be sold, ladies and gentlemen, it's Miss Lavelle's orders ... all these fine hand-picked objects ...'

So this was old Molly Lavelle's house. The schoolchildren waged perpetual war against the old autocrat in the overgrown orchard at the back of her house. I can just make out her pagoda-type summer-house over the top of her back hedge from my classroom windows. And now she was packing it in. The kids would miss her threats and summonses and long complaining letters to the principal. She was the only one left to give them a fight.

'Christ, did you ever see the like o' that monstrosity!' Terry was breathing in my ear.

The tray, with the suggestive temple dancer on it, had been knocked down to a self-conscious man who tried hard to look as if he really knew something about his purchase that nobody else had cottoned on to.

'Is it no good?' I asked innocently.

'No good? You can't give the things away. Now *this piece* has quality.'

The auctioneer had his hand on a tall grandfather clock with a brass dial.

'Are you going to buy?' I asked.

32

He looked at me in horror. 'Christ, man, it's *William and Mary*!'

I said, 'Oh?' and began to lose interest.

I tried to pick out all the people I knew. Dr. McRory – red-faced, point-to-point mad in the true Irish provincial G.P. tradition, Father McGreevey, the town's R.C. priest (I'd noticed his black Volkswagen outside with the plastic madonna screwed to the dashboard), old Maxwell, the grocer, who was on the School Management Committee, young Mrs. Uprichard, the vet's wife, the Sergeant of Police, the new Methodist minister, Sean Maguire, cinema proprietor, bookie and owner of Maguire's Select Bar Lounge in Irish Street, and *yes*, in the corner, smiling down into the local solicitor's face (trust him to know who to butter up) Mr. Trevor Clever-Balls Warwick himself, our vice-principal – very short hair-cut, Errol Flynn moustache and neatly knotted R.A.F. tie – nothing calculated to displease. He calls me Glass – always Glass, and is the arse-licker par excellence, first class, Croix de Guerre.

Terry nudged me.

'To the left of Father McGreevey,' he whispered behind his catalogue. 'The Merry Widow.'

My day was made, for my imagination had fed on this woman ever since I had first been told about her. I turned my head slowly and saw a lean, hard-faced woman, in her late fifties, with a skiing-holiday tan and a cigarette dangling from the corner of her mouth. Her eyes were screwed up against the ascending smoke from her filter tip and she was scribbling on her catalogue. Rumour has it that she takes home one of the first fifteen after every Rugby Club hop. Wilbur Todd, who makes up our three male teacher complement at the school and who plays wing three-quarter, once spoiled an otherwise good day for me by recounting in detail his own experience in that line. At the time I consoled myself with the thought that her taste must be in her mouth if she picked Wilbur Todd, but she continued to play an even larger part in my sexual fantasies. So this was the woman who, only three nights ago, had driven me home in her car, fed me, plied me with drinks, shamelessly undressed me in the pagan opulence of her bedroom and then slaked her lust on me in a thousand sinfully ingenious postures until dawn. Naturally I had to be disappointed, but, as I stared at her, already a new fantasy was beginning to form. Then she looked up and stared me in the eyes coldly. She blew out an arrogant, blue column of cigarette smoke in my direction and I ducked my head in confusion. The fantasy drifted away with the smoke.

Just a dozen people, that's all I knew, and those mainly by sight. I suppose the population of Annagh is around the twenty thousand mark, yet the only inhabitants I know are a few shopkeepers, a few parents and the 'characters' whom everybody knows. Not like Terry. He knows *everybody*. Not because he works in the bank in Scotch Street but because he's the sort who gets to know everybody and they soon get to know him. Ever since we had come in he had been nodding like a bloody mandarin.

Now he had left the packed fringe around the auctioneer and the sideboard he was fondling and was talking to a tall, heavily-built man with a black moustache. Terry was smiling and I wondered if he was giving him the old treatment. I was curious because I'd never seen him 'in action' before, if that was the phrase, because, according to him, *they* usually picked *him* up. *How do they know you're their type?* I often asked him, for the risk involved must be something deadly, especially in this benighted neck of the woods, where every stranger you meet either knows about you or else knows someone *you* know. Terry's theory is that 'the brotherhood', *his* term, have some kind of built-in radar. When I press him further he just shrugs and says, 'You just know, that's all,' so I'm no further forward, am I?

Something happened a few minutes later that brought it back into my mind with an unpleasant bump. I was standing near the door, where the crowd was thinnest and a couple of men at my elbow were talking quietly. They didn't notice me and the taller one said to his friend, 'Who's that over there in the yellow waistcoat?'

That pulled me to attention.

The other one looked up. It was the man who had bought the Indian tray.

'Oh, don't you know?' he said unpleasantly. 'That's Terence.'

The way he said the name made my blood run cold. The tall one laughed. 'Oh, a nithe boy?'

34

'Yith,' lisped the other one, and they both laughed.

Then, 'Who's that with him?'

'Sam Bradley,' said the one with all the answers.

The tall man looked shocked. 'The M.P.?'

'Yes, that's him.'

Then they both stared at the dark-moustached man and Terry who was smiling as animatedly as ever.

I moved off into the hall, feeling slightly sick. So I had been fooling myself that other people didn't know about Terry. I tried to be objective and see him as outsiders must see him, as these two men did. Did he *look* different? A little over-carefully dressed, I suppose, but what of that? And his voice wasn't thin the way Bertie Duff's was – Bertie who works in Maxwell's and flaps his duster needlessly over the shelves a hundred times a day. When he laughed and flung his head back, now there was a trace, but would that single gesture be enough to stamp him?

... that first drunken night of a holiday in Douglas on the Isle of Man. The first time out of Ireland for me and Terry too, for that matter. We had reeled back to our bedroom, we had booked a double for economy, and we had pulled off our clothes and flopped on top of the bedspread, with the sweat breaking out at every movement. The heat frightened us a little. We had never felt anything like it before. It was a 'foreign' heat to us.

I woke up – a cool breeze was bending the curtains into the room – and, slowly, I realized that Terry's body was pressed close to mine, spoon-fashion, not loosely, as by accident of sleep, but consciously. I could feel that even though his breathing was slow and noisy. The effects of the drink hadn't quite worn off and I felt drowsy in a dulled pleasant way. His arm was lying loosely across my waist and presently his fingers moved lightly inside my pyjamas. I lay there feeling drugged, at first tolerating the exploring touch out of sloth, and then enjoying it. I didn't question anything. I kept up a pretence of sleep, breathing slowly. Everything left my mind except the pleasure that came from the deft fingers.

Then the caresses ceased; I was turned round and pulled roughly towards him. His arms went round me and I felt the rasp of his male face against the side of mine. I think it was

35

that which brought me to my senses. All the pleasure drained away as I listened to the excited whispering in my ear.

'I knew I was right,' he was breathing. 'Oh I knew it. Why didn't you tell me earlier? There's nothing to be ashamed of. There's millions like *us*.'

I pulled myself away, mumbling something about a drink of water.

I dragged out the time at the wash-hand basin, swilling and rinsing and gargling, not knowing what to do and praying for a miracle.

When I got back his back was towards me and he lay well over on his own side of the bed.

For the rest of the night we lay with a wall of embarrassment between us and the next day on the crowded beach was the same. At tea-time I knew something had to be done – we had almost a week ahead of us. I still don't know how I screwed myself up to it, but I asked him point-blank if he was a homosexual. I had never heard the word spoken before, I'd only read it in books, but I felt any other word would have been dirty. I hoped he would answer me as seriously as I had put the question and he did, and for the rest of that week we talked. The flood-gates were up, all the secrets and private feelings he had been guarding for years he poured out for me and I listened, fascinated, by the strange new underground world of an in-between sex. Many of the things he told me I had read about, tantalizingly in novels or clinically in textbooks, but there were other things that struck me with hammer-like force. He showed me membership cards for a dozen clubs in London and the Continent, he listed me film stars, actors, writers and celebrities he knew about and some he had slept with, and he told me of local men, some of whom I knew and some of them married. As I say, it was a new world to me, with its own language and laws, and I was greedy for knowledge. That was the beginning of the *real* understanding between us and since then he has told me of every affair and adventure as it happens to him. And it was only now for the first time that it struck me that others might also know about his secret.

I was standing stock-still in the hall, and, realizing I must look odd, I moved forward into the drawing-room. A few people were bending over tables or turning up chairs for

36

woodworm. They were milling over carpets and stubbing out cigarettes where it suited them. I thought of the old lady and her pride in keeping herself to herself. Was she dead or in one of those homes for old people? Just as well she wasn't here anyway, among this bloody crowd of locusts.

'Hello, Frank,' a woman's quiet voice said at my elbow, and I turned to see Mona Purdy, the principal's secretary.

'I didn't know you were interested in this sort of thing,' she said.

She was smiling and I noticed she had her hair in a new style – most of it on top of her head. It didn't suit her a bit.

'Oh, I'm with Terry. Terry Butler. You know him?' I asked.

She kept on smiling. 'Everybody knows Terry. He's a scream, isn't he?'

I gave her a sharp look. Her, too?

She was studying me. She had grave dark eyes. She was a strange wee thing – about twenty-two I should say. I didn't know her very well, just the odd wise-crack across the crowded staff-room at lunch-time.

'I'm with Jack.'

'Oh, your husband?' I said, remembering some talk about her being married.

'Yes, big Jack.'

Christ, I thought, big Jack and little Mona!'

'He's looking at some silly old lawn-mower out at the back. He likes to fool himself that he'll get some gardening done. Some hope.'

I laughed politely. One of those married jokes a bachelor isn't supposed to understand. I felt it was my turn to say something, but what? There was a short embarrassed silence as we pretended that the people moving around us were so fascinating that conversation was out of the question. She was wearing one of those belted grey hairy coats that are fashionable now in a cheap sort of way, and I could see she had on her white back to front cardigan underneath that she always seems to wear in school. She's one of those women who isn't as interested in clothes as she should be.

'I suppose you're going out tonight,' she said suddenly, looking up into my face.

'Yes ... yes. I wouldn't know what to do with myself if I didn't go out on a Saturday night.'

37

She said, 'I used to be like that too,' with what seemed a wistful note in her voice.

'Oh, don't you go out now?'

'Sometimes. But most nights we just sit and watch television. Jack likes that.'

'Oh?' I said.

'I like it *too*,' she added quickly and I looked away. There was another silence and I could hear the auctioneer's steadily mounting patter behind us.

'Where do *you* usually go to on a Saturday night?' she asked and I thought, *What is this? Is she trying to recapture her lost youth or something?*

'Oh, a dance mostly.'

'You're going to one tonight?'

For the first time I noticed the mole on her left cheek and the down at the corners of her upper lip.

'As a matter of fact I'm going to The Pheasant.'

I laughed apologetically for The Pheasant is a plushy road-house not far from Kildargan on the main Belfast road. I'd got into the habit of dropping in to the bar there for a few beers and to see how the other half lives it up, but I didn't feel like explaining that.

'Oh, Jack and I are going there quite soon. It's wonderful, isn't it?'

'Yes,' I said, and at that moment, bless his old heart, Terry turned up.

'Ai, *ai*! And what are you two up to?'

He held each of our shoulders and peered alternately into our faces with a comic leer. He was being 'a scream'.

'Ah, I knew it. Look at her blushing.'

She was too, so I said quickly, 'Did you buy anything?'

He tried to keep the joke going but he was only getting half the response, so he answered my question instead. 'I bid for a nice old tea-poy, but it went too dear.'

'Oh,' I said. 'I thought that was an Indian soldier.'

Mona laughed, and rose in my estimation, but Terry looked blank. He really is very ignorant about a lot of things.

'Tea-poy – sepoy . . . get it?'

He had obviously never heard of the word so I said, 'Skip it.'

38

He looked at me quickly. 'He's clever, our Frankie, isn't he? Reads books an' all.'

There was an edge to his voice. Mona must have noticed it too because she dashed in with, 'You know an awful lot about antiques, don't you, Terry? I wish I did. I haven't a clue when it comes to anything like that. Tell me, is that sideboard over there any good. Jack's mother has one just like it.'

She pointed to a grotesque turreted thing – all ivory inlay and little bits of bevelled mirror. I tried to look serious as if I too were a genuine seeker after knowledge.

Terry swallowed and said, 'Well, it's hard to say, ah, Mona. Victorian stuff seems to have had its day so I suppose, ah, Edwardian will be next. It certainly is, ha, ha well made, I'll say that for it. Yes, they certainly knew how to put things together and it must have taken hours and hours of ...' At that point I sloped off, muttering something about not having been upstairs yet. He gave me a glare as I escaped.

The bedrooms were quieter than the downstairs rooms and, despite the open windows, that musty smell that old houses and old people have about them still lingered. I must say I felt a fool wandering about because everybody else seemed to know at least what they were after – young married couples prodding mattresses, dowdy old dears feeling curtain materials and cushion covers and experts running knowledgeable fingers along drawer runners. A bedside shelf of books caught my eye and in desperation I pulled out one at random. It was called *A Shrinking Violet* and was written by someone called Mrs. Olivia Oliphant.

I was looking at an illustration of the heroine, hour-glass figure and tiny, tiny hands and feet and the inevitable parasol, when someone said in a loud voice, *'Babs!'* Everyone in the room looked up to see a slim young upper-crust type advancing with outstretched arms on The Merry Widow. I hadn't seen *her* enter. In turn, *she* cried, 'Pete-*ah*!', and they met in the middle of the room. Then they sat down on the bed side by side, talking very loudly in that way those fuckers have of forcing everybody within shouting distance to listen to them, yet effectively ignoring everyone in sight. He had on a beautiful old suit in mellow brown check, jacket in hacking style, waistcoat with lapels and narrow cuffless trousers. His hat was just that elegant size too small for him, high up on his head, with the hair long and curly at the back. A sleek black setter came into the room and he said, 'Heel, boy!' and it crouched obediently at his boots. They both scratched its head. Then the long loud exchanges of the names of mutual acquaintances began to fill the air. I've listened to these people and they can keep a conversation going on this line alone – 'Have you seen So and So?'

Terry, of course, would say that's just my old working-class inferiority complex on the go again. He's lucky in a way because nothing like that ever bothers him. He's a great believer in the class system. He even gets angry when I make cracks about the Royal Family.

I felt a sudden rush of resentment at those two baying frauds and the way they had everyone in the room listening to what they had to say about Micky and Pamela and good old Tubby and once (I could hardly credit it) somebody's bloody 'pater'. I decided that I wouldn't touch The Merry Widow now, not with a barge pole, even if she did come crawling to me. Anyway, her legs were bad and she had no diddies worth talking about. Disgusted with them and myself, I went downstairs. In the hall, Trevor Warwick was chatting to a red-faced woman in a ridiculous hat and as I passed I nodded to him. He looked right through me. That about finished me, I can tell you.

I went out past the wee man at the door whose eyes lit up when he saw me coming, but I couldn't think of anything clever to say to him as Terry would have done. There was a rustic garden seat around the side of the house and I sat down on it in the full glare of the pale sun. It was a sheltered spot and when I closed my eyes the sounds were almost summer sounds – the soft rush of a distant car, a dog barking slow and rhythmically far away and the lazy hum of the people inside.

A feeling of unreality, of non-existence, came over me. Why was I sitting here on this strange seat with my hands flat on its dry grey wood and my closed eyelids redly filtering the light? There was no single answer, only a chain of repetitive, childish ones all leading backwards – because Terry asked me to – why? because he's my friend – why? because we grew up together – why? because we live in the same community – why? because my father brought my mother to live here when they first got married, twenty-seven years ago when they were young, fresh and hopeful ...

I was born a respectable two years after and, at decent intervals, Walter and then Jennifer. They borrowed our names from the current film favourites of the time – Walter Pidgeon, Jennifer Jones, and an earlier obscure character called Francis X. Bushman. *I'd* never heard of *him* and I thank God they didn't saddle me with the 'X', which I suspect stands for Xavier. I'm sure if I ever told the old fella that Francis Xavier is a Catholic saint's name he would want to change it right away. I sometimes try to shake Walter's and his inherited bigotries but Walter says 'Have you ever worked with them? I *do*,' and the old fella mutters something about '*them* gettin' in everywhere.'

I feel it my duty to persevere because I'm the educated one of the family, the bright light of understanding and culture, the pride of our Row. When I got the scholarship from Kildargan Public Elementary School they all dropped into our house to see the official letter and the one small clipping from the local newspaper. Of course, that was twelve years ago; now the change over from sticky primary school corduroys to crested blazer and cap can be made without anyone thinking it's marvellous. I can still remember when I got the Regional scholarship and felt, even at that early age, that I had been singled out, creamed off. Not that it wasn't enjoyable then, it was – all those dreams of being a naturalist or a scientist or a world traveller, and nothing to stop them coming true. But then when you know what you *are* going to be, you look back and find that a wall has been constructed in the meantime, and you can't get back. Even to your own family. I can't talk to my father, my mother, my brother, my sister, and I know that's normal in ordinary circumstances too, but what I *do* resent is this imposed thing making it even more difficult.

Like a bubble suddenly surfacing, an imagined twinge of my father's sickness gripped me and I thought of him. It was like a pain too, every time I remembered what my mother had told me about six weeks previously.

I had discovered her crying to herself in the glory-hole under the stairs. She was on her knees facing the great jumble of old Wellingtons, oil-lamps, broken toys, biscuit tins, war-time gasmasks, piles of years-old newspapers and paint-tins – all rammed tighter and tighter in there, over the years, like the charge in a gun. She was pretending to be dusting. I remember I reached out to help her up, and as the rough, work-hardened palm tightened on my soft one, I felt that emotion – one of the rarer ones – part pity, part anger, that comes over you when you see your parents crying or see what they've become through sickness or old age or sheer drudgery. It's not pleasant.

We went into 'the room', as we call it, our one good room for Sunday afternoons and visitors and she told me about the pains that gripped him suddenly in the middle of the night. She repeated what she remembered of what Dr. Mc-Rory had said, 'Angina something ...' and I had supplied 'Pectoris' and tried to convince her that I knew all there was to know about it and that it wasn't all that serious. I succeeded.

But the pain I felt every time I remembered was getting less and less. It didn't suit my conscience but that was true. Then would a time come soon when I felt *nothing*? Despair slid over me like a clammy hand. I asked myself what was wrong with me? Why couldn't I feel like other people, quickly, easily, the right emotion at the right time? Why must I have to wait to see how I am going to react? My father is my father. I asked myself if I should talk to someone. Terry? Should I tell *him*, should I ...

'Should you what?' Terry's voice beside me made me jump. I ripped out a string of curses and he laughed.

'Well, should you what?'

I must have been talking out loud.

'Well, for a start, should I have anything to do with a pig who comes up like that and scares the shit out of people?'

He put his fingers to his lips and rolled his eyes – yes, I must admit it, in a distinctly *fruity* way.

'Sssh,' he whispered. 'Little Mona might hear you using bad words and then Frankie would go down in Mona's estimation would Frankie.'

'What are you bubblin' about now?' I said more easily, because I had my eyes closed again and the sun was beating down warmly. I relaxed.

'As if you didn't know.' What the hell was he talking about?

42

'She fancies you.'

I said, 'Your bum's out the window,' and went back to sun-worship.

'Okay, okay, you'll see,' he said. 'You'll see.'

He let it drop and I could feel him soaking up the rays too.

Mona Purdy? Wee quiet Mona with the big sad eyes and no clothes sense? I had never given her much of a thought beyond the first routine mental undressing when I had met her in old Matchet's office about four months ago. Legs, bad shape, too short, of course she always wears flats – bust, should be bigger – behind, loose, not firm, and too low – teeth, slightly discoloured – hands, a bit red in cold weather . . . no, he just thought it would swell my head up. My voice was angry when I asked him, 'I thought you were going to buy somethin' in this bloody mausoleum?'

'Mausol— what?' he said, and I snapped back, 'You know you should open a book sometime. It might do you good.'

'Please sir, please sir, can I leave the room, please sir?' he piped and I had to laugh.

There was a pause, as we sat side by side, two sharks basking in our sun-trap. It was unbelievable for the month of February.

'What time is it anyway?' I said, too tired to look at my watch.

'A quarter past four, you lazy hoor.'

'Ter-*ence*, reely!' I lisped and then recoiled inwardly as the echo tallied with the tone of the horrible little man inside. Changing my voice, I said quickly, 'Well, what *are* you goin' to do?'

He winked. 'Relax, old son. I'm through here, if that's what you're worried about. This is no place for me. Too many fools here with more money than sense. We'll go.'

He rose and smiled down at me. 'You know, you're quite good-looking, did you know that?'

I chased him round to the front of the house. At the corner we slowed simultaneously to a calm walk up to the steps.

The wee man at the door came limping down to meet us. 'Oh, Mr. Butler, sir – ah, Mr. Bradley towl me to tell you that he had a wee bit o' business to transact an' – ah, he'll see you down at The Imperial when he's through. He towl me to tell you that – partickler like.' Then, as if he had been savouring the same joke all afternoon, he chuckled, 'Rhubarb up, Mr. Butler. Boy, but you're the quare geg. Rhubarb up,' and went off into peels of laughter. I could imagine him coming up to us in the middle of the street a week, or even a month hence, with the tears running down his cheeks crying, 'Rhubarb up!'

'Yes, Jimmy, rhubarb up,' said Terry, the way you humour a child and we backed away smiling and nodding.

At the gate I said, 'You might have given him a tip.'

Terry looked offended. 'What for?'

'Aw, forget it,' I said.

FOUR

THE Imperial is in Scotch Street opposite the Ulster Bank where Terry works from ten to three-thirty every week-day counting change into buff paper-bags and reluctantly accepting dirty rolls of notes from publicans, farmers, shop-keepers and cattle-dealers for safe keeping. He's got into the habit of washing his hands a dozen times a day and the first thing we did was go up the stairs and into the first-floor bathroom of the hotel.

'What was that about Bradley?' I yelled above the roar of the hot-water tap.

'We're meetin' him here for drinks.'

'Oh are we now? I don't want to meet any of your bloody M.P.s.'

He stopped washing his hands and looked at me in the mirror. 'What do you mean "any of *my* M.P.s"?' Oh ho, I thought, is that how the land lies?

'Just an expression, old chap, just an expression.'

He grunted and concentrated on his nails with a small nail-brush. As I zipped up my fly I thought that this wasn't like him. He had always told me about all his other 'friends'. Why the great secrecy act over this one? And an M.P. into the bargain. No it wasn't like Terry – not one little bit.

To test for reaction, I said carelessly, 'No, I don't think

I'll bother, thanks all the same. If it's all the same to you, I think I'll push on.'

He whirled round, suds dripping from his long hands. 'Och, Frank, please! Hang on for God's sake!' His voice was anguished. I pretended to think about it, knowing full well I had no alternative anyway, seeing as I had no way of getting home except in his car. 'Well I don't know now. 'Snot the sort of thing I go for. It's bad enough havin' to read their bloody speeches in the paper without havin' to sit and *listen* to one.'

'Look, he won't *mention* politics! He's just like you or me!'

I laughed scornfully and flicked dandruff from my collar. 'Tell me something. Have you ever met an M.P.?' he said.

I had to admit I hadn't. I had *seen* them, all right, on platforms or on the backs of red, white and blue festooned trucks at election times spraying the crowd with slogans from a megaphone and the solemn Orange bands standing by ready to blare away their party tunes. Once, when I was fourteen, I'd seen a drunken man who had shouted, 'Up the Rebels!' in one of the pauses, set upon by half a dozen angry bandsmen and beaten and kicked until he was rescued by the police. He was so drunk he laughed as they booted him about on the ground as if it was all one big joke. That was why they kicked him – not for what he shouted – but because he was making a joke of something that was very serious. The M.P. on the open truck had turned away from the disturbance and leaned down to talk to a supporter on the ground.

'Will you come, Frankie boy? For *me*?' Terry's pleading face was pressed closed to mine and his hand was on my shoulder.

I nodded resignedly.

'Thanks,' he sighed and we went down to the bar.

The walls down there are panelled in imitation oak and there's an enormous brick fireplace with a dwarfed grate in its maw. The place is only comfortably warm on a Saturday night when it's packed to the doors and you can write your name in the steamed-up mirror behind the bar. Now it was sub-zero and we made towards the glow of the fire like a couple of homing eskimos. The warmest corner was already occupied by two women so we sat down on a couple of hard Windsor chairs and stretched out our hands to the heat.

45

While Terry was up rapping on the bar for service, I studied the two old things who sat opposite. They reminded me of a couple of elderly frizzled buffaloes, both were wearing identical cairngorm brooches and they were contentedly sipping glasses apiece of colourless liquid. One of them looked about five years younger than the other, although at that age, I suppose, it doesn't make much difference. It did look though as if it meant a lot to *her*, however, for she was doing most of the talking, using her face a lot, while the other sat there glum.

'That's a *warming*-pan, dear,' I heard her say and the old sad one with the frozen face looked over my head at the wall behind me. 'They were filled with *hot* water and then they were slipped into the *bed*.' She looked pleased with herself for being so knowledgeable but there was no reaction on the other's face that I could see. It didn't seem to worry her, she was probably used to it, and she went on with her conducted lecture tour of the room's curiosities.

By this time Terry had winkled out Brendan the barman from his retreat. He came out, smiling, from the little back room, his hair wild, and spiky and a paper in his hand. He hadn't been sleeping, just wrestling with the racing-page of *The Independent*.

'Any hot tips the day, Brendan?' I said cheerfully as he set down a glass of stout for me and a vodka and lemon for Terry.

He looked cautiously over his shoulder before pulling up a chair. '*Maiden's Prayer* in the four-thirty. Do it.' He pulled out a paper from under his arm and stabbed a dirty finger at the scribbled inside page.

'Can't miss. Had it down the wire at dinner-time from Danny at Newmarket.'

Danny, his brother, is a jockey and went across the water when suspected of having been mixed up with the I.R.A. Danny is Brendan's hero and Brendan has built up the absent brother into a kind of legendary figure of the turf, although I very much doubt if he ever won a race in his life. Brendan is about forty and has a club-foot so he does his dreaming through his brother.

'Is there any word of him comin' home?' asked Terry slyly.

'No bloody fear o' that, don't you worry,' sniffed Brendan.

46

He leaned forward confidentially. 'I had a letter from him about a week back there. He wanted me to come across, he did, an' live with him. He's built himself a split-level bungie-low near the racin' stables, you know. Aye. Central heatin', big picture window – just like one of them places you see on the movies. Twenty-three inch TV, too, an' he's talkin' about gettin' a swimmin' pool.'

I thought of the Danny I used to know and it didn't tally somehow – shifty-eyed Danny, always hanging around Maguire's, the bookie's, and running across the street for a packet of fags for whoever would ask him.

As if he read my thoughts, Brendan produced a photograph from the inside pocket of his short white jacket. And there was Danny sure enough, leaning proudly on the bonnet of a car with the house itself in the background – a geometry of gleaming glass and rustic brick.

'Och, he's doin' powerful well out there,' murmured Brendan reverently, as he received the photograph back into his possession.

I finished my stout and glanced across at Terry. I knew he was thinking the same as I was. He nudged me under the table and, hypocrites as we were, we solemnly congratulated Brendan on his brother's good fortune. He smiled shyly, as if it was he we were talking about, and went back to the bar with our empty glasses, his good leg punishing the ground.

'What do you think of that for a yarn?' whispered Terry, when he got out of range. 'Split-level bungalow – me arse and parsnips!'

Although I had been thinking the same thing a few seconds ago, I said, 'Ach, I don't know about that. He *could* have done well for himself.' Terry snorted and went back to his glass. I felt angry because I knew that he knew I was just being contrary.

'Well why couldn't he have bettered himself? Tell me,' I insisted.

Terry grinned maddeningly. 'Now what do *you* think?'

Last week Wilbur Todd was in my empty classroom at break-time and he was leafing through a pile of compositions that the class had just finished. He's a thick-skinned bastard and I've never been able to get it across to him that

47

I don't want him shoving his nose in, but in he barges every day, picking up rulers, looking in drawers and cupboards and kicking over the kids' schoolbags. He's just out of training-college a year, he has blond bristly hair and he'll never be anything other than a big over-developed peasant who should have stayed on his da's farm where he could have perfected his latent sadism to the full on dumb uncomplaining cows and horses.

He held up one of these exercise-books, roaring with laughter, and started to read in a falsetto voice, 'My house has a living-room, a dining-room and a kitchen. Upstairs we have four bedrooms and a big bathroom with tiles half-way up the wall. The bath is lemon and the rug is blue. My bedroom has pictures on the walls and a white fluffy rug on the floor. I like to sit in my comfortable armchair in my dressing-gown before I go to bed each night and read stories to my Teddy. He likes bed-time stories.'

I couldn't make out what was so bloody funny. It was just one of the weaker ones I would give a 'C' with 'Try harder next time' across the bottom. He came to the end of it and began to laugh again.

A bit peeved, I said, 'What's the joke, Wilbur?'

He threw it down on top of the pile, still laughing, and said, 'It's Madeleine Quigley's.'

I saw the point immediately. She's a poor wee illegitimate waif and, as if that isn't enough to be going on with, she lives in The Dardanelles, the slum part of the town near the river. The walls of the houses down there are so old and have had so many coats of whitewash that the bumps on their surfaces are snow-smooth and pebbly. But behind the gleaming whiteness the houses are so bad and insanitary and rat-infested that the local town councillors turn pale whenever The Dardanelles is mentioned. Its exotic name was coined after the 1914–18 war when the youth of the area joined up almost to a man and got the shit shot out of them for their pains.

'There's no baths down *there*! They haven't even got bloody *lavatories*! Imagine writin' that stuff!'

His voice was beginning to get angry. It was curious the change that had come over him. If I hadn't been there he would have torn the pathetic thing to shreds. He stormed out of the room, his face red, muttering, 'I can't stand *liars*!'

and I said to myself – *Madeleine Quigley, I hope, for your sake, love, you never go into Mr. Todd's class.*

After that I began to take more interest in the kid. I would stand at the back of the class against the radiator and watch the scurfy little head as she bent over her work. She sat near the back for she was quiet and gave no trouble. I never mentioned the composition to her, just marked it and put it in the pile for next composition day. The apathy which I'd felt before for her had changed into – pity, mainly, I suppose, but there were traces too of the old deadly derision, the curse which we are all born with in this cold cynical northern province. But what was the use of trying to explain that to Terry, or anyone else for that matter. Better just to keep quiet and spend the time saved polishing and strengthening the old mask for everyday wear . . .

I looked across at Terry over the table. He was twisting the bloodstone ring he wears on his little finger round and round and round ceaselessly, and thinking of God knows what. I know him as well as anybody knows him, I suppose – but how much do *I* know? He hadn't told me everything about Bradley, for instance. Yes, what about Bradley? I felt curious – and at that moment, with immaculate timing, Bradley came marching confidently up the room towards us.

Terry jumped to his feet, which wasn't like him, with an unnatural smile on his face. I could see he was timing his introduction, but Bradley clapped him on the shoulder, taking him by surprise.

'Look here, have I kept you waiting, Terry boy? I'm very sorry, but it's this damned rate-payers' protest meeting I was chairing. It just went on and on and on.' Then he swung to me. 'Ah, you must be Frank. Terry's told me a lot about you, Frank.'

His handshake was like his entrance, strong and sure, and his teeth were square and white beneath his military moustache. Close up, he looked even bigger than he had done at the auction – a big, heavy, dark man with lidded eyes. Somewhere in his early fifties I would place him.

I had planned a cool, guarded approach and, if my hostility happened to show itself, I wasn't going to worry. Was I? *No.* To hell with him and his like! That was the plan. But I found myself gasping like a stranded goldfish when he turned to

49

4

Terry again. I became aware for the first time of his trick –
if it was a trick – of concentrating all his attention on the
person he was speaking to at the time, and when he shifted to
someone else it was like being deprived of the glow of a
powerful searchlight. I had had only about a second's worth
but already I felt I had been over-exposed. I thought of him
raking his audiences with well-directed shafts.

'No, really, Sam, we haven't been here long. No time at all,'
Terry was saying and Bradley cut his own apologies off clean
before Terry had the sentence finished. He saw me smiling
but I wasn't smiling at the brutally neat way he did it, I was
smiling because I had suddenly realized that no one had
thought it necessary to introduce *him* to me. It was taken for
granted that I knew who he was. Bradley smiled back and
said, 'Now what about a drink, . . . *Brendan*!' and Brendan
came hobbling up as if he had been poised since Bradley had
come in.

'Vodka and lemon and – you'll have a half 'un and another Guinness – and the usual for me.' He wasn't *asking*
me, he was *telling* me, but I didn't care, I was beginning to
thaw out under the powerful arc-lamps. It's painful up-
rooting your prejudices. After all, how many years does it
take nurturing them to full growth, but here was I well on
the way to perhaps admitting not all our politicians – Union-
ist ones – are complete and utter po-heads . . . I didn't need
to ask; his party was obvious.

'You teach here, Frank, don't you?'

I nodded and as Bradley scooped his change off the hover-
ing tray I slid a quick, telling glance at Terry. He looked
away.

'*My* nipper started at your school last week.'

'Really?'

I tried to look interested. They were all the same, *their*
brat was so different from everybody else's that you *must*
know him.

'I don't see much of the juniors,' I apologized. 'Their time-
table is different from ours.'

'Oh, but Warren isn't in the junior end. He's in – what do
you call the fella? – yes, Todd's class.'

Terry said, 'Och you should have sent him to a prep.
school. Annagh Primary, haw!'

Bradley ignored him. 'I wanted him to start his education at Magheraboe primary school the way I did. I don't believe in these expensive places.' Terry blushed. 'But I had to take him out of the place.'

We raised our eyebrows politely. 'Yes. The principal there now – a bad egg if ever there was one – got his knife into the kid for some reason or other. I might have overlooked the welts across the hands, I don't want him pampered, but he wasn't even being taught, by God. Can you imagine it, nearly ten years old and he hadn't got to *long division*!' He twitched his eyebrows angrily and tossed his whisky down at a gulp. I made a sort of a—tch, tch noise. He shot me a glance. 'Maybe you know him. Hoy is his name. Albert Hoy.'

'No, I can't say I do.'

'Oh well, you don't want to, believe me. Damned unpleasant affair, I had to go up to him and try and make him see sense. Didn't do any good. And bloody cheeky he was too, the young blackguard. Made some crack about me using my influence to get rid of him. One of these boyos with a chip on his shoulder. Anyway, I got the kid out of that, fast, and got him enrolled with you people last Monday. No, if there's one thing I respect, it's education and the right to education.' His face suddenly relaxed into a smile. 'God knows I had little of it myself.'

We relaxed with him. He had involved us while he had been talking, with such passion and conviction, that we had been hypnotized into believing that this was *our* concern as well. I could imagine his effect on an election crowd once he had found his range. And that poor bugger of a school principal – because I was on *his* side, although Bradley's version of the story would have swayed any jury – I felt sorry for him having to face an *angry* Bradley, in front of a gaping class too, if I knew Mr. Bradley. I decided not to warn Wilbur Todd. Then I reflected that Todd would make a suck of the boy anyway once he found out who his da was. Not that that would cut much ice with Bradley senior, he was too smart for that. I wasn't worried about myself at all because my lot are the ones who have failed the elven-plus – the scrap-heap brigade – and young Warren, I felt sure, would be grammar school material, his father would see to that.

Bradley ordered another round and waved my half-

51

hearted fluttering with a ten-bob note aside. Terry didn't make any move. This was the sort of situation he loved. He doesn't sponge deliberately, he accepts free rounds, free meals, free anything, as his right. The only way I can explain it is that his attitude is the same as a woman's when you take her out and whether that has anything to do with his sexual make-up or not I just don't know. He was sitting back in his chair with a silly grin on his face that said – *didn't I tell you you would like him?* He was quite definitely at the 'merry' stage. I was feeling it myself – after all, we hadn't had anything to eat since breakfast.

That reminded me and I looked at my watch. Bradley saw me and said, 'You're in no hurry, are you? Look, you'll both have a meal with me. I insist.' I was beginning to feel warm and pleasant inside and I wasn't going to argue any more.

Brendan came up again, his alacrity did peeve me a little because I'd always found him slow in bringing orders, and Bradley ordered three steaks with all the trimmings – medium, medium and rare for him. Admiration for the man grew in me. I wondered how far he *would* go. Not that he would over-reach into arrogance, I felt sure of that, even though Terry and I were almost willing plasticine in hands like his.

My steak was the best I'd ever tasted and big enough to satisfy anyone's greed. It divided itself neatly at a touch of the knife and no one tried to talk for what seemed a long time. Even Terry, who is inclined to be 'picky' about his food, had a genuine appetite for once. We had carried our half-empty glasses up from the bar and now they were filled again by the usual 'small, sweaty girl', as someone I knew once described the typical Irish waitress.

Then Bradley glanced at Terry and said, 'I think I'll go round the corner for a minute.' He stood up and Terry hesitated for a second before saying, 'I need to powder my nose too.'

I watched them go out in the mantelpiece mirror, Bradley – big, square and purposeful, paying no attention to the diners who stared at him because he was a noticeable figure, and Terry – dutifully bringing up the rear. What would he have done if I had joined them, for my dirty mind had long passed the two and two make four stage.

I'd never met anyone like him before. It was useless comparing him with people I had known; he was someone you accepted as new, original with a set of rules all to himself. It didn't strike me that I might never meet Sam Bradley again. I knew without any doubt that I would.

When they returned I examined them carefully, but beyond a slight flush on Terry's face, there was nothing to pick out. As Bradley dropped into his chair, he said, 'Look, Terry, I want you to have a look at that bit of junk the wife picked up last week. She says it's the rale McCoy but I still say it's just junk. Will you come up and run your eye over it for me?' Terry nodded, a bit too quickly, and Bradley said smoothly, 'Good. That's that settled.'

It wasn't until we were standing outside the hotel with the first street-lamps staining the pavements with their harsh sodium light that I understood the by-play. Bradley went up to a big sleek Humber with its bumper over the kerb and pulled open the door. Terry moved round to the other side. I said, 'What are you doing?' The fresh air had fuddled me and I swayed slightly. I straightened up and repeated more loudly, 'Terry, what are you doing?' A passing woman with a full shopping basket bumped against me and muttered something. She had evidently joined the conspiracy and I began to get angry.

'Terry!'

He ducked guiltily into the front passenger seat and Bradley came up and put his arm round my shoulders. I could feel the strength through the fine suiting and his voice said in my ear, 'Terry's going home with me. You don't mind, do you? We'll drop you off.'

'But what about his car?'

'Och, don't you worry about that. Don't give it a thought. I'll bring him back later and he can collect it then. All right?' He squeezed my shoulder until I nodded. 'Good man. Now in with you. I would have asked you up too, only I know a good-looking young fella like you has something better to do on a Saturday night than look at a lot of old furniture.'

I allowed myself to be shepherded into the cool luxury of the back seat. I leaned back and closed my eyes and we started off. My feelings of guilt about Terry driving home on his own, and in no fit state too, I bet, were off-set by resentment at his behaviour with Bradley. I was piqued at his childishness. Christ, a blind man would have seen what they were up to. Who the hell did he take me for? I made silent vows about this going to be the last time etcetera, etcetera, and then I put the whole thing out of my head as the realization of my own predicament came over me. How was I going to get into the house without anyone noticing my condition? An hour or so's grace would have seen me right but I had to get in straight away for I was going out. Was it four or five Black and Whites? Christ! When would I learn to drink intelligently?

The car sped on and the dashboard glow was a soothing comfort. We turned off the main Belfast road and Bradley said, 'You live in Kildargan village, don't you, Frank?'

'Yes,' I said. 'If you can drop me off on the High Road I'll tell you when.'

He grunted and then there was silence. Then he said, 'It's a pity about the mill closing like that.' A tiny balloon of fear somewhere in my stomach started to inflate, but I managed to let escape a strangled grunt. He thought I'd said, 'Yes?'

'Aye,' he went on, 'it's sad to see another going under Of course none of these old mills are an economic proposition any longer. Obsolete. Aye. Old Spence should have got out years ago the way things are. I was speaking to him only last week. Tells me after the auction he and the wife are going to live with his son Billy in Cheltenham – I think the place was – aye – Cheltenham.' He drove on in silence, and I thought the pair of them would hear the racket going on in my head. Two words from his conversation bounced about in the emptiness of my mind like deranged lead shot –'obsolete' and 'auction' – over and over again until they merged into one ugly, rasping sound.

Bradley spoke again. 'Yes ... Kildargan Mill will be another headache for the Ministry of Commerce. More bloody unemployment figures for those Labour gets to crow about. Of course that Swedish soft-toys manufacturer might be interested...'

I suddenly shouted, 'This'll do!' and Bradley jammed on the brakes. Terry's head shot forward and he snarled, 'Christ!' I began to fumble with the door catch. As the door opened the inside ceiling light came on and I saw them looking at me curiously over the top of their fat padded leather

54

seats. 'Are you all right?' Bradley's voice was fatherly – inquisitive. I grunted something about the air helping me once I got out. Bradley made a move to get out at his side but I waved him away and climbed out on to the footpath. I slammed the door savagely, shouted, 'Good night!' and began to walk strongly towards the light that shone down on the first house in the Row, hoping that they would bugger off.

The car sat there with its headlights burning full on, and I cursed Bradley for all the hoor's gets as I marched steadily away, head down, hands in pockets, shadow bobbing in front of me. Then the glare swung across the road back the way we had come and I turned, my hand on a cold iron fence-post and watched the red tail-lights until they disappeared over a dip.

They had thought I felt sick. I was sick all right but not the way they imagined. Soft toys. I had the clearest picture of the old fella sticking powder-puffs on rabbits' arses – going like a fiddler's elbow. Powder-puff ... glue ... rabbit, powder-puff ... glue ... rabbit, powder-puff ...

Now then, get a grip on yourself, you silly fucker, I told myself and I began to think hard, painfully, about what Bradley had said, and, more important, what it all added up to. What I couldn't understand was how the old man didn't know about this. Surely to God *he* had been told. After all, he was the head bombardier in the Works nowadays, wasn't he? And Bradley hadn't given the impression that it was any great secret he was letting me in on; he took it for granted that I knew all about it. Christ, I didn't know what to make of it!

I walked on up our poorly surfaced road (God knows how long ago *that's* been tar-macadamed) and I could see ahead of me that Curry's shop-blind hadn't been pulled down yet. Even with our single street-lamp under his eaves the light from the glass door had a force of its own. The side window was no guide to go by, as far as light was concerned, because, ever since I can remember, it's been filled to suffocation point with packets of tea, headache-powders, Drummer dyes, tins of boot polish, packets of pencils, boot-laces, spools of thread, faded writing-pads, bottles of Blue-Black ink and one large tin of Glacier mints. It's the sort of shop that stocks everything but never has what you want in an emergency. Believe me, I know.

As I drew opposite, the shop bell pinged and poor wee Mrs. Mallon stumbled out with what looked like a dozen large wrapped pan loaves in her arms. She's the only Catholic in the Row and her quiet, inoffensive nature is inherent. It doesn't stem from her minority position in our community despite what people say ('*If they were in among their own sort you'd just see how nice they'd be.*') Everybody likes her but it's the husband I can't stand – a dirty, drunken, surly brute responsible for her regular yearly pregnancies. There's about eleven red-haired little Mallons in all. That accounted for all the bread.

'Hello, Frank,' she said shyly, and I said, 'Can you manage that all right, Mrs. Mallon?'

'If you could just push the front door open for me, I'd be obliged to you.'

She lives next door to Curry's and I shoved the blistered door open and a smell of too many children and poverty hit me.

'Frank, you didn't see Hughie on the road?' (she pronounced it Cuey).

I shook my head and she said anxiously, 'An' he's no taillight worth talkin' about. Ah well, ah well . . .'

As the door closed behind her resigned keening I marvelled that she could still worry about him, for I knew and everybody else knew that inevitably he would come wobbling home on his bicycle when the pubs closed, always with a large bottle of lemonade up his coat for his dehydration in the morning; ramrod stiff in the saddle, face white and unshaven, the spittle dribbling freely from the corner of his mouth, and he would celebrate his rotten-mindedness by handing her out another black eye for people to talk about at early morning mass. That was about the height of Mr. Hughie Mallon.

'Oh . . . Frank, is that you?' Curry had come out of the shop too and had his hand up to his eyes. He wears thick-lensed spectacles but his hearing makes up for it – he doesn't miss a trick, for he could hear the grass grow.

He sidled up in his fawn carpet-slippers, his hands held in that pious way of his. He clasps and unclasps them all week as practice for Sundays when he preaches in the local tin tabernacle about a mile away. He fills up his old Wolseley with all his customers in the Row who owe him tick, then he transports them to this hall of his, and when he gets the door closed on them he builds up to an orgasm of hot gospelling. It takes him most of the afternoon. I know; as kids we were frequently bribed by lavish hand-outs of Bible pictures, missionary magazines, book-marks with texts on them and a mammoth bun-worry once a year.

'Did you get the phone message all right, Frank?'

'I did, yes,' I replied shortly.

'Ah, good, good. If I can do any wee turn now, I'm only too pleased. I can't say I know the young man. He has a nice speaking voice ... cultivated. What did you say his name was?'

'Butler.'

'Not the son of the retired bank-manager?'

'Yes.'

'Oh they're very nice people, *very* nice—'

'I'm in a bit of a rush, Mr. Curry.' I cut him off short before he had time to ask how I had managed to fall in with such 'nice' people. Nice is his favourite word. But he got in one last plug.

'You couldn't come to our little hall tomorrow, could you, Frank? Mrs. Emily Forgave of our Foreign Mission is giving the address. It should be very nice indeed and – you could bring Mr. Butler.'

'I'm afraid not, Mr. Curry. I'm – ah, I'm seein' a chap off at the boat.' God forgive me, it was the first thing that came into my head.

'Ah well, you're always welcome, you know that.' He smiled a sweet forgiving smile that said, *the way of the chosen few is always a hard one*. I mumbled, 'Thanks,' and moved on.

I hadn't gone a dozen steps more when I was hailed a second time, this time from the dark, shadowy hedge on the opposite side of the street. I had never seen so many people on the go.

'Excuse me, sir,' came a deep man's voice and I waited for him to show himself. He was a stranger and was wearing a heavy putty-coloured stiff raincoat buttoned up to the neck and one of those cap-beret things in grey felt.

57

'Excuse me, sir, but could you tell me where a Mr. McBride lives around here?' He was a little taller than I was and much heavier.

'That's the house there,' I said, pointing, 'but I don't think you'll find him in.' I thought of what Terry had told me about the arrest.

'Oh, that's all right, sir ... well, thank you, good night.' He stood waiting for me to go on.

When I was about ten yards away I heard him putting a key in the lock. Everybody else in the Row have got Yales – Tojo McBride never bothered changing his old-fashioned brute of a key. That's how I knew it was his door that was being opened. I must say I felt a bit curious but I decided it was none of my business. It's one of the things you learn early in The Red Row, not to interfere, or ever get involved, if you can possibly help it.

The way he kept calling me 'Sir' made me put him down for an official of some sort – very minor, of course – but he couldn't have been the man who read the meter calling at this hour. And then I knew what he must be! One of those plain-clothes detectives you always read about but never meet in real life. So I had seen my first plain-clothes man. Well, well! I wondered if he were searching for clues – the beam of his torch stabbing the cobwebby blackness – *what's that under the stairs, sergeant? I'm not quite sure, sir, it looks like – my God, sir, it's* – I reached our front door as the music shrieked to a crescendo and a voice said, *Listen again next week to the final instalment—*

A squall of wind arose somewhere out in the darkness and the first few spiteful drops of rain spattered on my cheek. I had my hand on the knocker when I remembered. I let the cold metal claw gently descend and tip-toed past the lighted front window and its lowered roller blind. They would be at their tea now – sitting round the table pushed up under the window.

It was a little after ten past six. The Backs smelt of wet ashes and soot, and the brown smell of the river was stronger than usual. Someone slammed the door of one of the privies in the block of ten that backed out over the swirling waters. Each one has its own private key which you carry with you on your visit. You traverse a jungle of sheds and hutches constructed from beaten-out oil-drums and old tin adverts for Camp Coffee or Ogden's Plug. Narrow pads slippery with hen droppings wind in and out maddeningly and, believe me, you wouldn't want to be in any great hurry to find relief at your journey's end.

I slipped into our yard and lifted the catch on the back door. My eyes were dazzled for a moment in the lighted scullery. I spent a second or two studying my appearance in our small mirror over the sink. Next, a cupped hand held close in front of the mouth and breathed upon revealed no smell of drink. I rinsed my mouth and poured out a couple more mugfuls from the white enamelled bucket into the plastic basin in the sink. The cold water on my face made me gasp but it took away any last lingering traces of muzziness. I dried my face on the roller-towel behind the door and pushed on into the living-room.

'There's a kipper in the oven for you,' were the first words of the old lady. Walter, Jennifer and my father were seated at the table, just finishing off, by the look of things.

'I've had my tea,' I told her and Walter nearly knocked me down in his rush to get at that kipper.

'What a gorb that boy is,' said the old fella, and he sounded quite cheerful for the first time in weeks. It was a pity his mood would have to be spoiled when he heard my news. He had just had a wash by the look of him and he'd changed into a pair of baggy old flannels and faded blue clean shirt and pullover in homage to the shrine in the corner, in all its twenty-one-inch oak-veneered glory, which he would watch religiously until 'The Queen' played out both networks. He looks forward to his Saturday nights with the house cleared of Walter and me, his feet up and his pipe going.

I said, 'Have you got a clean shirt for me, Mammy?'

'Of course,' she said, but as I moved to go upstairs where I knew it would be hanging ready over a chair, she snapped, 'You'll just have to wait till I'm finished in the scullery before you go in to wash yourself. I'm not goin' to leave the dishes the way I do every Saturday night. I haven't been off my feet all day. I think I deserve one night to myself.' The edge to her voice made even Walter look up from his plate.

'Ach a dear,' the old man mock-sympathized. 'Poor oul'

Mollie. You're killed, so you are. Dear dear.'

The door slammed behind her and we heard the foolhardy rattling the pile of dishes made in the sink.

'Somebody's in bad twist the night,' sniffed my father, a bit embarrassed that his olive branch had turned into a boomerang in front of us. 'She works too hard, that one. Still, you might as well talk to the far wall for all the good it does.'

But I knew it wasn't overwork that was the trouble. Her mood had grown out of worry. I felt another twinge of guilt at forgetting so easily. Under cover of an ancient *People's Friend,* which had been lying under my cushion, I studied him. He looked no different – no thinner, no sadder than usual. And then I also realized that involvement was looming up for the second time like some big black locomotive and me strapped to the rails ten yards from the cow-catcher, for I knew I had to get this mill closure business out into the open.

Attack was the best policy. But when I did open my mouth I merely said, 'How's the work goin', Daddy? Okay?'

He looked at me suspiciously. 'A bit slack,' he grunted and turned back to the hit or miss, top-twenty disc show on television – the faces in the audience looming up as the cameras stared at them long beyond the point where self-consciousness ended.

Jennifer, suddenly excited, cried, *'Eartha Kitt!* that was her in the front row! Did you see her?'

Walter laughed contemptuously. 'Don't be daft! What would *she* be doing there among the scruffy lot? You should be wearing your specs when you're watching tee-vee,' and wiped his fingers on the table-cloth under the table.

'It *was* her, I tell you! It *was*! Daddy, did you see her? Frank tell him it was Eartha Kitt. You saw her, didn't you? She had a sort of fur thing over her shoulders.'

'*Fur!*' hooted Walter. 'Fur under *those* lights? Do you know, what temperature it is in that studio?' he was just as childish as she was.

I said, 'You were right, Jennifer. I saw her too.' It was a lie.

She stuck out her tongue and said, 'Yaah!' He did the same and then began to run a comb through his oily hair. When the combing was complete he patted the sides in so that it wouldn't look so full there. A couple of babies! Jennifer came across and cuddled in to me on the settee and I ran my fingers up under her short thatch of fair hair at the back of her thin little neck. 'Maybe she'll come up on the screen again,' she whispered and screwed up her eyes. She really does need glasses, I thought.

After some time I said quietly, 'I heard today the Mill's closing down.'

The old man's head came round.

'Where did you hear that?'

'It doesn't matter where I heard it. It was a reliable source. I was told that it's going to be auctioned, lock, stock and barrel. Did you know about *that*?'

I saw that I had hit the spot. He leaned forward and turned down the volume, he didn't switch it off, just turned down the sound. The smooth disc-jockey smiled and crinkled his deep, dark eyes and moved his lips in dumb-show.

'Who told you?'

'It doesn't matter who told *me*. What's important is that nobody seems to have told *you*.'

He snapped back, 'I was told. I was told.'

We all gasped. '*What?*' I couldn't believe it. He *knew!*

'Jack Spence mentioned something about it to me a fortnight ago.' He tried to make it sound casual.

'That was bloody big of him I must say!' I erupted. I felt sick. It was Jack Spence with us but in the Works it would be *Yes, Mr. Spence, no, Mr. Spence, three bags full, Mr. Spence*.

'You watch your lip m'boy. You're not all that big yet.' Aye, he would just love an excuse for throwing his arms about so that he could continue evading the whole thing as he had been doing for the past bloody fortnight.

'All right, very well then.' All the calm reasonableness and sweet temper I could master were in my words. 'Let's take this one step at a time. Firstly, what do you intend to do? You're obviously out of a job.'

'The Mill's been there as long as *I* can remember. I'll get my day in, never you fear.'

I groaned loudly and his face got red. I thought I had ruined everything.

He said, 'Don't be the bloody smart-aleck *all* the time,' but there wasn't enough venom in the words to hold me back.

'What did Spence say to you? What were his *words*? Can you remember?'

I thought he wasn't going to answer because he turned away to look at the smiling 'celebrity' who was shaking hands with the panel. When he did speak his voice trembled slightly.

'He said he was worried about the slump in production, the Mill wasn't a paying concern any longer – hadn't been for months. There might be the possibility of – closure. That's all he said. A *possibility* of closure. Aye.'

Word for word, it was what Spence *had* said, I didn't have to be told that. The phrases – management jargon – had been rolling around in his head for two weeks until he didn't have to think about remembering them. I began to realize he wasn't fooling himself, as I'd thought, *he* didn't believe the Mill would continue in operation any more than I did. He was just running away from it. Drugging himself against the ultimate reality night after night with – *Wagon-Train*.

'My God!' I cried, 'and you can just sit there and watch *television*!'

At my yell mother came into the room with a dripping plate in her hand. 'What is it?'

'The Mill's closin' down, that's all. It's really nothin' to worry about. We're thinkin' of holdin' a party as a matter of fact.'

She turned pale. She dropped down into the armchair facing the fire, her wet hands limp in her lap.

'Is this true, Tom?' He hadn't even told *her*!

Jennifer started to sob half-heartedly; she didn't really know what it was all about, her instincts were warning her. Walter too had lain down the paper he had been reading. Under our combined scrutiny my father hunched his shoulders until his thin neck disappeared and stared savagely at the programme credits as they uncoiled across the still smiling faces of the television panel. I could hear him breathing hard through his nose. It's a habit he has when he's excited.

'Tom?' she repeated plaintively.

I went over and switched the picture off, and it dwindled to a bright pin-head. I thought he was going to hit me. His face tightened and he shouted, 'It's none of your business! Why don't you leave me alone?'

His yell took in all of us.

'But Tom—'

'Don't Tom me. Yap, yap, yap, from mornin' till night. Don't worry yourselves, any of you. The oul' cart-horse'll see none of you starve. He's never let you down yet.' But underneath the sarcasm there was no reassurance there. He saw it in our eyes. 'Anyway I don't know what you're all gettin' so bloody excited about. Nothin's definite. If you listened to all the oul' talk that's been on the go people would have had the place closed *years* ago.' He swung round to me. 'What the hell do you mean by comin' in here and upsettin' everybody with your fairy-tales?'

I closed my eyes, and in a martyred voice, began to explain, to reason with him. 'As I said before I can't give the name of the person who told me the Mill's being closed – and not only closed, but auctioned. I can't tell you who it was but, believe me, this person should know, if anyone does. Spence himself told *him*. He also told him that the family are going to live in England, so if that isn't enough for you, what is?'

If it hadn't been for the gravity of the situation I think I might even have enjoyed the effect I was having. There's a picture above our mantlepiece and it's a hay-making scene with hay-wains in the middle and far distance and a bulging haystack in the foreground. A ladder leans up against the broad shaggy mass and it's covered with hay, but it's so badly painted that it doesn't so much resemble what it's meant to represent as one of those slides you see in playgrounds or at the deep end of swimming pools. I kept my eyes fixed on the top of the slide, and as I made each point I moved my eyes down a fraction at a time. When I reached the grass I spoke directly to him. 'Did Spence tell you to look around for another job?'

'*I tell you there's nothin' settled yet!*' He was shouting again.

My voice got quieter. 'You realize he can do what he likes with the Mill *and* you any time he wants to, don't you? Unless of course the Union might help—'

'What Union?'

'You mean you're not in a *Union*!' said Walter in a shocked voice.

'What would I pay good money to them layabouts for?

63

One o' them, oh, a fast talkin' spiv came roun' the Works about a year or two ago, but Spence soon chased him—'

I murmured, 'I'll bet he did,' but he ploughed straight on, his voice rising again. 'There's too much talk of Trade Unions these days. A lot of lazy boys the lot o' them – a hard day's work would kill them. I've got along without them so far and I'm damned sure I don't need them now.'

We were all surprised when Walter burst out, 'You wouldn't be earnin' what you are today if it wasn't for the Unions. They had to fight for every penny from the – the capitalist bosses!' He turned red and stammered out the last phrase as if expecting a roar of ironic laughter. Aha, I thought, you've been spending your dinner-hours listening to the speakers on the blitzed waste-grounds in Belfast.

My mother added her pennyworth. 'Oh, Tom, what about the house? Mr. Spence owns the Row.'

With all our high-flown talk none of us had thought of the reality of *that* one. I suddenly got the idea of a protest meeting and as the idea caught fire it started getting tied up with a film I had once seen. A shot of the great house at nightfall with the angry glow of a hundred torches washing its walls. The murmur of the crowd becomes menacing as the door remains closed and their cries are ignored. But who is this that comes forward as the first stones are being lifted? Who is this pale determined figure who detaches himself from the crowd and climbs on to the steps? He raises a hand and the noise dies for they know he is their friend and they respect his education and intellect. He is the son of their foreman, a young teacher but now a leader of men ...

I said, 'The first thing to do is to get organized and plan your first move.'

Walter said, 'Hear, hear.'

'I think a spokesman should be picked,' I continued. 'By the way, how many hands are there altogether?'

The old man's face was tight and his lips trembled. He said, quietly, 'Twenty-five.'

I couldn't believe it! I had no idea the place had gone down as far as that.

'Surely to God you must have seen this comin'?' I said.

'Yes, Tom,' said my mother. 'Why did you keep it to yourself? You might have told me.'

Walter said, '*I* would have come out on strike. That would have fixed him all right. They think they can treat the workers like dirt but this is the twentieth century.'

Jennifer sobbed, 'Oh, Mammy, what are we going to do?'

The old man rose to his feet and moved in a direct, furious line to the door at the foot of the stairs. If Walter hadn't lifted his legs smartly he would have trampled right over them. With his hand on the knob, he turned and shouted, '*Why the hell can you all not leave me alone?*' Then he went into the bedroom.

Whenever he comes up against any big problem he goes to bed. I suppose it's cheaper and less harmful than drink, and there's always the chance that everything will have sorted itself out in the morning. But that was only wishful thinking in a case like this. It wasn't something you could tread down into the subconsious there to be sorted out. I looked around at the four of us huddled round the fire and it took me back to the time when Walter and I were still at school and we sat like this whispering after a row or when one of us had got the strap that used to hang behind the door of the glory-hole.

Jennifer said, '*I* don't know what I'm going to tell Marlene Milligen on Monday,' and we all looked at her. 'We've been saving up to buy a pony between the two of us.'

We laughed, not so much at the thought of the pony in The Row which would have been about as incongruous as a Rolls-Royce, but because of the way she said it. We were still laughing when the stair-door banged open and the old man stood there, eyes staring in his head with rage and his hair sticking out – the pullover had disarranged it as he'd pulled it over his head to get ready for bed.

'What's so bloody funny? *Well? What's the joke?*' He thought we were laughing at him.

No one said anything. He came a step into the room and banged his fist on top of the sideboard and Walter's lunch-box which was sitting there jumped in the air.

'Don't you worry, my beauties, I can do without the lot o' ye. I'll be able to manage, never you fear. *Do you hear me?*' We kept our heads down. That made him angrier.

'All these bloody years knockin' my pan in for you lot. An' what do I get for it? I could have spent my pay-packet in

5   65

Ned Boyle's but I didn't. I brought it home here every Friday night instead and threw it on the table – to fill your bellies and put on your backs.'

If he said one word about my education I wouldn't let him off with it. But he had spent himself. The anger sucked itself out of him and he stood there keeping his eyes still blazing with an effort of will. He had become pathetic again, back to his normal shrunken look which I'd first noticed a few years ago. You realize it most whenever he puts on his one good suit, that used to fit him, but now flaps about him.

I had a great desire to get up and gather his smallness in my arms, to tell him that we all loved him for everything he had done for us and that we only wanted to help him, but as usual I sat where I was, ashamed of my feelings. I suppose if I were French or something I *would* have done it but in this bloody latitude the only time you would ever get even near such an action is when you're drunk.

Mother, Jennifer, Walter and I stared into the red coals until the door clicked behind him. We looked at each other. Then I got up and went into the scullery to wash myself.

I thought of what Terry had said as we'd left his home in the afternoon. I'd laughed at it then. Now I could see his point. It *was* enough to make you want to leave home.

FIVE

AFTER the third stout had curved its smooth way down into my stomach I felt easier, relaxed. All the knots were unravelling and the worries of the past two or three hours were beginning to shrink to manageable size. I even *laughed* quietly to myself, wondering if the old man had reached the same stage on his side of the big double bed – sleep for him – drink for me.

The thatched, horseshoe-shaped bar and the long room with its white-capped tables and tiny red-shaded individual lamps were deserted; the waiters were probably having a quiet smoke somewhere because it was still early. The people who motored out here the fifteen-odd miles from Belfast to dine and dance and lose their inhibitions left it as late as they could.

Half closing my eyes, I looked down the polished length of the room to the big brass jug of greenery on top of the piano and found it a pleasing, friendly sight. The only object that didn't soften round the edges under my warm gaze was Madge who had reappeared behind the counter. I knew that was her name because I'd overheard the customers talking to her. I had dropped in here for the past seven Saturday nights but I knew, after I'd ordered my first, even if I turned up at the same bar stool for the next twenty years, I would never get to calling her by her first name. Not that I was all that mad-keen, for she was unattractive in a dark nervy way. I had decided, observing her from my stool, that her looks must have soured her whole personality. Thus, she was to be pitied and not despised because she so obviously disapproved of me. So that took care of poor neurotic Madge.

I had dropped in to The Pheasant the first night, more out of curiosity than anything else, and liked the atmosphere and the sensation of being in the same room with all the thousand and over a year types who were dining and dancing (if you could call it that) yet being apart and able to observe them over a drink. I had only an hour or so because at half ten when most of them were just starting on their scampi and the old Chablis, Madge was pulling down the tamboured bar-shutters and calling, 'Last orders, p-lease!'

Still, I felt it was better being here than the alternative – the old sweaty tribal rite of the Saturday night jig. I had gone right off that. Especially the birds picked up before the band played 'Good night, Sweetheart'. Not from snobbish reasons, but I suppose I'm getting too old, or better still, too tired, for fumblings on the way home in the early hours of Sunday morning that never get you anywhere anyhow. And as well, too many bloody teenagers with their death to the over-twenties attitude.

I sat on my stool, heels together on the tubular chrome, knees under the edge of the bar, a half-empty glass of Guinness convenient to my right hand, and saw my Saturday night stretching out ahead of me, full of infinite possibilities. The clock with Bols across its face said eighty-thirty and Madge polished glasses and tidied bottles and laid out her cocktail-sticks and drip mats. I felt sorry for her in a way, because it's damned hard to keep on avoiding someone's eye if they're your only customer.

When a fat, red-faced type in a Prince of Wales check suit that didn't quite reach county tailoring standards came up and stood beside me you could almost hear her sigh of relief. 'The usual, Mr. Rooney?' she cried eagerly, hand already on the gin spigot.

He grunted, two fingers feeling for change in the front slit pocket of his not tight enough cuffless trousers. I mentally catalogued him as someone who had a bit of land and went in for pigs in a big way on a gentleman-farmer basis. It was a pity his hands, like his clothes, gave him away, because they were just a shade too red and scrubbed for a man who did none of the actual manual labour himself. I couldn't help feeling sad that Madge could be so blind to his true position in the social scale yet be so bloody discerning about mine. Porky suddenly snorted, 'Cheers,' and without thinking I said, 'Slainte!' to the mirror behind Madge's head. There was a silence that told me I hadn't been included in the toast. He probably put me down for a Papish, into the bargain. But the way I was feeling just then, I didn't give a fart for him or Madge or what they thought about me. That nice warm glow centred just behind my belt-buckle was hotting up to something that promised me a full evening's enjoyment and I knew nothing could spoil it.

One or two young couples – the middle-aged ones came later – had sat down at the tables and were holding hands under the cloth, and the regular pianist had swung into a nice bouncy 'April In Paris'. That was another of the reasons I liked the place. I liked listening to the pianist; he was very good – much better than the usual 'Selections from *The Student Prince*' ham you almost always find inflicted on you at dinner-dances.

His bass player was tall with thinning fair hair and a Ronald Colman moustache, and as the taped tips of his fingers tub-thubbed up and down he would lean over the pianist, who was short and dark, and they would grin at each other. The only time anyone took any notice of them playing was when they stopped for a break or some tight old bag requested something from *Oklahoma*. I had often wanted to speak to them as they passed the bar on their way out for a pee and a smoke and tell them how much I'd appreciated their playing but I never found the courage somehow. But that night I felt that I might do that very thing ...

I sat on my stool, *my* stool and looked calmly and resolutely around the select part of The Pheasant road-house, the part reserved for those who matter, discreetly separated from the common public in their own downstairs bar with their own low-class version of Madge to serve their drinks for them.

It was now ten past nine and people were coming into the bar in twos and threes and you could hear the cars arriving in the car-park and the quick rev-up before switching off and then, after a pause, the slam of the doors. It was a funny thing but they all seemed to arrive about the same time, which didn't make it easy for the poor bugger of an attendant. I thought of him outside, in his peaked cap and the trollopy blue coat with the gold buttons (*Standing room only in the two and nines!*) rushing like hell from one car to the other, bursting a gut to make himself look as if he was giving each driver some invaluable personal service. And he was about the same age as my father too. God, but I'd hate to have *him* depend on tips for a livelihood ...

I called out loudly, 'A Scotch, please,' and Madge unfolded her thin arms from below her miniature breasts and grudgingly poured it. I drank half of it before I set it down. There was no time to be lost. Something could still be salvaged from the debris. How had I got myself into this state anyway, that's what I wanted to know? Where had all the joyful anticipation gone?

I didn't want to admit to myself that in less than half an hour – time had started to accelerate for some reason – I would be turfed out into the cold, keyed-up and excited for something that I knew wasn't going to materialize. If you sat down and logically worked it out, you wouldn't bother your arse going through the door on a Saturday night, because nine times out of ten it ends up the same way, but who would want to use logic on a Saturday night? This was the night when people smashed out of their work-day shells and you got as much fun out of watching how they did it as you did with your own sensations. I listened to the noise rising steadily to its climax when the clock would strike ten-thirty.

At the far end of the bar was a party of six people, husbands and wives in dinner-jackets and ancient evening frocks, and their English voices were rising in direct proportion to the din around them. I wondered how long it would be before their faces would redden and their neck muscles vibrate like fiddle strings. Beside them were three heavy middle-aged men whose faces were well flushed and who kept pushing each other aside and waving pound notes when Madge held her tray out. I couldn't hear what they were saying in competition with the other braying lot but you could sense their quivering restraint. You felt it would erupt after closing-time in a burst of horseplay in the lavatories or in their driving on the wrong side of the white line when they got out of the car-park.

Music from the dining-room kept inserting itself in gaps in the noise. I couldn't recognize the tune but the throb and the drink that had reasserted itself – cheers! – were taking their effect. I scanned the room – the expanse of authentic, craftsman-carved, oak beams and rough plastered indirectly lit walls – and on the way winked slowly and carelessly at a brassy blonde while her partner was trying to catch Madge's attention. The blonde winked back and raised her glass. She had big cheek-bones that stood out like chestnuts under her skin and a hard thin mouth but the rest of her was soft and compensating. Her dress was black but on her the colour looked too obvious, like green for red-heads or white for brunettes.

Pleased with my childish success and grinning stupidly, I focused my eyes on the reflection before me. I was drunk. But not too drunk. Just drunk enough for the thoughts to come flying on each other's tail – jagged, fragmented lumps of verbal shrapnel. I'd noticed this before many times. Thinking in sentences is impossible when you're tight. And when you open your mouth that's the way it comes out. But I wasn't going to open my mouth, so what? The face grinning lopsidedly at me in the mirror was the old familiar one. Dark hair, *enough* forehead, one eye sadder than the other; nose? hard to say, teeth – white – rigorous daily brushing; chin –

70

weak in profile, beginnings of a double there, neck could be longer – much; pale blue button-down shirt, navy knitted tie – squared ends, light grey flannel suit – narrow lapels, three-buttoned, single vent, trousers? playing it by ear now – no turn-ups, seventeen inch bottoms, Chelsea boots – black, very *very* swish!

'Time, please!'

Good God, there must be some mistake! What a cruel joke to play on a Saturday night! *Your bloody clock's fast, Missus!*

'Now, drink up, please, gentlemen. We don't want the po-leese round now, do we?' Madge at last into her own. A tough smile on her ruled lips but none in her shoe-button eyes. Putting bottles away, snatching up empty glasses, bolting the counter-flap.

'Another Scotch, please. Make it a double.' Ignored, by God! The dirty, rotten – Someone talking to me at my elbow. At a time like this! Blue suit, Cherry Blossom toe-caps.

'Yes?'

'We haven't met yet. I'm Jack Purdy. Mona's husband.'

'Oh?'

'Yes. She's over there.'

'Where? I can't see for this crush. Trying to get a drink, as you can see. *Service!*'

'That's what we wanted to talk to you about.'

'Oh?' A bottle in the glove compartment? A pub back room where they serve you after hours? Could be interesting.

'Would you like to come over to our table?'

'Okay.' Might as well. Nice chap, shy, a bit awkward, but nice. Big, square, that tight, curly fair hair so many outdoor men seem to have ...

'*Mon*-a *dar*ling!' Christ, get me, kissing hands. Easy. Mustn't antagonize nice hubby. Needn't have worried. Laughter all round. Christ, I'm drunk, but wonderfully in control; no one suspects.

'Frank, meet Jack. Jack, meet Frank.'

'Pleased to meet you, Frank.'

'Same here, Jack ... *Hey*, we've already done this!' More laughter all round.

Bar emptying. Madge shooting steel-tipped glances in our direction. Bugger her! *Menial*.

'Frank, we have booked a table here, haven't we, Jack? We were wondering if you would like to join us.'

Don't know what to say. Haven't bargained for this. Unlimited drinking until two in the morning, but menu in French, *very* expensive. Emergency folded fiver in ticket pocket – been there for three months. Hmmm ...

'Well, okay. But are you sure it's all right? I mean you only booked for two, didn't you?'

'Jack, see somebody, will you? There's a dear.'

Eighteen stone of captive husband on its way. God but he's big when you're looking up from these low chairs. Aaaah ... Warm, rich feeling from the navel downward. Mona looking distinctly attractive. Can just see their soft contours flowing to confluence when she's bending over the ash-tray. Freckles on shoulders. *And* moles. Yellow patterned dress. Cool. Misjudged her. Life really in top gear. Smooth bliss. Nothing to stop me now – a beautiful vista of uninterrupted pleasure ... wine and women. Mona really got something, but what? Lightly snaffled sex, I think. Wonderful potentiality. Frock tight across her stomach, but *nice* tight. Knees showing. Light dark down on forearms. Repeated on upper lip. Always liked dark women – exotic, opulent, jewel in the navel, fluttering gauze, abandoned pleasures, *watch what you're doing with that fan, old girl* ...

Jack back. Earnest face. Anxious to please Jack. 'They're setting another place.'

'Good. Let's go.'

'The night is young. Toujours l'amour – tonight for sure!' That's me, mad impetuous fool.

Mona and Jack still laughing at table. 'You're so quiet at school. You never talk to anyone. Stuck up.'

'*Me?*'

'Yes *you*.'

'Would you look who's talking! Miss Minnie Mouse hiding behind her Remington.'

'But *I* thought—'

'And *I* thought—'

More laughter. Jack ... Benign sun-face. Have fun, my children, ho ho ho. His skin is beautiful, like a girl's – hair

72

coarse, blond, sofa-stuffing, scissor-blunting, almost a crew-cut.

Mona laughing again. '*Now* what are you laughing at?'

'You.'

'Me?'

'Yes, *you*. You're so funny, Frank.'

Pretended anger. Gales of laughter.

'Oh you're a scream. You really are.' Can't lose, can I?

Waiter smiling as he presents '*New Statesman*'-sized menu. 'Like to order now, sir?'

Mmm, consommé – that's the thin, yes, the thin; no fish course (God, salmon mayonnaise ten and a tanner! no thank *you*) – sirloin for me (had it before, but no matter) – rare with French fried onions and chips, that's that.

Mona pointing to menu. 'What's *canard*, Frank?'

'Duck.' Good old Senior Cert. French.

Mona listening to the music. Eyes closed, long lashes, mouth relaxed, soft lips . . . 'Do you mind if I ask your charming wife to dance?'

'Not at all. Go ahead.' Have fun, my children. Ho ho ho . . .

Three other couples on the floor. Middle-aged, punishing themselves to the applause of their friends at ringside table. 'That's the stuff, Ben. *Swingin'!*' 'Good old Doreen, let's see you twist!' 'Not too close now. I'll tell Fred, May.'

End of quickstep. Bom, bom, diddy, bom bom, *bom, bom*. Curse it!

Ah thank you, Mr. Pianist, and a slow-fox too. 'You Do Something To Me.' Very appropriate. Soft accidental pressure of her right hand *and* silk-covered stomach. Accidental? Pressure relaxing. Now dancing round past beaming Jack. Wait for it. Ah, tightens again. *Very* interesting little woman. *Very*.

'I like your husband. He's a nice chap.'

'You think so?'

'Yes.'

'Good. So do I.'

Pause. Who needs to talk anyway? Soft insistent pressure. Risk slight lowering of right hand to root of buttock. No girdle. Ecstatic flexing to slow, slow, quick, quick, slow. More forward thrust – the hussy! Eyes closed, lips sensual. Careful, Jack coming up again, watching us. Smile, that's right.

Good old Jack. A true sport if ever there was one. Dally now near the piano. Vertical rhythmical bouncing to a count of one, two, three . . .

'You're a good dancer, Mona.'

'Thank you. So are you, Frank.'

'We seem to dance well together.'

'Mmm . . . We do, don't we?' Had a few jars that's obvious. So has he, more power to his muscular elbow.

Stirring animal in his lair. She's bound to feel it! Disgraceful. Should be a law against it. Question in the House . . . Does the Member for South West Antrim realize that at this moment certain of his constituents are dancing closer than the regulations permit, not to mention blatant contravention of the Public Acts of Indecency Bye-law, Section 9, Paragraph 3a? Give that man a seat in the Cabinet!

End of set. Reluctant disentanglement. Certain looks exchanged. Meaningful.

'Your wife's a good dancer.'

'Well, that's a thing I couldn't say much about, I'm afraid.'

'Oh?'

'Jack doesn't dance.'

'Oh – you're not missing all that much, Jack, really, I can tell you. It's a ridiculous pastime when you come to think of it. Two people pushing each other around the floor and being bumped to bits . . .' Why don't I shut up and sup my soup? . . .

White cloth, gleaming silver, smiling service, music – aah! A memory to cherish. Man over there, napkin tucked in under chin, either ignorance or the gesture of an eccentric. Which? Latter. Old golden brown tweeds, soft moustache, startled iron-grey eyebrows, frail little wife-woman at his side, both top-class people. Three classes. Top, they know who they are. Middle, they don't. Bottom, they do. Mainly middle here, and slightly below centre.

'Would you like wine, Frank?'

'Of course! Let's have wine!' Elation. 'A meal without wine is like a day without sunshine.'

'Who wrote that, Frank?'

'It's a TV advert.'

'Oh, so it is! I know the one. The people all sitting round with long faces and then the waiter comes in with a bottle of

74

wine on the silver tray. You know the one, Jack. You're bound to.'

'Is that the one where they're in the garden wiping the sweat off their faces?'

'No, that's the orange squash one, silly! It's the one where you see all the faces close up and then—'

'I think a claret would be correct, seeing you're having duck and I'm having steak. Okay?'

'We'll leave it to you, Frank. We know nothing about wines.'

'Waiter, a bottle of Number twenty-three, please.'

'Very good, sir.' Pause.

'Frank, where did you learn about wine?' Earnest round face, beads of moisture on upper lip, small gold filling, ear-lobes pierced – funny, never noticed that before ...

Sudden pull on wrist. Watch the soup, silly wee bitch! 'Oh, I *have* to dance this! You don't mind, do you, Jack love?' Beseeching wet kiss on Jack's honest, open face. 'Pl-ease, darling?' Oh Christ, what a slabbering match – in public. 'Can you bossa-nova?'

'Can *I* bossa-nova.' Prolonged girlish giggles. How does the bloody thing go now? Ach hell, slow foxtrot with plenty of facial expression and exaggerated hip-action should see me through. Floor crowded now. Wonderful thing, drink. Gladdens the heart, emboldens and relaxes. Three cheers for drink! Sorry there. My fault. Not at all.

'This is the best night-out I've had for years. Are you enjoying it too, Frank?'

'Yep.'

'Are you sure now?'

'Sure, sure, *shoo*-er!'

More giggles and renewed forward pressure of the abdomen. Ooops, reaction. She *must* feel it. Wonder would she perform, extra-maritally, as they say in the *News of the World*? Lo-ovely thought! Smiling bass player shaking maracas *and* playing bass. Bloody marvellous! Jungle rhythm. Abandoned woman swaying over there, green mascaraed eyes closed. Ripe for orgy. Partner – old fellow – waxed moustache. Looks tired. Time he was in bed. Past it, poor chap. Not like me. Young lusting animal. Away again, begod. Bloody big head I've got. Have to catch myself on, settle to

75

something serious. Twenty-four after all. Old. Should have an aim in life by now instead of – 'Mona, have *you* an aim in life?'

'Can't hear you! Music's too loud! What did you say?'

'Pain like a knife. Here.'

'Is it a cramp? Let me rub it.'

Caressing my stomach suggestively. By God, if I play my cards right . . .

Back at table. Deferential waiter. A little of the French beans, sir? Burst of sentimentality. 'Your good health, Jack. Here's to a pleasant friendship.' I like you, Jack, and I'd like to carry our friendship to the point of riding your good wife and, Jack, do you know, she might just let me. Hooray for adultery! *Christ, what have I done!* A glass of Number twenty-three over the table. Shameful purple stain spreading. Waiter up like a shot.

'Soon fix that for you, sir. Just spread a napkin over it like that.'

God, what a wonderful place! Civilized, that's the word, civilized. And people around at other tables, not really bad. Pop, popping out of shells all over the place. Hooray for Saturday night! A halo and a knighthood for the boy who invented Saturday night, bless his soul!

Trip to gents' suddenly imperative. 'Excuse me, friends. Call of the great outdoors.'

Giggles from Mona. Full as a po that one. Eyes all silly and wild. Jack stiffly correct over second course. Pale slivers of canard disappearing into good-natured mouth. Good healthy farming-type appetite. Never asked him what he does. Must before I forget.

'Jack, before I go, one question.' Mustn't sway. Both hands on back of chair. Look serious. More giggles from Mona. Wonder does she laugh in bed . . . *Oh Jack it tickles. I'm sorry, Mona, I was born that way, you know, I can't help it.* 'I didn't ask you what you did for a living, old chap.' Like to be open and direct. Comrades together. No secrets . . . mutual sharing of each other's humanity. That's what drink's for after all.

'I'm a rep.'

Means representative. They don't like being called commercial travellers any more, but that's what they are all the same. Living out all those dirty yarns about putting farmers' daughters up the pole. *Jack* wouldn't of course.

'Pharmaceutical.'

'Interesting . . . Well if you will excuse me.'

Careful studied progress across waxy floor. No accidents. Cornered once by revolving quartet of whooping fox-trotters near dining-hatch. 'A Foggy Day in London Town.' All the good old standards. Ah me! *Wonderful* pianist. Lost in this place. Must congratulate him *and* the bass player.

Bar shuttered. Lights out. Sad looking. So quiet. No sound of Madge. Stairs. Easy. Right leg trembling, pins and needles in foot. Must have been crossed over left under the table. Never noticed it.

Gents' cold and echoing. One lavatory door closed – *Engaged* slid across. Steadying hand on the clammy white tile. Only a foot from the flushing Niagara. Funny thing the bladder. Must be *bloody* elastic.

Up the stairs again. Easy! Nearly tripped. Then – good God, might have gone in with fly open!

Deep breath, then into the lighted, noisy pool. Sucked in near the door, whirled round, cast up like a piece of driftwood at table. Jack and Mona staring dully straight ahead. The married look. Practising their telepathy. Both sets of eyes light up. Never fear, Frankie's here! The catalyst cometh! 'Jack, any chance of gettin' a drink?'

'Jack's just ordered a round for us, Frank. Come and dance with me.'

'Of course, darling, anything you say.'

Wall-lights dimming. Very slow beating of bass. 'I'm In The Mood For Love.' Slow spinning of wrap-around couples, silent, serious suddenly. Mona clinching with audible sigh. Must have put on fresh charge of perfume. Her hair tickling. Whoever said that women's hair was soft and—? Both arms around my waist. God she doesn't *care* any more! Women! And you can't go by the look of them either. The prim ones with prayer books would tear the Y-fronts off you and the ones you'd think were dynamite are all innocent Sunday-School teachers with pure minds and virginity.

'Stop it, Frank, that tickles.'

'Ma chérie, vous êtes ravissante. Vous êtes—'

'You're mad. You're blowing into my *ear*.'

'—magnifique, formidable – uh—'

'You're stuck. Ha ha!'

'—terrif-ique.'

'That doesn't count. Here, stop it! Don't forget, I'm a married woman.'

Coy flutter of eyelashes. God, you can't trust one of them. 'How long?'

'Two years, three months, three weeks, four days and – twelve hours and—'

'*You're* stuck. Ha, ha!'

'Oh, Frank, I'm drunk. But it's wonderful. *Wonderful.*'

'You *look* wonderful.'

'Thank you. You look nice yourself.'

'Wait till I tell them in school on Monday.'

'Wait till *I* tell them in school on Monday.'

'Excuse me, sir.' Waiter at my elbow.

'Yes?'

'Your friend told me to tell you, sir, that he's not feelin' too great and that he's gone outside for a minute or two. He'll be as right as rain when he gets some air. Nothin' to worry about. It could happen to a bishop.'

Mona's face suddenly pale and moth-like. 'I'll have to go to him. Och the poor dear. I'm so *selfish* and I never gave him a thought. He wouldn't say, that's just like him, he'd suffer in silence. Oh Jack.'

Oh Christ! I'll never understand them – never.

'Look, Mona, I'll go and find him. You sit down and I'll bring him back with me. Okay?'

'No, he'll want me. I *know* he will.'

'Stay up here. I won't be long.' Sharp with her. Only way. God, you'd think nobody'd ever been sick over a feed of drink before.

Heigh ho, down the stairs again. 'Jack . . . Jack.' Head out of front door. Black as the inside of a bagpipe. Rain blowing in solid icy sheets. Ah – cloakroom attendant. One half-crown and a shoal of tanners in his begging bowl (which he put there himself – his little confidence trick). 'Did a tall fair-haired fella in a blue suit go outside about a minute ago?'

'Not past me, sir.'

Never find him if he's out there in *that*.

'Have you tried the Gents'? He could have gone in there, sir. I can't see the door, you see. That big wooden pillar blocks my—'

'Hey, Jack, are you in there?' No answer. Third door – *Engaged*. Softer – 'Jack?' Muffled groan. 'Are you all right? Open the door, there's a good lad.' Nothing. 'Now catch yourself on, Jack. Mona's worried about you. Open up.'

'Aaaahh ...'

'Come on, open the door.'

'Go away ... aaahh!' And leave me to die in peace.

I know the feeling, yes, I know the feeling. A hermit's death with no inquest, please. No flowers, just a simple ceremony.

'Jack, put your fingers down your throat.'

You never know when it's going to hit you. When you least expect it. Terry Butler says, take a glass of milk before and after. Tried it *once*. Never kept it up. Jack's too late for that now.

'Aaaagh.'

Words beginning. 'Scampi, I think, not sure, tartare sauce, oh God, never again, drinkin' on an empty stomach, no tea worth talkin' about, shoppin' in Belfast for a bl-oody fridge, rush, rush, rush, she *had* to come here tonight, oh yes, oooh! we usually sit in and watch the television, don't like this place, too flashy, but she *had* to come, I don't know why, some damned urge. Don't bring her down here, do you hear! I don't want her to see me like this. *Frank, do you hear me, mind?*'

'Okay, Jack, okay. Try the fingers. It's the only way, mate.'

Drastic, but effective. Knew a fella once, at College, used to drink about six pints. Two fingers, sick, rid of it, fill up again with more double x. I bet he's an alcoholic by now. Crafty bottle of hard tack in the stationery cupboard ...

'I'm away up for Mona. She'd better drive you home.'

'She can't drive – ooh.'

Bit of a let-down that. 'Well, we'll rig up somethin'. Don't worry. It happens to all of us.'

'Oooh, aaah, *oooh*!'

Up the stairs again. Inquisitive cloakroom boyo, head out, likes to be in touch. Seen some queer things, I bet. Exuberance of dancers beginning to trickle away, sleeping on their feet some of them, don't know when to give up. Except for one long table near the back wall. Looks like somebody's birthday or the office treat. Giggly girls from Accounts department and that funny Mr. Smith From Upstairs. Christ, he's making a *speech*. Waving a glass around him.

'Did you find him, Frank?'

'Yes, I found him. Now don't worry. He'll be all right. Just had a wee drop too much to drink.' Now for it. 'He says you can't drive.'

'No – oh I see what you mean. *He* won't be able to drive, will he?'

'Hardly.'

'Oh, I'd better go to him. This is terrible. It's all my fault. I made him come. He didn't want to.'

'Yes, he told me.'

'Oh.'

Gone all red. Why?

'Yes.'

Four Scotch and a gin-and-tonic on the table. She's downed one when I was below. Cheese board on table too. Can't remember having any of that. What time is it anyway?

'What time is it, Frank?'

'A quarter to one.'

'Can you suggest anything, Frank? This is terrible.' (Second time that.) 'We've spoiled everything for you, Frank.'

'Balls – sorry.'

Pale wee smile. Pathetic really.

'Frank, I hate to ask you this. You've done so much as it is. But could *you* drive us home?'

'Well, you see—' Awkward situation. My old crock just enough juice to take *me* home. God knows where *they* live. No petrol at this time of – Sunday morning. God, most miserable time of the week, Sunday morning. When the suicides reach for the sleeping tablets. 'Take our car.'

'But what about—?'

'Could you not stay at our house tonight? Jack could run you over here to collect your car in the morning.'

The way things always turn out! Uncanny. But arse about face as usual. Invitation to sleep in the same house as willing bird (I think so), with husband laid up. Wouldn't have dared

80

dream a thing like that. But, as usual, everything wrong. Wrong time, wrong circumstances.

'Well it's the folks at home, you see. I don't like to—'

'Oh, of course, it's so late and you don't want to disturb them, that's it, isn't it? Is it too late for a taxi, do you think, Frank?'

Must make some gesture. Recover self-respect, don't want her to think me some kind of lesser animal. 'Look, I tell you what. I'll run you home in *your* car and bring it back in the mornin'.'

'Oh would you? Oh, Frank, you're a darling!'

Affectionate squeeze of right biceps. Poor kid. Quite nice really. Wonder what sort of bus they own? Bound to be better than my old scrap-heap. Can park *that* well out of sight behind some trees, so it won't give the place a bad name. Collect it early in the morning. The morning, that's a laugh. Now the bill. Easy to catch waiter's eye, two in the back of his head at this time of night. Leaves pink slip on saucer. Withdraws tactfully. Considerate of customers' feelings. Doesn't wish to intrude on a private moment of grief. Good God, four pounds seventeen and eightpence! Well, there goes the emergency fiver, farewell sweet prince, you felt very re-assuring there just under my third rib . . .

'How much is it, Frank?'

'That's all right, Mona. I'll look after this.' Be nonchalant. A common occurrence this, really.

Now the tip. Ten per cent, I think. Three half-crowns on top of the blue note. Symmetrical. Delightful still life.

'Frank, I'll get Jack to square you up when we get home.'

'Never give it a thought. Don't be daft. Ha ha.' Don't sound *too* offended. She might say 'Are you sure now?' *God dammit, I'm not mean.* I'm *not!* It's just that – oh, I don't know, what's the use?

Downstairs in the bogs again. Jack swaying in front of the hand-basin, scrabbling in the water. Scalds himself. Pulls hand out in slow motion. He'll feel it in the morning. Spurts in more cold. Basin overflows around his trousers. You'd think he'd be sobering. Strange.

'Come on, Jack, old chap. We're for home. Give me your arm.'

'Home? Whatyoumean?'

81

Eyes, red, streaked, wild. Mouth – loose, wet, hanging. Face – colour of white pudding.

'You're a decen' bloke, Frank. Know that? Decen'. Like you. Very much. Mona likes you. Thinks you a great guy. Honest. No kiddin'. Frank this, Frank that. Frank says this – she's right too. Good lad. Thought you might be stuck-up. Mona says you're very clever, so I thought – stuck-up. But you're not, you're just ordinary, nice, decen' bloke. Decen-bloo—'

God, what a weight! Helping me and no more. Through doors. Cloakroom boyo. 'I'll call Jim, sir, to give you a hand.'

Mona fluttering over. 'Oh Jack, Jack, are you all right?'

Must deflect her. 'Had he a coat?'

'Oh yes, yes. Jack, where's your cloakroom ticket, dear? Your cloakroom – ticket – darling – for – your – coat.' Spelling it out for the child.

Swaying giant gestures brokenly. 'Tick – ticket?' Let's feel in his breast pocket. Right first time. Arrival of Jim, shining oil-skins over blue Odeon uniform.

'Despert night, that, sir. Wicket. Where did you park the car, sir?' Drop at end of his nose. Rain? Door open. Deep breath. Bucketing outside. Good for the old best suit, I must say. 'Right, sir?' '*Right.*'

Gasp from Jack as first clout of cold rain hits him on up-turned face. Mona ahead in darkness leaping from puddle to puddle, calling, 'Over here! Beneath the trees!'

In with him into back seat. Falls like bag of turf face downwards on tartan rug. Push feet in. Door slammed. 'Okay now, sir? Will he be all right, sir?' Pale blob of face at streaming window. Can just make out the concern on it. Tip him, poor bastard. Face disappears. Rain pocking away like mad tattooist on roof. Glass alive – running, melting.

'Is he all right back there?'

Bending over, down into black well, her skirt lifting, two inches of soft vulnerable white flesh above stocking tops. Urge to touch. 'Well?'

'I can't move him.'

Jack lying on his face, nose flattened, breathing muffled, one hand limp as halibut. Turn him. God, what a weight. Face away from us. Moans, 'Home yet? I'll sleep here.' He sounds better. Just craves oblivion.

82

One of the newest Fords. I bet he changes it every year. Dashboard comes to life, a dozen lighted eyes, a new car always exciting at night. Gears easy. Same as mine. No time to move *that*. Let it stay . . .

Oh, that's Lord Glass's yoke, sir, out there, won't drive anything else, sir, loaded of course but a bit of an eccentric, if you follow me, goes his own way, one of the great men of our time, sir, he'll be remembered, aye, he'll be remembered . . .

Switch the key, into gear, and away. Handling the smooth, heavy projectile of a car, sliding out between gate-posts on to liquid black gleam of main road. 'Left or right?'

'We live on the Dublin Road, outside Annagh.'

That means left. Road in front of headlights being sucked inexorably into somewhere under the chassis, expelled at back. What a car!

'Do you feel cold, Frank? Do you mind if I switch on the heater?'

'Not atall.'

Beginnings of soft warmth on left ankle. Spreading tendrils up trouser leg into secret regions. Very pleasant. Can steer herself, this. Flowing – that's the word – over the asphalt. Old demesne wall on right rippling past.

Encased in warmed, glowing shell. Fifty, up to steady sixty. Effortless. My 'new experience in motoring', as the Ads say.

Snores beginning to rise from back seat and a new rectangular glow from the dashboard. Radio. Aha, a foreign station to drown husband's off-guard night sounds. Montmartre accordions coming in waves and outside – the Belfast–Derry Road. Flicking past the sleeping ribbon development, every little bell-button a glow-worm in the dark. A bungalow near the bus. What more to ask from life?

A touch at my side. Mona inching up the bench seat. Nice. Very. A passion for closeness, this one. Stare straight ahead, into the night. Admiring my profile? My good side, the left.

'Frank . . .'

'Yes?'

'The heater's not too strong, is it?'

'No.'

'The driver gets the full force of it. Jack destroyed a left shoe when he first got the car.'

'Oh?'

'Yes, the heat did something to the suede.'

'Thanks for the tip.' Mutual laugh. Polite.

Passed parked car, two inside wheels high on grass, side lights, two heads together, *cafuffling*. Back seat better. No gear lever. *Our* heads close now. Companionable wee thing, Mona. Hope she doesn't talk any more. Don't want to answer. Only spoil nice floating sensation.

Through Annagh. Empty wet streets. Shop signs flapping in the wind. Circular Esso stand flat on back outside Murray's garage, metal legs helpless in air. Under the fluorides. Long shadow of car shrinking to nothingness, then leaping long again. One solitary policeman in Co-op doorway. Trying locks?

'Have we far to go now, Mona?'

'No, it's the third bungalow on the right.'

One – two – three. Swing in through posts. No gate. Sort of grill in ground to keep cattle out. Rattle, rattle, *kerump*. Arrived. Storm roaring up as engine dies.

Out with him between us, limp weight. Up garden path, into trim hall with brass gong over the telephone. Green carpet, contemporary house-proud smell. Steering Jack into bedroom. Felling him neatly on to the candlewick. Shoes off, loosen collar. Sleeping where he fell. Dead to the world. Embarrassing atmosphere suddenly. Her pink nightie there on chair? Try not to let her see me gaping.

'Don't look too closely, will you? Everything's a mess.'

'Nice place you've got here. It's new, isn't it?'

'We built it about two years ago.'

Why *must* houses be like this? Everything to put you off marriage. How do people *live* in them. Not a decent honest-to-god colour anywhere. All the life sucked dry.

In the hall again. Our eyes sliding past and around each other's. The flame of an hour ago snuffed.

'Well, he'll be all right now.' (Uncle Frank speaking, bluff, harmless old Uncle Frank.) 'Do you think you can manage?'

'Oh yes. Would you like a cup of coffee?'

'No thanks.' Let's get to hell out of here. Into that lovely car for a dare-devil Le Mans drive home.

'I'll just see you out then, Frank. Mind the step.'

Head-down dash to the car. In behind the wheel. Sud-

denly – Mona in beside me. Breathless. Rush of words –
'Frank, I'm awfully sorry about tonight. It's rotten the way
things turned out and now this, putting you to all this trouble.
I just don't know what to say ...' A born apologizer, sorry
for everything, never happy any other way. A bit like myself. Now I know how irritating it can be for other people.
Feeling tired for the first time. Stop her yammer, for God's
sake. Unthinkingly, put finger to her lips. Certain amount of
roughness in gesture. Clutches my finger, my hand. Trembling. 'Frank.' Throaty whisper. *Good God, I don't believe it
... it can't be ... it ...*

Soft, soft lips, eyes closed, falling slowly backwards on to
seat, my weight following, left hand and arm underneath,
her arms round my neck, fingers searching in my hair, don't
leave her lips whatever you do! Her *tongue*, no resistance.
(*Always happens like this when you're off-guard. The touch
on the lips did it. A touch can set them mad, send them over
the edge. Yet I never saw it. So quick, so quick.*) Move to
ear, blow a moist monsoon into her left ear, swirling round in
the pink shell, *oh, Frank, oooh*, sighs welling, my right hand
route-marching to right breast, sliding under flowered
rayon, under white cup, fingers gently pressing, walking
down, one hand now holding warm, most satisfying of shapes.
(*Moment of decision, whether to slide out left hand from
underneath, transfer it to right knee. Separate the men from
the boys, this. Women are lucky, don't have to make such a
decision. Well, she's married, nothing to LOSE, after all,
nothing to protect, intangible has become tangible. Might
even be scornful of celibate shilly-shally. Put it off a little
longer.*) Kneading the warm flesh, nipple subsiding, lips on
eyes, nose, cheeks, risk 'Ah, Mona, darling.' Passionate reaction, renewed kisses, her own tongue probing, wonderful
... Right, now for it ... Rock slightly, under guise of passion,
hand slid out, let lie for a moment, docile, circulation restored, sensitivity restored – *now*. Volcanic disturbance
underneath, legs together, like scissors' snap, hand pushing
on chest. (*Christ, wouldn't it sicken you! I HATE women.
Damn, damn their devious bloody souls! Now it's all ruined.
But what else could I do? It became a point of honour. Like
pulling up your horse at the last jump.*) Her weeping now,
me feeling bloody stupid, lying like this, meaningless all of a

sudden. (*They always make you feel as if it's YOUR fault, if you're daft enough. I really think they blubber because they're ashamed of themselves. Women hate their bodies. A constant affront. A constant reminder of what they really are. Blind intuitive bits of flesh. Jelly-fish, by god. Yes, jelly-fish, vaguely striving after higher things.*)

'Mona, now don't cry.'

What do you do? Embarrassing. *Her* car too. Never know how they're going to take it. By all that's holy, six miles back to Kildargan, if walking's called for! No laugh, no laugh, still sheeting outside.

'Oh Frank, oh Frank.'

She doesn't sound angry, thank the Lord. Still ashamed of herself, aye, that's it. Well here goes, nothing else for it – 'It's gettin' late and my old Ma'll be thinkin' I'm lost.' (Good God, even mustered a laugh, just shows you what you can do when you try.) Act as though nothing has happened. This is the way all civilized people say good night, didn't you know, sort of thing?

Looking at me very odd now, watching closely for a flicker of ridicule. Thinks I'm pulling her leg. Never even got my hand on it, sez he . . .

'Frank . . .'

'Yes?'

Whoof! Flinging herself on me again. Arms throttling. Must be beside herself. Pent up. God help big innocent Jack in there on the bedspread, his size elevens dangling in space.

Hard kiss on the lips then – 'Good night, Frank,' and out the door like a liltie . . .

Half-way home before I know what's hit me. Thoughts breeding like maggots inside my skull, on each other's backs, all beginning with Why? and not an answer to one of them . . .

Sympathetic speedometer at thirty-five. Ach to hell. Just time for a fast close to the evening. Forty, forty-five, fifty, fifty-five, sixty, sixty-five – slow down for the bump under the beeches, then skimming up the short stretch from the High Road to The Red Row. All dark, quiet, asleep, swing in up the Backs, engine breathing. Light on in Tojo McBride's backyard. Bedroom window bright. Between lamp and roller-blind, curtain or bag or something hanging in the middle straight down. Car parked neatly close to our end wall so milkman can turn in the morning. Lights out, doors locked. Time? Two-thirty or thereabouts. In. Back door on latch. Usual arrangement. Shoes off, in the hand, into darkened house. Thin streak of orange under *their* bedroom door. Old lady reading. Pile of Dornford Yates and Howard Springs beside the bed. Old fella's back turned to crinoline lady lamp. Wonder has he things sorted out yet? *I was a sleep fiend, I had to have eight hours of it a day or I couldn't be lived with, honest, doctor, it's insidious, this craving, can't you help me? take these before going to bed, my good man, guaranteed . . .*

Watch! Creak on third tread. *On the third tread the time will be . . .* No bloody sleep for me tonight, can tell that for a start. Too many ideas in the old nut chasing each other round and round and round.

SPRING

ONE

On a Monday morning in April I came through the swinging glass doors of Annagh Primary and teetered gingerly across the ringing, still-drying expanse of terrazzo. My shoes had just come from the menders the day before, and this, combined with my custom of always keeping my eyes sharp right when I come into school, made my entrance that day doubly perilous.

I should explain that on the wall facing the door is an 'object' which I find so depressing, especially on the first day of the week, that I can't bear to look at it directly if I can help it, so I have developed this habit of eyes right or eyes left but never eyes front in the hall. The 'object' is a large, very home-made looking map of the world which gets more like a diseased mottled wall-fungus every day. Trevor Warwick's class made it for a project about a year ago but it hasn't any of the nice artlessness which is so refreshing about the things kids usually do for you. This just looks as though it's been pieced together by a very painstaking adult with no taste or imagination. Sticking out of the Northern Hemisphere is a large label which reads – OUR SCHOOL IS HERE. You follow its sharpened end to a blob on the map which is meant to represent Ireland. It always reminds me of those things you find scribbled on the fly-leaves of school textbooks – *My name is Bertie Brown, my abode is 10 Slieve Croob Parade, Annagh, County Antrim, Ireland, the British Isles, Europe, The Northern Hemisphere, The World, The Universe* ... The thing affronts me. What makes it worse, of course, is that visitors to the school always comment on it admiringly and ask how long it took to make. People are like that I find. They're always more impressed by the amount of work spent on a thing than whether the time was justfied or not.

'Salonika' Gorman, the caretaker, was standing among the

coat-racks, propped on his mop as usual and he nodded me across. 'Mr. Glass. Here a wee min-ute.'

'Salonika's been his nickname round the town since he made the mistake of talking too much in a pub one night about the only action he ever saw during the 1914–18. That's how nicknames start and stick in this town – like tar. Thank God they haven't daubed me yet. Gorman's a dirty-minded old sod. And he still shocks me with the stories he tells – all set in some 'kip-shop' or other (his favourite locale). It's his whiter-than-white hair and baby blue eyes that make you doubt your ears when he begins one of his elaborate spiralling obscenities.

I completed a cautious right-angle on the echoing cream tiles, and crossed to him, picking my steps. I was sure it would be – *Did you hear the one about the* ... but with a different excitement in his voice, he said, 'Mr. Glass, have you seen the new bit o' stuff? She's in wi' Ernie now.' I only found out a short time ago that, to most of the other teachers, he refers to the Principal as Mr. Matchett and I'm sophisticated enough to resent this as another form of the familiarity which some of my pupils try on from time to time. The biggest fear in a teacher's life – familiarity.

'Oh?' I said, giving him as little to build on as I could.

'Aye'n' a great wee bum on her,' he leered. 'I wonder who she is.'

'Search me, Tom,' I lied and he looked at me with his washed-out, red-rimmed eyes. His veined old hand moved involuntarily up to his buff plastic, kidney-shaped deaf-aid. He's very conscious of its newness and he hates it being there behind his ear but it was either that or lose his cushy caretaker's job through growing deafness.

One of the juniors just then entered after a struggle with the heavy door. Gorman studied him the way a ferret does a leveret, then roared, '*Clean yer feet!*' when the child was about four feet past the recessed mat. He was only a baby in the smallest size burberry you can buy and his mother had dressed him with loving care. He scuttled back to the mat and began trying to wear his tiny soles away in a backward stroking action. Gorman growled, 'Wee huer's get the lock o' them. They'd have me workin' here half the bloody night, so they wud.' I used it as an excuse to laugh, and the laugh got me round in a U-turn away from him across the treacherous floor.

As all the electric bells in the school began to vibrate in unison for nine o'clock Assembly I wondered what the new student in Matchett's office would be really like – plain and conscientious or pretty and slack? I was half-tempted to have a look for myself but that meant going into Matchett's office and Mona would be there behind her typewriter and she would raise her eyes when the door opened and then lower them again quickly when she saw it was me.

Of course the whole thing was bloody ridiculous; for we had hardly exchanged a couple of words since that night at The Pheasant. Had it really happened? That was the question I asked myself every time I saw little Miss Prim. It was that thought and only that that kept the tiny flame of interest burning.

Without thinking what I was doing I rapped the gun-metal grey door beside me and turned the handle. Matchett raised his mottled brown dome from a notebook the student had been showing him (she was at his elbow) and his bright diminished eyes twinkled behind the thick lenses. Mona's desk was empty. I mumbled something about the scripture reading for Assembly as he rose to his feet.

'Ah, Frank,' he said. 'I want you to meet Miss McCurdy, our new student. She won't be in your class though. I'm putting her in with Todd. Miss McCurdy – Mr. Glass.'

She smiled shyly and didn't offer her hand and I felt grateful that I hadn't stuck mine out. Old Matchett was in good form. He likes having the students. He's very conscious of his position as Principal of an eight-teacher school (such dizzy bloody heights!) so when he gets hold of a nice new impressionable student or teacher, for that matter, he bores them with long stories about his tough rise to success – the hard way. Still he could be a lot worse, the old eejit . . .

'I think Miss McCurdy will be happy here, don't you, Frank?'

'Yes,' I said, 'they're a nice bunch of kids here,' and smiled at her. She smiled back, emotionally. A turn-up for the book, conscientious *and* pretty.

Her bum *was* nice too, trust our war-hero in the hall to pick the salient part of the anatomy first go off – a trim, controlled affair, tucked into a shortish grey, pin-striped skirt. She had dolly blonde looks and round her neck she wore a thin gold chain which disappeared behind the vee of her man's bottle-green pullover to plummet down into God-knows what warm mysterious clefts. I thought of something I once read about a practice in Odessa they had of giving ivory charms a fraudulent patina of age by keeping them for a period of time between the abundantly sebaceous breasts of Jewesses. Then, I realized with a start that my absent-minded gaze was making her blush and, equally embarrassed, I dragged my eyes away from her.

As I was leaving, Matchett said, 'I'd like a word with you later, Frank, when you're not too busy.' Then he smiled warmly to show the student and I that there was nothing to worry about.

All the same, as I steered myself cautiously back on to the terrazzo in the corridor outside I felt a flutter of doubt. My reaction was a conditioned one. After five years of teaching among my fellow teachers, who all, every one of them, look on inspectors – and the principal – with equal degrees of suspicion, I could think of nothing else but – *what does the old weasel want?*

Three late-comers burst through the glass doors behind me and glared simultaneously at fat Kelso out of Warwick's class, who was standing to one side, one arm locked casually over the top rail of the coat-racks. As they sprinted despairingly past, Kelso wrote down their names in an exercise-book.

About a month ago Warwick had sold old Matchett the idea of a perfect system. It wasn't hard because anything with the remotest connection with the grammar-school set-up goes down very big with him. Kildargan is one of the few primary schools in the area with a uniform (the crest of the blazer as 'Docendo Discimus' in cheap, red letters under something that looks like a diseased turnip) and we have sports days, prize days, open days ... we have the worst results in the eleven-plus too, but we have lovely tone for a school of our type and size ...

Kelso saw me watching and grinned cheekily as much as to say, '*You* have no authority over *me*,' and I went down the big main corridor to Assembly cursing quietly to myself.

To my left I could see into the school's two rows of class-rooms jutting at right angles from the corridor I was on like two widely-spaced teeth from a comb. Between them a rectangle of grass that never seems to get cut at the right time. In each tooth there are four classrooms, identical except for the colour scheme of the walls and woodwork. Mine is the end one in the second block – the furthest – done up in two shades of blue. I noticed that my blackboard still had writing on it, and I made a mental note to change the 'board roster. Devlin obviously could not be entrusted with it.

Hetty Morton, who takes Primary Five, was going over the hymn on the piano in the corner, near the platform of the great high-ceilinged Assembly Hall but her stiff-fingered chords weren't rising high enough above the noise of three hundred children from four to fourteen. The figure's important because if the number falls below two-forty some one of us teachers is out of a job . . .

'Mr. Glass, isn't this your week for Assembly duty?' Vice-principal Warwick at my elbow. That pained smile on his nondescript features and a knot in his tie the size of a bloody pea. His brain's about that size too. My mouth opened and shut a few times. '*I* took over for you. Okay?' And he walked off to his own class, who were lined up against the end wall, great intimidated bloody louts the lot of them.

As if to further underline the difference between his lot's subservience and mine, who were lined up at my elbow, one of mine, wee Bothwell, piped up cheekily at the head of the line, 'Have you seen the blackboard, Mr. Glass?' I took him by the fleshy part of the ear and needlessly asked him to repeat what he had just said. His eyes filled with tears and I felt sorry and released him. I like Bothwell. Like all cheeky kids he's very sensitive and shy underneath. To make amends I said, 'Eric, away and change the water in the flowers,' and he dashed off. Damned if Warwick didn't stop him at the back door of the hall! I could see him questioning him and then reluctantly letting him go. Some day, some day, I'm going to stick my fist down that fucker's throat!

'Silence!'

Matchett had entered. I knew he had paused – posed dramatically a minute just inside the double doors before

92

calling for quietness. Then, as I also knew he would do, he
stood on for a further moment with a look sliding around the
hall meant to be cold and quelling. I always feel like laughing at that point because the *Look* never really comes off. I
think it must be the glasses. He just looks daft, instead of
awe-inspiring. Still you can't really dislike the old goat
because he's one of those chancers you have to laugh at. His
front is a harmless one. Nothing like Himmler Warwick's for
instance.

Hetty Morton struck a venomous opening chord and Matchett, I knew, was calling her all the names of the day as he
scrambled on to the platform, because she deliberately
sabotages him every morning before he's time to bring his
Look to that satisfying dramatic curtain, by coming in too
soon. This bloody school rattles with vendettas, really. Old
Hetty hates Matchett for some imagined injustice in the past
and she doesn't speak to him. I know it's incredible but she
doesn't speak to him. Any contact is carried out in the form
of notes or messages passed through an intermediary. Mad,
I tell you, mad! But that's what happens to teachers. The
job exaggerates any hidden leanings you have towards cranki-
ness. Warwick's a power-maniac, Wilbur Todd's a sadist,
Hetty Morton has a persecution complex, big Fat Pat – Pat
Ferris, who is our 'Games Mistress' and who also takes the
backward class, has tendencies, I *think*, towards nympho-
mania (no personal experiences there, but still . . .), Mrs.
Connolly hates her husband, Primrose Bultitude is a Plym
(Plymouth Brethren) and a religious fanatic. That leaves
Rose Matchett, Ernie's wife, and Mrs. Reid who takes P.2
and 3. Given time, I *know* I could hook them on to some peg.
All my workmates have got kinks, and it isn't, despite wide-
spread opinion, because teaching attracts people like that,
It's just what I have already stated, the job really does
develop unfortunate tendencies. My own? Can't really focus
it down to one simple textbook phrase like the others. Of
course that's only natural because you're too close to yourself to see properly ... edges become blurred. With other
people it's into the pigeon-hole and a label round their necks,
neat, and I suppose over-slick ...

'Sir, sir! What number is the hymn, sir?'

My lot were all leaning forward looking at me. Damn it, I

93

had forgotten to tell them the hymn selected for the week. It had gone right out of my head on Friday.

'Three hundred and sixty,' I growled to Crowe and he passed it along the row. I cursed them for not having the common johnny to put on an act, for they nudged and whispered and rustled the hymn books until I lost my temper and tip-toed up behind the row and, picking out one at random, nipped him by the ear. Quinn turned his head with that hurt look in his eye and I moved quickly on up to the far end. Then I relaxed against the radiator which stretched in an unbroken line under the huge side wall of glass, and the heat flowed through the taut seat of my trousers.

Rose Matchett moved quietly up besides me from her class of nine-year-olds and, out of the corner of her mouth, said, 'Have you seen the student?'

'Yes,' I whispered in return, Bogart fashion, my eyes roaming the rows of faces as Hetty reverberated into the final chorus.

'Is she in with *you*?'

'No . . . Todd.'

She made a silent 'oo' sound with her mouth and glanced across me to where he stood singing lustily at the head of his class. We exchanged looks and smiled. She feels the same way as I do about him and we have moments of rare understanding when he says something pompous in the staff-room and our eyes meet. She's about fifty I would say, a little light-weight sparrow of a woman with carelessly rouged cheeks and a stringy tendony neck. She smokes like a train, and her outspokenness is continually embarrassing Matchett, who is torn between having her on the staff or keeping her at home out of harm's way. I think it's the extra pay-packet coming into the house that makes up his mind for him.

'*He* won't be nice to know today,' she nodded up to the platform where her husband was singing away. *Sets a good example for the children, you can't expect them to do it if you don't do it yourself*, he would say. He's full of little bits of *Readers' Digest* psychology like that.

'He'll have to have something tempting for his tea tonight.'

It was the sort of thing that would have infuriated old Matchett if he could have heard it. She brings him down beautifully when we're all in the staff-room . . . talks about his little domestic failings when he's present and it makes him writhe. He hates being reminded, in front of us all, that his feet smell, or that he takes stewed prunes every morning as a laxative, or that he wears long white Interlock combs all the year round. Good old Rose, she really keeps us all sane, because, going back on what I have just said, *she's* the only normal one on the staff. She's less like a teacher than anyone I've ever met.

I still looked blank so she dug me with a sharp old elbow and hissed, 'Mrs. Purdy's off sick.' Then, 'Do you think it's—' Her eyes gleamed and I felt a sudden stupid, instinctive feeling of guilt. Then, the singing around us came to an end in a long 'Aaaaa-men'. Matchett called out 'Heads bowed!' and as he began, 'Our Father which art in Heaven, hallowed be—' I stared at the floor. Morning sickness? I thought, *No. But why? It was very possible*. It was the first time she'd had a day off since I'd ever remembered. Amazing, but I was *disappointed* she wasn't there when I went into Matchett's office and saw the covered typewriter ...

The monotonous rumble ended and the lines began to peel off in shuffling formation towards the two doors, front and rear. The restrained, worshipping atmosphere showed its artificiality in the way it was sliced off abruptly. The classes talked noisily, punched each other, swung school-bags, laughed, or recited pieces of tables, scripture or poetry to each other. Four boys from Warwick's class dashed up to the Bechstein and wheeled it on squealing castors out through the door and down the echoing corridor. They were taking it to Hetty Morton's class. She had some of the seniors for music on a Monday morning.

I felt unprepared for the day's work. It was the kids that made me feel like that. The sheer animal cruelty of their energy tires you. They can't understand an adult's screaming need for a slow build-up to things. *They* don't know any other way to live. Bang, bang, bang. In, out ... I saw myself in twenty years as a Mr. Chips-type figure, moving carefully about, consolidating my fragile energies, with children flashing past like frenzied minnows round a senile old trout.

My lot were lined up outside the classroom door waiting for me. I walked up the whispering line and felt that strange current emanating from them. It's there for the first half-hour or so of every day. Experience tells them that it's no use, that it's going to be a day like any other day, but they keep hoping *something* will come up to change the routine, bring excitement into the humdrum. Some days the feeling is stronger than others and you have to wrestle with them mentally for the first period until they give in, finally convinced that it *is* just going to be another Monday, Tuesday, Wednesday . . .

The door was locked and Bothwell was inside making a meal of arranging the jam-jars of crocuses and snowdrops along the window-sills which Lily Burns brings in as peace-offerings. He was pretending to be absorbed in his task and oblivious of the angry faces pressed close to the glass, stretched into gargoyle masks against the steamy panes.

I rattled the handle impatiently and he raised his head absent-mindedly. I had to laugh at his artistry – the innocence of those big bush-baby eyes of his. He even managed a little start. He twiddled the key in the lock, then, just as it clicked, he gave a quick glance to the blackboard and then to my face. I had forgotten all about the chalked scrawl I'd caught a glimpse of earlier. From that distance it had looked like one of the new algebra equations I'd just started on Friday afternoon. I looked up at it casually and the first thing I noticed was that it wasn't ciphers but words. The top word was MONA in thin, uncontrolled capitals and I felt as if somebody had pulled out a plug somewhere and all my blood was being replaced with ice-water. The whole thing read

MONA
L.
MAVERICK.

Bothwell was looking at me through the glass and waiting. I realized my face was giving the game away but I could only stare back. Then he turned, ran over to the blackboard, grabbed the duster and, with short quick strokes, rubbed it clean. He stood on his toes and his thin white wrists seemed to stretch further and further away from his stained windcheater sleeve.

I could hear the class muttering behind me. They wanted in. My hand was still on the brass handle and I twisted it, and the first boy in the line pushed past. His rudeness was only a tiny pin-prick and the thought of grabbing him by the neck and hauling him back to the end of the line only flickered half-heartedly at the back of my mind. The rest of the class filed past, stopping their chatter only as they passed me, resuming immediately they got inside so that I was standing in a little pool of silence surrounded by their noise. Lily Burns was last and I stared vacantly into her round bespectacled face as she bobbed apologetically past. She blushed and I followed. The door closed. Bothwell was at the board stroking the duster against the edge of the channelled shelf that holds the chalk. A fine mist of white dust was falling lazily around his feet. He stopped as I came towards him and we looked at one another. Then he walked down into the body of the class, pushing and scolding like the rest as they painfully settled down for the day's work.

Surely to God they had seen it! But there wasn't one smirk that I could detect as I opened the drawer of my table and took out the roll-book. Bothwell couldn't have resisted pointing it out to them, or could he? That look we had exchanged had enough of the 'we men-of-the-world understand these things, don't we?' in it to make me hope that he had held himself in check. Yes, he was enough of a complex wee get to enjoy denying himself the treat of having about ten short minutes of glory. But that didn't make any difference anyway because the bloody thing was clearly visible through the glass ... or was it?

I turned my head. Misted – *on the outside*. Cold panes in contact with breath-laden corridor air. A scientific fact ...

I looked down at my bunch, my elbows on the table and my hands clasped before my mouth, and gradually the noise and fidgeting ceased. My silence at the head of the room couldn't be ignored indefinitely. The last die-hards turned round from the desks behind and heard their own voices ringing startlingly loud in the quietness. There were a few laughs at their embarrassment and then a long silence unbroken except for the steady, starting hum of the central-heating fixture near the front of the room.

Then, out of my abstraction, I realized the danger of what was happening and I stammered, 'Get out your New Testaments,' and to my relief the noise soared again. When I thought of the concentrated, probing scrutiny of those thirty-eight pairs of eyes and what they might uncover telepathically, I went cold for the second time.

Jack Kerr, one of our former teachers and a 'mis-fit' (he's a police inspector out in Uganda now), always referred to them as 'the enemy'. 'They're the fucking enemy,' he would say, 'and don't you forget it, Frank, old turd, the fucking enemy. On their own, away from the herd they can be nice, even human, but en masse, in class, animals, fucking animals, potential teds to a man bent on kicking in some poor old shite of an old-age pensioner's rib-cage. Don't forget it, mind.'

I liked Jack. Didn't care a damn for anybody or anything. Those qualities I would have liked myself, he had them all. Wilbur Todd got his job when he left. Old Jack still writes the odd letter to me every now and then – full of uproarious stories about 'the fucking nig-nogs,' as he calls them. I often wonder did he leave one set of 'enemies' here for another with black skins . . .

The room was all silent again and I came back from the depths of darkest Africa to see all their eyes on me. They could 'smell' there was something up. The atmosphere was tightening. It was up to me to slacken it right quick.

'St. Luke, Chapter 10. Verses 25 to 37. Read quietly. I'll be asking questions about it,' I rapped out and my voice had lost its soprano quality.

I stared out the last remaining rebels until they got tired of glaring around the room looking for moral support that wasn't there. *Another native rising crushed in the bud by fearless Frank . . .*

It was not twenty past nine. I had a good uninterrupted ten minutes or so in which to untangle my thoughts. So . . .

Anybody could have written what was on the blackboard, but the odds were on somebody sitting in the desks in front of me. It was easier for them to get the key, or more likely, to be there 'tidying up' on Friday afternoon, because, as I remembered, I'd left them at three sharp because I'd had to go to Belfast. God! I went frozen again to think of *that* being there all week-end. The cleaners look upon anything left on the blackboard as sacred. I do believe if some wag had chalked up a big dirty penis and accessories of the public lavatory variety, they wouldn't have noticed, or if they had, dismissed it as some sort of biology diagram or abstract art cod. I wished to hell someone *had* drawn a cock. That would have meant I wasn't involved, because the class's half-hearted attempts to nickname me had up to then stuck at *Maverick*. I was *Maverick*, in honour of their fast-talking, fast-shooting, dude western hero on television. I remember I had felt flattered in a way when I first overheard it but the name hadn't stuck. It wasn't a good one, it hadn't that inevitability that all the best nicknames and dirty jokes have.

Yes, I was definite about it, some little fly bastard with his nose in the story of the 'Good Samaritan', sitting in one of those single, flat-topped desks out there was silently chuckling at his own little private joke and he wouldn't be found out either, he knew that damn well. *Mona Loves Maverick*. The age-old message. But surely no one could have known about that Saturday night at The Pheasant, so why? The chalk artist must have *some* reason for what he did. I thought about that as the class went on with their 'silent reading'. *Mona Loves Maverick*. Not Maverick loves Mona. Any significance there?

And then it came to me, and I laughed out loud, changing it like lightning into a violent attack of coughing as the eyes swung up from the small black print to stare at old mad Glass who had gone all nutty this morning. I saw it all. *I saw it all.* Somebody switched on the magnet and all the little bits rushed tingling and clinging together . . .

I remembered what Terry had said at the auction . . . *she fancies you* . . . and about *her* asking me that same afternoon where I was going to that night, and then out of the blue her turning up and Jack saying she had plagued him into bringing her and that time she had blushed . . . Suddenly I couldn't wait until she came in the following morning so that I could see her again and look into her face and study her as someone I had somehow overlooked before.

I got up from the table and walked into the little room where all the exercise-books and paints and brushes and stuff is kept, and I closed the door carefully behind me. Then, putting my head up into one of the strutted corners between the shelves so that the class couldn't hear me, I laughed aloud for a solid minute. *I could not get over it.*

There was a tap on the door and I straightened myself up.

'Come in,' I said, and opened one of the exercise books for a bluff.

Bothwell poked his head round the door and the noise behind him died, but not quick enough.

'Well,' I said, 'what is it?' His eyes flickered to mine and then away.

'The Roll, sir,' he hinted softly, and I boomed, 'Of course, Eric! Thank you for reminding me!'

He skipped out of the way, thinking I was coming for *him* as I raged past out into the sunny, humming room and I felt like beating my chest and roaring, 'Me Tar-*zannnnn*!' until every drawing-pin on the ice-blue walls popped out.

Triumphantly taking the war into the enemy's camp, I rolled off the names so fast they couldn't get their 'Presents' out in time ... 'Adams, Allen, Barbour, Beggs, Boomer, Bothwell, Burns, Caesar, Carson, Calvert, Connor, Crowe, Cuddy, Dickey, Duffin' – and on and on and on until the last name Young shot like a hurled brick into silence. Then I laughed at their frightened eyes and slowly, hesitantly, they began laughing with me, back at me, until the room was filled with the sound of their voices.

When they were all caught up in it, even the nervy ones – Long and Caesar and Hamill and Lily Burns and Marlene Tate too – I thumped the table and shouted, 'The book!' and the laughter changed to cheers as Bothwell darted like a hare from his seat to the store. He came out in a flat-footed Chaplin waddle, face straight and the class roared back into laughter again. Bowing, he handed me the thin red book and I took it from him delicately, entering into the game with him. Then I opened it, smoothed the pages flat, settled the flats of my forearms along the table and looked straight ahead until the room settled down at its own pace into silence.

In a calm, unhurried voice I read aloud 'Chapter one' and the class shivered. Then: *'Squire Trelawney, Dr. Livesey, and the rest of these gentlemen having asked me to write down the whole particulars about Treasure Island, from the beginning to the end and keeping nothing back but the bearings of the island, and that only because there is still treasure not yet lifted, I take up my pen in the year of grace seventeen – and go back to the time when my father kept the "Admiral Benbow" inn and the brown old seaman, with the sabre-cuts, first took up his lodging under our roof . . .'*

The story unreeled in smooth shining coils and the class shivered as they felt it tighten and grip them. They sat still in positions that had set hard after the first paragraph. Only eyes that gleamed or fingers that moved with nerves disturbed the thick heavy covering of bodies and faces before me. This was the thing I would miss most if I ever gave up teaching. There never was an audience like this, rapt and ravenous, tearing at the words even before they came out of my mouth.

I read to them like this a half-hour a day. This year I've got through *The Thirty-nine Steps, A High Wind in Jamaica* and Hemingway's *The Old Man and the Sea.*

As I watched their faces then I knew this new one was going to be a winner. The first chapter unrolled with oiled mastery until at the climax, where Dr. Livesey, cool and nonchalant, in powdered periwig drawled, *'If you do not put that knife this instant in your pocket, I promise, upon my honour, you shall hang at the next Assizes',* they could restrain themselves no longer and cheered and clapped until I was beginning to worry that Warwick might come in from next door. Bothwell jumped out of his seat and soundlessly conducted a frenzied bout of fencing with an imaginary opponent in the aisle and when he had finally delivered the death-blow and stood panting, I said quietly, 'Thank you, Bothwell,' and everyone laughed. I began to read immediately and the laughter died at once. At the end of the chapter I closed the book and said, *'Chapter two – Black Dog appears and disappears* – tomorrow at the same time.' The class sighed 'Aaah' like a great wounded balloon hissing its last and then, before any further noise could flare up, I snapped curtly, *'Now* I want you to do a little arithmetic test on the past few weeks' work to see what you've learned, or, better still, what you *haven't* learned.'

When the board was filled with neat sums – *One to twenty and check your answers* – I sat down thankfully at the desk, anticipating the enjoyment of a half-hour's grace to think. You don't get many half-hours to think when you're a teacher. That's what makes it such a tiring job. You get home at three and your fatigue angers you, because what *did* you do all day? It's the continuous assaults on your privacy that floors you. There's no refuge, no locked doors behind which you can draw a deep breath and count up the score. You're like a man running a coconut shy, gathering up balls and hurling them back over and over and over again and, believe me, those little bastards down there bent over their jotters have arms that are tireless.

On the wall facing me the red second hand of the electric clock jerked soundlessly, and all the heads were down. In the fourth row, third seat back, beside Fatty Gault, twitchy McKittrick was battling with his hysteria. Just him and his sum and no help from his mates. I knew what he was feeling as he glanced from side to side helplessly, appealingly, while the figures smiled back at him unchanged from the rule paper. But how much sympathy can you give? I felt lazy and slow today. Why should I go down and silently forestall his mounting terror with a hand on his shoulder and a whispered, 'Stuck? Where?' I put him out of my mind and looked across the matted grass to the other classroom block. Four clocks identical with mine stared across from four bald, bare walls, each painted in a different relaxing, pastel shade.

Over there were the babies, living in their scaled-down world, their desks Lilliputian, even their toilet bowls were for pigmies. I thought of the urine smell unsuccessfully kept at bay by the sickening one of Jeyes' Fluid and sour milk from the stacked crates, and vomit. Whenever anyone's sick the call goes out for Salonika and he comes limping along grumbling, with a bucket of sawdust and a shovel and brush. I don't know how those infant teachers stick it, kids either dirtying their trousers at their desks or ceaselessly on the trot to the toilet. God, it's a raw physical world over there all right.

Mrs. Connolly, with the youngest class, is there, dark and intense. She takes everything to heart. She always gives you the impression she's just on the edge of a breakdown, one push and she's over. She's English and she married a Catholic, not realizing what a mixed marriage means here. She's never forgiven anything or anyone for her mistake. I must admit she terrifies *me*, too bloody brittle by far.

Mrs. Reid, on the other hand, who takes the next couple of classes, is about the same age as Matchett, same hypocritical old school too, and smiles all the time. Her nickname is 'Smiling Through'. She sits at her desk knitting woollies for her grandchildren while her class parrot 'Two and two make four', or the alphabet or 'The Cat is on the mat', all day. She scorns Madge Connolly's modern methods of teaching next door. You can see the undisguised contempt on her face as poor Madge staggers in of a morning loaded with fir-cones or empty cocoa-tins or spools or jam-jars.

Then one classroom further up is Primrose Bultitude – Cleanliness Is Next To Godliness Bultitude. God help any poor kid who skitters on *her* floor. She wears a fresh blue nylon overall every day of the week and she's something called Froebel-trained. I don't know much about her teaching because she guards her methods jealously. Her kids are all cowed, scrubbed and terribly nice. You can't tell the little boys from the little girls because they're always bringing in posies of wild flowers or skipping or playing shop in the playground. Everybody's 'nice' in Miss Bultitude's world; nothing 'nasty' is ever allowed to enter. I don't think she likes me much. Not since the day in the staff-room when I foolishly made some crack about the well-known money-making propensities of the Plyms . . .

McKittrick was chewing his pencil now, so I said, *Oh what the hell*, and started down towards him. The usual full whiff of stale lunch sandwiches and sweaty feet and unwashed bodies met me. As I passed Muriel Cuddy, our glamour girl, waves of cheap perfume dulled the smells around for a moment. She was wearing an almost transparent blouse with a low square neck-line and her skirt was one of those short tubular affairs that pull the knees together and shoot out the buttocks. As she leaned forward, the black straps of her bra could be seen clearly through the thin blouse cutting into her flesh. I restrained an impulse to put a not-so-fatherly hand on her shoulder and stare down her fantastic cleavage, while inquiring innocently if she was having any difficulty.

I walked quickly on and shoved McKittrick over in his desk with a dunt of my backside and edged in beside him. 'Well?' I said quietly. He silently pointed to the first sum, the only one on his blank jotter page. The fool had been sitting there staring at it instead of going on with the next one. I said, 'Well?' again and he jabbed his pencil-point at the smudged pence to pounds calculation on the first pale-blue line. I repeated. 'Well?' for the third time and the pencil shakily formed a 20 underneath and drew a line.

'What is the sum?' I whispered.

'Pence to pounds.'

'Well then?'

'You multiply by twenty to change the pounds into shillings . . .'

'Do you? *Really?*'

He looked at me and I noticed the soft fair bristles on his skin. He had been trying out his da's razor. 'It's the other way about, isn't it?'

'It is.'

He stared at the paper again until I said impatiently, 'Well get on with it then,' and needlessly his pencil tore and scratched at what he had written until it was obliterated.

I waited until he had started afresh. Then I stared out of the window, over the flat green felt roof of the opposite block up to the bare black trees on the other side of the road until the swept blue sky with its fast-moving blobs of cloud halted my gaze.

A well-scrubbed sort of a day with the country roads bone-hard. I thought of the town spread out in the drying air, tight and close around the junction of the Dargan River and the main Belfast–Derry road and then loosening and shaking itself out like bright confetti into the green fields. The railway skirts the energetic centre of population and separates also Protestants from Catholics. Out on *their* side on the Dublin Road (the name lingers from the time when that city was the navel of this whole island) is their Chapel, black and manifest and, close to it, St. Brigid's, our counterpart. Its architecture, like all Catholic schools, has that certain grey stone solidity, verging on the monastic, that emphasizes the bond between their education and their religion. Our schools on the other hand have no fixed character. Annagh Primary is simply a flat, low E-shaped structure of glass, brick and speckled-green felt; it could easily have come out an outsize filling-station and no one would have been any the wiser.

I began to think about Catholics, not about Catholics I know because I don't really know any, but about them in general. Anything I found out about them has been second-hand, because, living in a community like this, one where the

104

proportions are seventy-five for us, twenty-five for *them* (an inflammable mixture) division starts early – separate housing estates, then separate schools, separate jobs, separate dances, separate pubs ... a people with a past and no interest in the present, because they have been frog-marched back to that past so often that they have long ago given up any claims to right now. A musical, entertaining people (like the Jews) with no neurosis about cleanliness or material wealth ... I envy them their calm, inner knowledge of what they are, who they are and where they come from, but not their degrading, daily struggle to keep dignity in a country dedicated to keeping *them* 'in their place'.

Then my thoughts veered back to Mona. I would wait until I had a chance to look closely at her in the morning. In a silly way I was certain I could penetrate with a glance to the secret core of her regard for me ...

Rising through my thoughts was a persistingly growing outside irritation which should no longer be ignored. I opened the visor of my clasped fingers and realized that most of the class had finished the work on the blackboard and were watching me. 'Right!' I said, rising to my feet, and the H.B. pencils clattered into the grooves beside the ink-wells. 'Betty Duffin – number one.'

I forced myself to appear interested in the results. I even had McKittrick out to the board to demonstrate one of the ones he had left undone but all the time I knew this was one of those days when no progress would be or could be made. Some consolidation maybe, but nothing new.

Clapping my hands for silence, I continued the mood I felt I had introduced at the start of the morning – one of new beginnings, a fresh page to be turned. 'Now listen to me,' I said, 'I've not been happy for some time about the seating arrangements, so we're going to switch around a bit.'

The people in the back seats looked alarmed. Some of them, I knew, had spent weeks manoeuvring themselves into those coveted, safe positions outside the radius of my power or in beside bright sparks who were either willing to pass answers across or who could be easily persuaded to co-operate. The bright sparks tried to look apathetic. They couldn't afford to show pleasure for they knew that retaliation would be swift.

Several aggrieved, 'Och, sirs', came from the back row. Ignoring these, I said, 'All out to the front row. And bring your bags with you.'

Bull Ramsay kicked Sloan Ritchie, his seat mate, under the desk, but I pretended I hadn't seen it. I wasn't sure of Ramsay. He was big and surly and his da was supposed to be a terror who bashed teachers who laid hands on *his* family. *Never fear*, I thought to myself, *there are other more subtle methods of reprisal, you big overgrown potential shit-shoveller you*.

When they were all lined up at the front, the boys swinging their hams of hands self-consciously and the girls giggling, I sat on my table with my feet on my chair and considered. I started off with the extremes. Ramsay in the desk immediately in front of me and Sally Beggs in the far back at the window. It became harder as I reached the no-man's land in the middle row where the extremes blurred. But at last it was finished, just as the clock on the wall said it was time for morning break.

Milk was handed out and straws from the Education Committee's grey cardboard cartons laid on each desk, and I went over to the window and looked out until the last gurgle and suck sounded behind me. A clatter of hob-nailers on the floor and the room was empty – except for me and the forty vacant desks.

It was as if all the life-blood had pumped out into the play-ground and I was left with a carcase only distended with slow chalk dust-dropping air. The noise from the playground seemed distant, foreign. I looked around me at the dull walls with their pinned rows and squares of lino-cuts and poster paintings of circuses and snowmen and bonfires. Only last week's had any life left in them. A fortnight and they recede into the wall, dust-covered and dead. Everything you do is like that. Dying in a week, dead in a month. I'd been trying for a month now to stop them using the word television for television *set*. I know it's ridiculous. No one else seems to worry about it, but that's not the point. The point is that I haven't succeeded. They keep on saying, 'We've got a tele-vision at home,' or 'Our television has a twenty-one inch screen.' I wonder am I getting a complex about it?

The door opened and Ernie Matchett poked his head in.

'Good,' he said, 'I see you're free.' I smiled and waited for him to come to the point. 'Two things, Frank,' he said briskly, rubbing his knuckles. He closed the door behind him and I saw his eyes taking in the work on the blackboard. It would be just like him to deliver a little two-minute lecturette on the importance of neat blackboard work, but he resisted it and sat on the edge of my table. I faced him. I hadn't risen from my seat on the low broad window-ledge. At one time I would have stood up when he came into the room; now I just can't be bothered.

'A new boy. I want you to take him into your class, Frank.'

I realized he was expecting some reaction, possibly a hostile one, for he knew my class was overloaded as it was. But it didn't seem to matter one way or the other, the way I was feeling, so I smiled again and said, 'Oh?' He resumed gratefully, 'Yes, Frank, I've tried him out with Todd but he's too far advanced for P.7 You'll help him along for the first few weeks or so until he gets into the swing of things? He's from some wee country school up in the hills. Oh, and by the way, he's the son of – uh, the M.P, Bradley.'

He lowered his voice for the last few words, miming them, to impress me with the importance of my new pupil.

'Yes,' I said, casually, 'he mentioned something about it to me not so long ago.'

'You *know* him?' He was impressed.

'I *met* him. Yes. He told me all about the kid. Warren, that's his name, isn't it?'

'Yes, it is.' He looked like an incredulous and slightly disappointed quiz-show host whose victim had just answered the jackpot question without going through the preliminaries.

He was absent-mindedly half-way to the door before he realized there was something else. He turned and faced me, and I could see that this time he was not going to be denied his long lead up to the subject, the leisurely meat of the text, followed by the slow summing-up. Nearly all his statements are built like that.

'Frank,' he began thoughtfully, taking off his glasses, and his pale naked eyes leapt at me. 'Frank, I never asked you this before, but have you ever thought about your future career in teaching?' (*Christ*, I thought, *redundancy! But it couldn't be me. Todd was here last, and last in, first out, that's the rule.*)

'You're twenty-six now?'

'Twenty-four,' I corrected.

'Twenty-four. No matter. It's not old, but still in this game it's about time you started thinking about the years ahead. Obviously you're not going to be an assistant all your life. But getting back to the age business, uh, well *I* had my first school at nineteen. Granted it wasn't much.' (*Yeah,* I thought, *one room about the size of my book-store and a communal earth closet at the bottom of the yard.*) 'But in the County – I started off in Monaghan, you know—' I tried to look amazed but abandoned it. *Oh, dear God, would the little lay-abouts never come in from their break!* – 'it was something of a record, yes, and the fact that I had been a *monitor*' (he kept flicking out keywords for my reaction like a lion-tamer with a whip, but I was too tired now for a performance. I just smiled. My face was beginning to hurt) 'well, added to the achievement. What I mean to say is, Frank, uh, never get the impression that a principal doesn't take an interest in his staff. I know there are some who don't care but I'm afraid I'm not just made that way' (oh God, he was properly lost now. How would he get back to the beginning?). 'Frank, as I'm sure you know I'll be retiring at the end of May. That's what I wanted to talk to you about' (at last! But why? I asked myself). 'I wanted to talk to you about the vacancy – the principalship.' He smiled at my look of amazement. 'Surely now, Frank,' he chided, 'you don't expect me to believe you've never considered having a shot at it.'

'No, I didn't,' and it was the truth too.

'Frank, Frank, son, if you don't push yourself nobody else will.'

'Mr. Matchett,' I said, 'what chance would *I* have?'

It sounded coy but I didn't mean it that way. 'You'd be surprised. I'll tell you one thing. Warwick thinks you a threat to *his* chances, anyway.' He nodded. 'Yes, I know that for a fact.'

I looked at him as he swung his old man's grey tweed-covered leg from the edge of my table. He was smiling paternally and for the first time I didn't find it irritating. I'd misjudged him. It was a new experience for me to accept

108

what he'd said on face value alone, without any rapid double-think. I was going to ask him why he preferred me in the job to Warwick, because that was obvious, otherwise he wouldn't have left me in the dark, but I decided not to put him into an embarrassing position. Still marvelling at my sudden change of feeling towards him, I said, 'But leaving Warwick out of it, surely there'll be plenty of outside applications from people, well, with degrees?'

'I'm sure there will. But Frank, this is a tight clannish wee town as you know. You can take it from me that the local committee will only put a man first on the short list if they know him and respect him and have some idea of what he can do.' I felt like laughing. That was me ruled out on all three counts.

'Well, if that's the case,' I said, shifting my weight on the window ledge, 'Warwick's home and dry.'

Matchett looked at me with a gleam in his eye. 'What makes you think he's so popular about the town?'

He was enjoying himself, and, for the first time I began to realize just what his motives in all this might be; a case of the dead hand changing the course of future events? Warwick had probably shown his hidden contempt too early as Matchett's retirement loomed, and he, Matchett, had decided to spoke his wheel for him.

It was accidental that I came to be involved. Naturally my feelings towards Matchett began to lose some of their warmth as these thoughts raced through my head ...

'I lived here for twenty years, Frank; I know the people. When I came here first I made it my business to get to know them. It took some time. Take a word of advice. Use your head as I did. Join the golf-club and *meet* people, the *right* people. Any drinking you have to do, do it there; no one carries tales from *there*. Take a Sunday School class. Have a word with the Reverend Forsythe and offer your services to the Boys' Brigade. Get on to the town's third rugby team. Get *involved* with things ...' He saw the smile on my face and misunderstood. 'I know, I know, but do you think I *enjoyed* doing it?'

What I was really smiling at was the thought that not one item on his list had anything to do with teaching or life inside those walls.

109

The door opened and the class began to file in, abating their noise only slightly because they have no respect for Matchett. I could see them looking curiously at the two of us. They were 'smelling' things again.

Matchett got off the table and stood stiffly behind my chair until all the desks were full. Then, in an unnecessarily harsh voice, he barked, 'Settle down. *Quickly!*' and glanced down at the class. He waited until there was quietness. Then he looked at me with a look that said – *That's how it should be done, young fella.* I was torn between a desire to laugh at his pathetic bluff or to be angry at his attempt to lower me in front of my mob. But it was one of those times when tiredness with other people and their complicated motives had conquered.

Still wearing his 'stern' face, he turned to leave, having successfully quelled another potentially dangerous blackboard jungle incident. God's curse on his twisted old soul, he couldn't resist it, for when he got to the door he said loudly, staring pointedly at the sum on the board which McKittrick had been covering with twisted little aids to his counting processes, 'Oh, Mr. Glass, might I suggest that these people in P.8 are much too old to be writing down their carrying numbers. Even Miss Bultitude's babies have left *that* behind.' He closed the door quietly, almost tenderly, behind him and I noticed that Bothwell was smiling to himself.

TWO

LUNCH-TIME. It was my turn to patrol the echoing Assembly Hall, weaving my way at a slow pace among the maze of lino-topped trestle tables. The noise of cutlery and incessant talk was rising to its climax and, in proportion, the women-servers' faces at the hatch seemed to be getting redder and hotter. A few yards removed from the children's tables was the teachers' table and I could see my colleagues eating their Irish stew. I wasn't in any great hurry to join them because any appetite I had was taken away by repeated exposure to the smell of the food and the eating habits of my charges. For the second time I had asked a red-haired boy from Todd's class was he practising sword-swallowing and the sycophantic laughter of the rest of the table had followed me on my tour.

The floor-to-ceiling windows on the right-hand side of the hall were beginning to steam up so I told the red-head to open a top window or two. Then I changed my mind and told him to get on with his dinner, I would do it myself. The long green cord felt impossibly thin against my palms as I pulled and the row of hopper windows opened smoothly. Rubbing a hole in the steam I looked out and saw that Dr. McRory's gardener was digging over the potato patch at the back of the house.

My eyes travelled hopefully up to one particular window where I had once seen the Doctor's wife undressing one day last summer, but the curtains were pulled. She drinks like a fish and her lipstick is laid on in a crude straight line across her mouth. She had been swaying that day behind the glass and it had been like a laboured strip-tease in slow motion. When she had her waist-slip up over her head she had fallen and I thought the show was over but she climbed back up again and I watched with cold flesh and sweating palms as she took everything off. Then, after she posed for a moment or two, just as if she'd known I was watching, she moved off sideways. I couldn't do a tap of work all the rest of the afternoon. Since that day, when I see her in the town, I stare yearningly at her across the street, hoping that, miraculously, she will return my hot gaze and then, after momentary consideration, beckon to me with a moving vermilion fingernail, and we'll go off in her station-wagon Mini back to that room at the top of the house and then I'll draw the curtains and then we'll ...

'Please, sir, please, sir, can I leave the room, sir, I'm not feeling too well, sir.'

The voice cracked the idyll into small pieces. I looked down at the white, wedge-shaped perspiring face, then propelled him on his way and with the sex feeling still on me I crossed to the teachers' table and sat down.

There was a space beside Pat Ferris and as I dropped breezily into it I put my hand on her big fleshy thigh saying,

111

'And how's Pat, eh?' and then squeezing.

I wondered what it would be like with her. The way I was feeling just then I could have faced her with hungry relish, fat and all as she was. She's an amazing sight in the playground in her tight white shorts and man's outsize tee shirt and her lanyarded whistle bouncing between her mammoth breasts. I've noticed that when she's out there, racing with her class until all her exposed flesh turns maroon with effort, something happens to my boys' bladders. I suspect that they hang about the toilets watching fascinatedly the extravagant way she flings her surplus flesh about.

'The best, Frank, the very best,' she answered heartily and giggled as I gave another squeeze. I pressed her suspender button in until I had a horrible picture of it sinking further and further into the yielding quagmire flesh until it disappeared from view. That's what would happen to me too, I thought ... Sunk without a trace. I smiled at a yarn that came into my mind and Pat whispered, 'Share it.'

'Too dirty – even for you,' I whispered back and she dug me playfully in the ribs.

At the head of the table Warwick was gargling silently from his glass of water which is set before him reverently every lunch-time; he looks after his teeth. The birth-mark on his left cheek seemed to have got smaller somehow. I noticed him watching us and I thought of what old Matchett had confided to me earlier. Could this man in the neat, blue pinhead suit with its pocket full of pens, and the R.A.F. tie and the hard white unmalleable collar fear *my* influence?

Facing me, dark intense little Mrs. Connolly suddenly said, 'Mr. Glass, do you believe in astrology?' I halted my loaded fork in mid-air. 'We've been having an argument about it. Mr. Warwick, Mr. Todd and Mrs. Reid think it's all nonsense, and Miss Ferris and Miss McCurdy aren't sure. I'd be interested to hear what you think.'

They were all watching me and there were two red areas of colour on her sallow cheeks. I had to be careful. I have this ridiculous fear of her, I don't know why, and I keep on her right side whenever I can.

'Well, you know, there might be something to it,' I compromised. 'Some very famous people swear by it. So I've heard.' Her face relaxed and I realized I'd fallen on the

112

right side of *her* fence at any rate. Warwick sniffed and looked away, Mrs. Reid's knitting-needles resumed work (I do believe that bloody woman knits when she's in the lavatory), the student blushed, Todd dug his spoon into his triple helping of cabinet pudding and Pat nodded her head encouragingly. I gave her leg another quick squeeze under the table. 'What started this off?' I inquired innocently.

Mrs. Connolly snapped open her handbag belligerently and unfolded what looked like the middle pages – probably a supplement – of a woman's magazine. 'What is your sign, Mr. Glass?' she said, very business-like. Her voice had taken on a curious lilt. For the first time I recognized it as Welsh.

'Scorpio, I think,' I said.

The student came alive at the end of the table. 'Mine is too!' she cried and I smiled at her with one of my intense looks I'm always practising on women across streets. It seemed to affect her – perhaps it was the close range – for she dropped her darkened eyelashes and reddened. Todd looked up from his plate and stared at her speculatively with his little eyes – food and sex, his twin preoccupations.

Warwick sniffed derisively and pulled out his folded copy of the *Times Educational Supplement* which he keeps in his inside pocket for after-lunch reading. He never wastes a minute of his precious time. If he's not improving his bloody mind he's doing press-ups in the staff-room. His life is run by mottoes. Now it was 'Waste not, want not'.

I said, 'Mr. Warwick, what's your sign?'

He looked at me with contempt. 'I wouldn't know, Mr. Glass,' and fluffed out his newspaper.

I looked around the table for support but no one seemed interested. Then, 'When is your birthday?' I blurted.

He looked at me this time as though I had asked to see his private parts. 'October the third,' he grunted.

Mrs. Connolly read in a quiet voice, 'Libra – the sign of the Scales gives you the most refined sense of balance, harmony and justice. You take a detached view of things, and are the least involved in and committed to the world around you, although you understand it so well. Yours is the most sensitive nervous system, the lightest step and gayest personality. You're most easily distressed with the pressures of modern life and bear its crowds, noise and speed only at the cost of great inner tension. You should take more physical exercise to balance your intense mental activity and build yourself up to protect your over-sensitiveness.'

Over-sensitive? I wanted to shriek in the silence that followed, and roll over and over on the floor in the grip of uncontrollable laughter. Astrology – balls! He sat there at the head of the table looking at his paper and smiling to himself. 'Smiling Through' was smirking too. She's a fan of his. Everyone else seemed to be thinking about what they'd just heard and marvelling. Their straight thoughtful faces and silence maddened me. I searched each pair of eyes for the faintest flicker of lurking laughter but there was nothing. *What was wrong with me?* Hardly knowing what I was doing, I squeezed Pat's thigh viciously. She gave a sort of squeal which changed into 'Whea-at – what about my sign, please, Madge?' All the eyes turned on her big open honest-to-goodness face. She blushed and said, 'My sign is ... Virgo.' I gave a great burst of laughter and Pat looked as though I had slapped her. Scrambling out of my place, I muttered something about looking after the top tables who had finished their dinner, and nearly tripped getting my foot over the top of the form.

THREE

AFTER lunch, the long slow afternoon dragged itself on and on. My heavy meal had made me drowsy, and I kept having to get up from my table and stride briskly about the overheated room to shake off my doziness.

The class were painting. My three choices of subject were on the blackboard. *Space-flight, A Spring Walk* (that was for the girls and Bruce Sherlock) and *My Wildest Dream*. I thought the last would be flexible enough for even the grousers who are never content with what I give them and who always say that they can't possibly paint about *any* of the subjects. But someone said he wanted to paint a stage hold-up because he could only draw horses, and by the time I'd explained that he always could imagine himself as the hold-up man or even the shot-gun guard or driver and then that would be *his* Wildest Dream I was tired and cross.

As I was patiently explaining this, someone whispered, 'Maverick', in the back row. I heard it quite distinctly but I pretended to ignore it and the ensuing soft explosion of laughter. From then onwards the formerly docile class seemed to change itself into a treacherous and surly mob. They had sensed my mood and had reacted automatically. If I can explain it this way, it's like bouncing light waves off some heavy implacable mass way out in Space which has no life or emotions of its own but only comes to life when you send out to it. Sometimes freakish things happen in the intervening space – your signal can come back weakened or re-doubled in strength. This was one of those times when the return was double the output.

It was like a nervous chain reaction. Paint-pots spilled, people who usually enjoyed painting began to lose interest and doodle listlessly, smirks settled on the faces of the dangerous ones and the nipping and pinching of the girls began under the desks. As my prowling up and down became more and more feline and intense the atmosphere of the room kept pace. Some of the stupider ones began taking risks as the strain increased. The clever ones expertly gauged their latitude and watched delightedly as their sillier class-mates went too close to the bars.

Bruce Sherlock was the first to be mauled. His giggling at one stage shot hysterically above the hum in the classroom and, when he saw me looking at him, he hid something quickly below the desk. I was going to ignore him but his coy look enraged me. Strolling casually down I fixed my benign gaze on him so that when his ear suddenly felt my finger and thumb he yelped, and rose, with head to one side, as I pulled. A chorus of disapproval boiled up and my face felt hot. The girls' eyes flashed at my cruelty as I stared coldly, incredulously around. My anger at *them* streamed out through my grip and Sherlock began to whine. 'Well, Bruce,' I said, 'I'm glad you're enjoying yourself. I like to see my people happy at their work.' I half-hoped for a giggle from the class but they were silent.

'Let's see what you've got below the desk, Bruce,' I said,

115

releasing his ear so that he fell into his seat sobbing.

I didn't know what to expect. It might be a nude pin-up and then how could I carry off the situation? My fingers touched a sheet of paper, an exercise-book page and I withdrew it. It looked blank until I turned it over. On the other side was a pencil drawing of two facing figures, male and female, unclothed. Both had pronounced sex organs; the male, particularly, had the usual disproportionate penis. There was an unfinished caption below the figure's feet. Under the male was printed MAVERICK (the same block capitals as Bothwell had erased from the blackboard that morning) then AND and under the female an M. The artist hadn't had time to finish the last word. I crumpled the drawing and put it into my pocket.

I walked around the room pretending interest in the carefully coloured-in pencilled outlines of space-ships and galleons and toffee-apple trees and clouds. Each shoulder stiffened as I bent over it and Bruce Sherlock's sobs followed me reproachfully. I reached Ramsay. As I glanced down at his mean effort I saw the resemblance between his pipe-cleaner figures and the two on the paper I had balled up in my grasp.

'Winston,' I said gently, 'have you been drawing on exercise-book pages?'

He dug his pencil point into his sheet of sugar paper and muttered something. It sounded like, 'Don't be daft.'

My anger had been rising steadily because I was now sure he was the one who had written the message on the blackboard, but his heavy sullen power and the thought of his father checked me. His ears glistened with brilliantine and I felt I must grip one of them. The muffled sobbing behind me and the class's watchfulness were reminders of my duty. I must be fair at all costs. Children have a sense of fairness to the point of neurosis. I, as an adult, have to play their game, although it seemed at times the other way round.

'Winston,' I repeated, praying for some miracle that would save the situation, 'Winston, you didn't answer me.'

He showed his teeth and gave a long drawn-out, 'Aaaach.'

I drew my hand back and hit him with the flat of it across his broad hairless neck. It was a beautifully satisfying blow and he fell out into the aisle. He lay looking up at me, his

116

eyes blank with shock, and I moved quickly, threateningly to stand over him. Silently I dared him to get up and see what else I would give him. I got as close to him as I could because I knew if I drew back to allow him up he would let fly with his heavy hob-nailed boots. With one part of my mind I was conscious of the comedy in our attitudes as I followed him on his scrambling, creeping course up the aisle, almost stepping on him, but the other part screamed out in gigantic flashing capitals the consequences.

He managed finally to pull himself to his feet and, knowing it would have to come, I stepped back. His mouth was wet and ugly and his eyes stayed fixed on my feet as if he feared my using them. Low enough for just me to hear, all the four-letter words I've ever heard or seen written up on lavatory walls dribbled from him in a steady stream. We stared at one another like two enemies, trapped and facing each other in a pipe, and only one way – forward, but I didn't want to make the first move. As the seconds screamed I prayed he would act; even if he kicked, it would solve my problem because I could follow up *his* move. If he didn't and we stayed frozen like that the class would soon begin to titter and he would join in and I would be defeated utterly by the rising wave of derision.

Finally in desperation, I said, 'Well?' It sounded like the croak of a dying duck. I kept on repeating meaninglessly, 'Well? Well? *Well?*' at him and moved closer each time. When he broke I was unprepared, for his eyes hadn't moved from my feet. He jumped back with a clatter and snarled, 'I'm goin' to get me da for you. I'll bring him up. He'll *do* you!' He was near to tears and I felt shocked at his weakening. Then he ran for the door and its slamming sounded very loud in the quiet room. The class stared back at me with white faces as I fought to control my inward shaking.

'Well,' I said, 'that's that. Now get back to your work, and finish off. You know how long it takes us to get cleared up after painting.'

They began to whisper to each other but, ignoring it, I sat down at my table. Good God Almighty, now I was for it! I was scared of two things and I didn't know which was worse – Ramsay's tough of a father or the legal consequences if I had injured his son in some way. *Never hit them on the face*

117

or head, Matchett warns like some wily police chief briefing his rubber-hose squad, *especially if they wear glasses, and the hands are bad too if you leave welts. Grab them by the hair if you have to. Personally, of course, I'm against all forms of corporal punishment. It's not worth it.* I tried to recapture the feel of the blow. It had knocked him out of the seat and there was a dull red mark still on the back of his neck as he'd slammed out. Every hair-raising story I'd ever read in the papers or heard of damages against negligent or brutal teachers streamed across the surface of my mind like an unbroken ticker-tape. A voice at my elbow crimped the flow. 'Can I lift the paints and the brushes now, sir?'

It was Bothwell and his voice sounded friendly and normal. That was a shock. He was looking at me with his round brown eyes in that intense way of his, as if, with a glance, he could pierce through to what I was thinking.

I looked up at the clock. It was three minutes to three. It would take at least five minutes to store away all the drawings and water and poster paints and the thirty-eight squirrel-hair brushes.

He must have thought my glance at the clock signified something else for he lowered his voice and said, 'Ramsay's daddy's out of work, Mr. Glass. He'll be up after school, so he will.'

I looked at him and felt warm love for the small neat figure in the wind-cheater and jeans. He would never grow much bigger and I could imagine him as a dapper little adult wielding the same power, as he did here, over his pals in the factory or shop where he would most certainly end up, and he would always be conscious of his difference to those around him because of his quickness and wit. It must take a life-time of teaching to produce a single prime minister or even someone who will eventually finish up with a bigger salary than your own. So far I've only produced a generation of whistling message boys whom I keep seeing down the town on their carrier bikes. They always grin sheepishly when they see me, as if it's not their fault that all those essays about *'What I want to be when I grow up'* have turned out to be a joke on soft old Mr. Glass.

As Bothwell and his picked crew of helpers bustled around I decided that I must get away before the bell went. *But how?*

118

I asked myself, as the red hand jerked. A minute to go.

I could just see young Ramsay racing home, building up a story as he went, even managing a show of tears for his old man's benefit. And *he* would be buckling on his brass-studded belt just about now, spitting on his calloused palms and screwing his cap on to the back of his greasy head. He would have one of those hawker's handkerchiefs round his thick neck too. It was no time to worry about losing face before the class (God knows I'd done enough of that for one day) so I beckoned to Bothwell and took him to one side. 'Look, Eric,' I said, keeping my eyes well away from him. 'I have to go off early today.'

'Yes, Mr. Glass, I understand.'

His voice was soft and sympathetic like a tolerant doctor's whom you've just told you've caught V.D. If he'd called me 'old chap' I don't think it would have thrown me. In one of those rare moments of honesty between teacher and pupils, I added, looking at him straight, 'Eric, you know why, don't you?'

He nodded when I looked at him. 'Aye, I do, Mr. Glass. I know why.' Then, 'He'll forget all about it, don't you worry.'

'Would you—?' I began.

'Yes,' he said, 'I'll see that the room's tidied up. And – the next six problems on reduction of money for homework?'

I nodded, feeling something suspiciously like a lump in my throat.

The bells sounded in the building behind me as I reached the parked cars. They stood lined up on a square of tarmac about fifty yards away from the main entrance doors of the school. They were pointed at the second set of gates where tradesmen's vans entered. I looked over my shoulder at the bunch of waiting parents with prams outside the glass doors. Ramsay wasn't to be seen.

The starter rattled and I twitched guiltily at the racket and gave another quick glance backwards. Ramsay was coming through the gates half-pulling a tall thin man by a corner of his stained trench-coat. The man looked pale and sickly and his shoulders were dropped forward as the cold easterly wind and his son propelled him down towards the waiting crowd on the concrete steps.

119

I nursed the car out between Matchett's new Renault and Todd's red M.G. and up to the gates. It stalled noisily with the bonnet a foot outside the pillars. Jerking knobs on the dash as if it were the keyboard of a Wurlitzer, I twisted my head round and saw young Ramsay pointing. He began pulling the man in the trench coat again, this time along the narrow path below Matchett's office window leading to the car-park. They reached the cars and came up the smooth molten-looking black slope towards me. Helplessly I watched them in the mirror. I was a blind organist now, but no re-assuring music came from the engine.

The man in the trench coat didn't look dangerous – I could see him clearly; he looked as though he was recovering from a bad illness. He looked tired as he allowed himself to be dragged along by the loose end of his flapping coat.

Remembering something that Walter had once told me about clearing a flooded carburettor, I stamped the accelerator down and, praying, I gently pulled the black knob marked *S*. The car began to vibrate, so hard, that it was seconds before I realized my prayer had been answered. Then I slipped in the clutch and the car flew out into the road. Only a desperate jerk at the wheel saved me from certain death against the facing brick wall, and it wasn't until I braked at Gregg's Corner with the bonnet edging into the High Street afternoon traffic flow that I knew who and where I was.

Three high diesel-driven lorries piled high with Lough Neagh sand for Belfast building sites slowly passed and in the passenger seat of the second I saw Teresa Mallon from our Row. She was hitching lifts again. If her father found out that was how she travelled home from St. Brigid's he would break her back. She had no idea that anyone was observing her. I felt an odd sensation watching her, so unguarded, as she laughed brazenly across at the lorry driver. She was wearing a pale pink lipstick and a head-scarf in an attempt to make herself look older and wickeder. It was obvious where she was going to end up – in some home for Catholic Girls In Need Of Care. Poor Teresa, she never wore knickers until the age of ten, and the boys would look up her clothes every chance they got. 'Any hairs on it yet, Teresa?' they would cry and then some one of them would call out, 'More hair on a

120

gooseberry,' and they would all laugh as she tore past in a fury . . .

I slipped the car into a slot in the traffic behind the lorry and its exhaust fumes quickly seeped in through my open window. Behind was a long congealing column. At this time of the day it was always bad.

On the opposite side of the street two men were unloading sand from a parked tractor and trailer. They were shovelling it over the low Methodist Church wall on to a mounting pile. The sand was damp and each shovelful held its shape as it flew through the air. Their rhythm was soothing and the driver of the Vauxhall behind sounded his horn impatiently when the space between the lorry's tailboard and my bonnet began to widen. I jerked past the man in the white coat with the board who stops the traffic when the school-children reach the street. He touched his peaked cap and I knew he was wondering why young Mr. Glass was so early the day.

The pavements had the usual complement of harassed women shoppers with string bags and trailing children, red-necked farmers in for the day and single policemen, bus conductors and one or two off-duty Air Force men from the nearby Base. Everyone moved briskly because of the cold needling wind.

It was one of those days when my heart bled for the three poor buggers of salesmen who stamp their feet on the concrete floor of Pollock's Car Sales across the street.

In the Market Square on the low parapet around Annagh's single statue – a 1914–18 heroic lance-corporal with braced puttees, jabbing bayonet and one artistically torn shoulder strap – were two red-headed tinker children. Their feet swung in front of the legend IN MEMORY OF OUR GLORIOUS DEAD. They didn't look all that awed by the bronze ferocity poised above their heads. They were trying to light a butt on a pin. One of them had on a pair of women's flat-heeled shoes. *God help the poor wee gets, weather like this*, I thought, as the blue of the sky on the other side of the windscreen lightened to an even colder, steelier tone.

The wind was sucking papers out of the litter-baskets fastened to the meshed guards round the thin trees in the Square.

FOUR

I LIFTED the latch on the back door and walked into our small kitchen-scullery affair where my mother does the cooking.

'You're early the day,' she said.

She was standing in the corner pressing glacé cherries on to the tops of a trayful of buns. A baking smell hung heavy.

'Now leave them alone,' she said, as I stretched out a plundering hand, 'they're only out of the oven,' but she let me break the neat pattern on the tin tray. Juggling the hot bun from hand to hand I went into the living-room.

I didn't know what to do with myself. It's the same every day. Those three hours of extra time after school check the day's free-running flow, yet, God knows, I should be used to it by now. Three hours a day, fifteen hours a week, more than a month out of the twelve wasted, idled away, dozed away usually on the sofa in the parlour with the blinds drawn until life picks up again with Walter and the old fella coming in from their 'hard day's work' at six.

'Frank,' came my mother's voice from the scullery. I sat where I was, staring at a copy of *Motor Sport* Walter had left, ignoring her.

'Frank,' it came again as before, an exact disinterested echo.

I gritted my teeth. It always maddened me that trick of hers. She never would say straight out what she wanted; just kept calling until *you* went to *her*. She wouldn't win this time.

But in spite of myself I found I was waiting for her next call. The pause stretched like elastic, then it was me who snapped and I yelled, 'Well, what is it – *What is it?*'

She came out of the kitchen with dough all over her hands and wide innocent eyes. 'Frank, son, there's no need to shout.'

I flicked the glossy pages and the new models whipped past angrily.

'Frank, I want you to – now, don't look like that. Why is it that you're so disobliging? I don't understand you. What good does it do you? You'll never get through this world like that.'

She was driving me to whimpering impatience. Her slow soft voice piled on the agony. 'What is it you want?' I said as quietly as I could.

'That's better. Why couldn't you have spoken to your mother like that at the beginning?'

Standing there before her I felt like a sea-wall taking impassively all the waves pouring on, over and around it. I waited for a lull.

'Your father left his pills behind him when he was here for his dinner. I want you to take them up to him at the Works.'

'Pills? What pills? I didn't know he had to take *pills*!'

She pointed to her apron pocket. 'My hands are all dough.'

I slipped my hand into her warm pocket. The pills in the amber bottle were little navy ones. The label gave nothing away, just *One to be taken four times a day after food*.

'Mammy,' I said, 'is he any better?'

She began to cry gently, without passion. I looked at her, despising myself. She had been carrying her worry around with her like a weight on her back. It was there in the morning when she turned her head and saw him lying beside her in the bed and it was there last thing at night too. But I had forgotten after the first shock of the news had died in me. Remembering how I had felt then was like remembering an old toothache – the experience being rubbed away to almost nothing so that I knew I would be just as unprepared if it came gnawing again. And who had I suffered for? Him? No. I had suffered for myself, anticipating *my* anguish when I might have to watch him in agony. Christ but it's difficult to be really *honest*! One hundred per cent honest. Maybe it's impossible. Could be . . .

'Take them up to him,' she said and she had stopped crying as quietly as she had begun. 'I'll put a wee bit of brown paper round the bottle so that he won't know I've told you. He made me promise not to tell you or Walter or Jennifer.'

*   *   *

The wind was colder, more insistently probing now, as I stepped out, closing our front door behind me. I began to pick my steps. About twice a year a dozen or so lorry loads of brittle grey clinker (they look like the sweepings from some lunar landscape) are carelessly slopped down and left like

123

that to be flattened by weather and our feet as best they can. Nobody gives a damn any more about Kildargan. It's an embarrassment, an eyesore. What they would really like to do with it would be to advance a battalion of bulldozers on the place and raze it to the ground, or, better still, push it all into the fast, obliterating river. *They*, I suppose, are Annagh Rural Council and any of the other embarrassed influential types living around us and looking down into our damp hollow with their noses between finger and thumb. I never really think about them much – they're just *them* to me.

All around me as I crunched towards the Works were the signs of Kildargan's declining years – the missing slates, the starred panes, the rust, the rot, the swinging doors on sheds and warehouses that once were needed.

I crossed the dead parade-ground area where lorries used to turn. Three or four bicycles lay against the mill wall.

The building towered above me, cutting out the light. It is four storeys high and as long as the Row but wider. Its walls are of the same brick and its ugly windows are framed by squares of grey stone. On the blue slates of the roof once had been painted in enormous white letters SPENCE SPINNING COMPANY. During the air-raids, men on ladders tried unsuccessfully to scrub it out. From a distance it looks like a great stranded upturned liner. Nothing will ever right that leviathan.

I went over to an arched door near the piled bicycles and the latch felt greasy under my thumb. I pushed and the noise rolled out thickly, enveloping me like a bag dropping over my head. I marvelled that walls could contain such power. They should be bulging rhythmically with the heart-beat of the great beast within. Now I knew why my father had to have the volume on the television up to an unbearable pitch.

All over the room before me great vertical wooden beetles rose and fell thunderously, like organ pipes in motion, on to revolving rollers. The linen jerked tauty on to the rollers, and under the cascading blows. I remember what these monsters used to look like to us boys at the week-ends when we gaped through the dirty panes. Then they were poised dangerously still, blunt stalactites, some a bare fraction of an inch from the rollers, others drawn up to their full apex and the rest somewhere in between, but never two of them together. It was the multiformity that thrilled us most, I remember.

As I hesitated on the steps a bent old fella passed directly in front of me with a dripping oil-can in his hand. I pushed on over the brink and the noise foamed up around me. I felt I would never get it out of my clothes, that it would cling there, spoiling them the way smoke from a paraffin stove does for a very long time.

Catching up on the old lad as he was sighting his oil-can quiveringly at the insides of a churning machine, I shouted in his ear, 'Tom Glass!' He ignored me. I shouted louder, '*Tom Glass! Where is he?*'

He turned and put his hand to his ear. I repeated it again for him, exaggeratedly mouthing the words. A tiny flicker appeared in his eyes, a million light years away it seemed, and he pointed. I saluted, smiling at him as if he were a foreigner who knew no English.

Traversing the oily passage between the thudding rows was like walking a tight-rope. I felt that one inch to either side would edge me eventually under those terrible clubs. I walked until I came up against the end wall.

It was of flaky whitewash and covered with scraps of pencil-written words, sentences and drawings. The words were the familiar ones and the drawings were of the inevitable female shape – fat cello bodies with two dotted circles and the great scribbled crotch. I stood in front of this record of God knows how many workers' lusts and I wondered if my father had ever written anything there. That scrawled wall made me realize that I was in a world where he spent half his life yet I hadn't entered it to that moment.

The feeling of being a stranger and intruder was strengthened a minute later when I came upon my father. He sat on a bench pushed close to the rest of the wall I had been staring at and in his hand was a chipped brown mug. There were four other men with him, sipping their tea and eating their thick sandwiches slowly, meditatively, the way such men do. One of them looked up and saw me. He nudged my father who stood up swiftly. I saw concern on his face and embarrassment.

'What's wrong, Frank?' he said. 'Is your Mammy all right?' He had to shout to make himself heard. At the same time he didn't want the men on the bench to overhear. That's where the embarrassment came in.

'You forgot these,' I called out, reaching out the tiny parcel to him.

He took it and felt the outlines of the bottle through the paper. Then, quickly, angrily, he pushed it into his overall pocket. 'She needn't have bothered. It's all right.'

I yelled, 'She was worried about you,' and watched his face. He moved his head jerkily from side to side and muttered something I couldn't hear. He kept his eyes away from mine.

The men on the bench were watching me curiously. They had their caps off and their hair was clapped sweatily into their skulls. I couldn't get over how old they were. My father must have been the youngest there, except for the one at the end who would have been about my age and who looked not quite right in the head. They all had a derelict air about them. They looked as if they had been working there for years and years for no other reason than that no one had ever told them to stop. For the first time I really understood why the mill *must* close down, why it was useless for this ludicrous garrison of old done men to continue holding on.

It was a miracle that it hadn't happened yet, and two months had slipped past since Bradley had first told me that all was going to fall under the auctioneer's hammer. But the place still shook and rumbled from nine until six and my father still went out each morning and returned each night.

'Are there only *six* of you?' I yelled. He shook his head and pointed upwards. I waited but he didn't explain.

I looked at his thin face and the few wisps of grey hair plastered across the dome of his skull. There is a bump on the top like an egg trying to push its way out through the skin. His hands look too large and heavy for his meagre body. When he strips you realize how disproportionate his body is; his forearms have a Popeye look about them. They have been developed at the expense of the rest of him.

I blurted out, 'Are you all right?' and his eyes narrowed.

'What do you mean?' I cursed myself.

'Oh – nothin',' I stammered, 'I just wondered if there was anythin' you wanted me to tell Mammy, that's all.'

The suspicion disappeared from his eyes. He shook his head, waiting for me to go and leave him with his little forgotten band, his tiny brigade. He might even *like* it here, I thought; *his* castle, *his* fortress. I had forced my way in here.

126

I wasn't welcome. Visitors from the outside – the *real* world – weren't welcome here. I took a last look around me, at the rearing, plunging beetles, the peeling smoked walls, the greasy flagstones and the piles of oily waste lying in the corners and walked away.

When the outside door closed behind me and I stood in the open air the song of a solitary bird somewhere, anywhere, seemed the cleanest, clearest sound I'd ever heard.

SUMMER

ONE

THE last day of June – the last day of school. Standing waiting in the Queen's Arcade looking into a shop-window, a tobacconist, the rows of shiny briars and cartridge-cased havanas staring back and the Belfast shopping crowds rushing untiringly past.

The Queen's Arcade, know it? Mona had nodded quickly in the school corridor and I said in a rush, *Four o'clock then,* and walked on, for I had seen Warwick watching us from his classroom door.

I looked at my watch again. Eight minutes past. And no sign of her. Christ, why hadn't I said which end? My God, and I hadn't said which one! I just wasn't any good at this sort of thing.

Reluctantly I began to saunter back to the Austin Reed end. There were a couple of workmen down there slung up under the arched roof fixing a broken pane, and I had caught one of them nudging his mate and pointing down at me as I was shaking my watch and holding it anxiously to my ear.

A broad country woman in the wrong sort of coat for her figure, it was checked brown and white like a tubular tweed draughts-board, suddenly backed out of a hat shop across my path. She had two big parcels under each arm and she looked like a panniered donkey. She should have had on the old-fashioned black they wear still, day in, day out, all seasons, women like her. Black against whitewashed walls, with King Billy or Robert Emmett staring down. Black figure in Irish interior – after Goya . . .

I wonder why you keep me waiting, Charrr-maine, Charrr-maine, the clever glazier boyo sang above my head as I pretended interest in a marked-down overcoat.

Where the hell *was* she? Maybe she couldn't make it. It would be just like the thing after all the elaborate plans I had

128

made. I felt the bundle of strange keys in my pocket. She *had* to come. I had plotted this for a full week, dammit. It was to be the end of all the hole-in-the-corner snatched meetings we'd been having ever since I had balled up courage one day, after the blackboard incident, to squeeze out, when we were alone in Matchett's office, 'What about coming out with me some of these nights?' and after I had waited with a sickly sheep's grin for a count of ten inside my head, she'd said, 'Okay', and smiled over the carriage of her typewriter at me.

We'd met many times since that. In the back seat of my car, in Matchett's dark office twice when she'd been 'working' late, once in the back seat of *her* car, the night Jack was at the Round Table (I should have felt the stirrings of something masculine and mean at that but I hadn't) but always – *Duck your head quick, there's a car coming! We can't, Frank, somebody might come. Be careful! I can't! Pll-ease, Frank! Don't!* but there would be no excuses today – if they were excuses and not just the caution of a married woman. I put my hand into my other pocket and felt through its cellophane the imprint of the rubbery ring. A piece of putty fell near my foot. I moved away and the voice above yodelled, *I wonder where blue birds are mating, Charrr-maine, Charr-maine, Charr-maine.* Silly tit!

My view back along the Arcade was marred by hurrying people. I had forgotten how much of a bottle-neck this place could be in the afternoon. Someone touched me and I saw Mona's reflection beside mine.

'Where are we going?' she asked as I took her arm gently above the elbow and steered her carefully up the Arcade.

We stepped out of the cool tunnel at the far end into the blare of the sun, exhaust fumes and hot pavements.

The June heatwave was in full course and people were violently reacting all around to its implacable ferocity. The men raced resentfully past, their dark suits just that shade not lightweight enough, enraged at the thought of others on cool green links. And the women strolled easily, their faces smiling sleepily in shadow under pale wide hat-brims, enjoying the undress the weather permitted and the rousing sensual heat on bare limbs. I thought of the senior girls who were out on the grass after lunch. They all wore tight little shorts and when they sat down in squadron on the turf and I moved amongst

9   129

them their legs seemed to widen like petals opening to the sun. I thought of those little areas of delicate darkening disappearing skin where their shorts tightened into a vee over their fat beautiful little mounds and my hand moved quickly to take up a position of security in my trouser pocket ...

'Where – are – we – going?' We had reached the car. She knew it so well by now. I smiled mysteriously and held a finger to my lips. 'Get in, lady, and ask no questions,' and the first hint of a smile thawed her pale face.

'Frank?'

I knew I couldn't keep it from her any longer but I couldn't tell her point-blank what I had planned, for it would sound horrible there in the street. 'I'll tell you when we get there. It's a surprise. You'll see.' I smiled at her. 'Now be patient. Leave it in my hands.'

'Will I like the surprise?'

She was like a child. I patted one of her prim little white gloves. 'Baby must be patient.' She snatched her hand away in a mock tantrum and we laughed together. I was glad. She'd keep a mood going if she felt like it, I'd found that out, could stretch it on and on endlessly. The last one had been about a week ago. I remembered the black stillness that had suddenly seemed to settle on her when we were embracing in my car. She'd turned to ice in an instant. Stupidly I had gone on caressing her with edging, progressing fingers as if I hadn't noticed. What I should have done was driven her straight home. I knew this with half of my mind, the other half, the greedy half, was interested only in extending the graph of bodily exploration. And the graph had not reached a zenith yet. I was irked by a feeling that it should. Today was to be the day when the line would soar straight, true and triumphantly to the top.

'I hope nobody saw us back there in the Arcade,' she said.

The car had finally broken clear of the traffic and was speeding past a tiny park where old men and women from a nearby Home sat brooding on benches.

'Oh, I don't think so, Mona,' I said.

She laughed at my solicitude. 'You're keeping in with me today. You must be looking for something.'

I glanced at her. 'Maybe I am.'

She blushed and dropped her eyes to her gloves in her lap.

I felt a nibble of desire. A good omen. How easily and naturally we were sitting side by side, almost like a married couple out for the day. You could grow fat on this. I felt flattered, even a little incredulous, that she still seemed to find me so attractive. I certainly wasn't going to waste it. And as well, there's never a fair balance, I'd discovered; one always feels and suffers more than the other, and this time *my* name had come out of the hat first . . .

'Frank, I meant to ask you, have you heard any more news about the post?'

Now it was my turn to grin, at *her* sudden change of topic.

'I thought you knew.'

'Knew what?'

'I'm second on the short list.'

'Oh, Frank, but that's *wonderful*!'

'Not really, you know. Warwick's first. He'll walk it.'

'Oh you're so easy-going I could kick you. Really.'

I laughed. 'Well, I suppose it would be nice if I did land it. You could always be my secretary.'

With a faint blush she said, 'I don't think there'd be much work done,' and then, 'Oh, Frank Glass, you're hopeless – as lazy as you're long!'

Her unconscious wifely tone warmed me and I had one of those dangerously sentimental moments when the thought of marriage and all that slippers-by-the-fire cosiness seemed very, very attractive. Like what Jack has, I reflected. I played silently for a moment as we drove with the idea of the ambitious but affectionate wife pushing easy-going me. It was pleasant. I found it so. Another man might not find it that way, but I did.

I wouldn't have given Matchett's job, for instance, another thought after he'd mentioned it to me if it hadn't been for the new experience of hearing outsiders supporting my claim and, strangest of all, seeming to actively *care* about my chances.

The staff had split into two factions, one supporting me and the other Warwick. It was embarrassing and flattering at the same time. Of course the flattery had worn thin since then for I had quickly realized what their support really meant. I was now certain Matchett was out to balk Warwick because of some real or imagined slight and poor old Hettie Morton,

131

who would gladly crawl on her knees a mile to do Matchett a bad turn, was also on my side because she imagined Matchett was rooting for Warwick. That was a laugh.

'What's the joke?'

'Oh, I'm just thinkin' of the whole rat-race I've let myself in for. My god, the dirt! I mean I haven't really put myself out at all yet but already Warwick and me – we're like a couple of rival M.P.s before an election. You know, kissin' all the ugly babies and tellin' their fond mums how bonny they are. And makin' promises. Knowin' full well that if we *do* get in it'll be kiss-my-arse to the lot of them.'

'Charming,' she said and laughed.

'Well you know what I mean,' I said.

She slipped off one of her gloves and I felt her small warm hand exploring affectionately in my pocket. 'Frank, you're only a baby. You *have* to do these things. *Everybody* has to do them. If you want to get on, that is. This sort of thing is nothing to what Jack had to do to get *his* job. He hated being nice to people he couldn't stand too. But it had to be done. If *you* don't do it someone else will.'

The mention of Jack seemed to lower the temperature in the car. It was like that framed text that old Curry has in his shop in great staring gold letters about 'The Unseen Guest at the Head of Every Table'. We drove on in silence. I noticed Mona quietly withdrew her hand but I passed no comment. I began to worry again about my plan. Keep her in the right mood, I prayed . . .

We were threading our way through the quiet streets at the back of the University. Every turn, every cobbled back entry, every emasculated knobbly tree, I knew as well as I knew Kildargan. My three years at Training College had left me with the memories of daily, but usually night forays into this square mile of red brick Victoriana which in four generations had see-sawed from comfortable good-toned respectability to seedy anonymity.

We drove along past the borders of The Holy Land, past Palestine Street, Jerusalem Street, Damascus Street, Cairo Street. We passed a gable-end on which was scrawled in faded white paint 'TO HELL WITH THE POPE'. The letters had dripped like action painting. It would be lovingly re-painted when the Twelfth of July came round. God knows how many thicknesses of paint there were. Oh yes, we are a great crowd for writing on walls. Our national bloody pastime. Back at Kildargan, for instance, some religious fanatic had just nailed up tin squares on all the lovely old beeches as you come into the straight stretch at the bridge, all with the same message in black letters 'THE WAGES OF SIN IS DEATH'.

They appeared just after Tojo McBride's suicide. Poor bastard, nobody'll ever know what made him string himself up from his light fixture, but I blame people, people in general, around our way. It only leaked out afterwards how he'd been treated just before his case was to come up at Annagh. He was discovered gently swinging that Sunday morning, the Sunday morning I'd come home in Jack Purdy's car. *Then,* as I'd come up the Backs, I remembered, I'd noticed something behind his back bedroom blind. Since then I had been obsessed with the thought that if I'd stopped then to investigate he might still be alive. And then I think – *but would I have been doing him a favour?*

'You're very talkative today, aren't you, Frank?' I laughed weakly and was grateful when she didn't press the point.

We drove on. We crossed the Ormeau Bridge, over the scummy, black water with two swans breasting the thin waves and waited at the traffic lights at the Embankment end.

I found it hard to make conversation. I'd think of something to say and then crush it back when it echoed tritely in my head. She'd already decided that my silences were due to shyness, a melancholy, on my part. I had an idea too she felt sorry for me, seeing me as a lonely one.

We were getting near the area where the house was. Mona looked at me curiously but didn't say anything when I slackened speed and began peering out at the names of roads and avenues. This part of town was unfamiliar to me. 'Situated in a select and secluded residential sector convenient to buses, schools and shops,' was how the estate agents had described the big old detached stucco house I was looking for. The snooty office-girl in the blue nylon overall had handed me a closely typewritten foolscap sheet of particulars of the property and the keys which were now in my pocket. I dropped the sheet of paper without reading it in the first litter basket I passed. Something of the elation I'd felt when the idea and then the plan first came to me, reappeared (I'd been sitting in

133

the staff lavatory at the time as a matter of fact and I couldn't stop myself laughing). I found myself chuckling again. It was like a wonderful joke you can't keep to yourself. Mona was smiling too and staring straight ahead at the clipped privet streaming past. Good girl, *bloody* good girl!

'Was that Dunstable Drive we just passed, love?' It was a stupid question for she wasn't looking out for anything.

She laughed out loud. 'I've no idea, you nut.'

I giggled with her. We were like two kids. It was a lovely friendly moment, a rare moment, in our relationship, for we had never been *friends* before. She leaned over as close to me as she could from the other bucket seat. 'Nut,' she whispered and her dark springy hair touched my cheek. I took my hand off the gear lever knob and put it on her knee. She closed her eyes as I squeezed gently.

I wanted to yell aloud with anticipation. Who the hell cared now about all those frustrated manoeuvres in the back seat of the car, all the territories my fingers had reached and then found freshly fortified against my advances the next night we met. This, today, was going to be the triumphal, unopposed entry into the beleaguered city. Already I could feel the rose-petals falling on my victor's face as I marched through the gates, and the garland around my neck and the welcoming cries of the young maidens ringing in my ears ...

Half-way down the quiet avenue of large old houses I had turned into, a 'For Sale' sign showed between two sycamores. We had arrived. The tyres rubbed softly alongside the kerb and I kept my eyes straight ahead.

'Who lives here, Frank? Do I know them?' She was looking around her with curiosity at the other houses.

'Out,' I said briskly. Should I bring my old raincoat with me from the back seat? I decided against it. Might introduce a sordid element. Carefully I locked the doors. She was waiting for me a few steps away, facing across the road. I said, 'After you,' and opened the gate. I pretended to look surprised at her surprise when it came as if what I was doing was the most perfectly natural thing for two people to do on a June afternoon in Belfast in a quiet suburban avenue.

'Well?' I said. 'What's wrong?'

I would wait until realization came to her, unaided by me. It was part of the game, because it had become a game, with rules being invented as it went along and the rules had to be observed.

Slowly she walked through the gate and I let it snap back on its spring. 'I didn't know you were interested in property,' she said quietly. There was irony in her voice. But she still hadn't realized.

The house looked shabbier than the photograph in the estate agent's window which had first decided me; there were green streaks under the gutters and the paint on the front door was blistered in bubbles. The nearest house was screened by a sagging garden shed and a piece of incongruously new rustic fencing. The garden was a wilderness.

'Needs a lot of work done to it, Frank.'

I smiled and picked out the Yale from my bunch. There was a smell of damp and decay when the door opened. Inside was dark-brown painted walls and ceiling and four faded circulars lying on the mat. The bare grey stairs went up straight ahead.

'After you,' I said, and she hesitated a second before stepping in.

I began to close the door. It stuck the last inch. Her eyes seemed to be boring into my back as I shoved. The door crashed shut with a bang that shook the house. Something dropped to the floor and broke in one of the upstairs rooms. I felt a right fool and coughed nervously. That made two explosions.

Mona still hadn't spoken. Her bottom lip was trembling. My God it suddenly struck me! *She was frightened*. 'Och, love,' I said, and moved towards her, my consoling arms outstretched.

She backed away. *She backed away!* I couldn't believe it.

'What's wrong? What is it?' I said, stopping in my tracks.

Good God, this was becoming a bout of blind man's buff. She had her back against the meter cupboard under the stairs.

'Frank, why did you bring me here?' she whispered. Her voice *proved* she was frightened.

I felt like saying, 'To do you in, my darling, what else?' following it up with a blood-curdling laugh, but thought better of it.

Trust my luck. I ought to have known something like this

135

would happen. It was always the same. You built something up, a plan, a scheme, or you over-anticipated something that was going to happen, and every damn time it went wrong in that it rained or somebody died or you had mumps or you were stood up – but why go on?

'Mona, pet,' I wheedled. 'Come here and don't be the silly wee girl. Now catch yourself on.'

But words were no good. They were treacherous things. They could be read a hundred different ways. Wasn't that why I had kept quiet so long? I had the idea that if I could once touch her, hold her, communication would be possible and so around the musty hall we circled like two dancers in some complex figure. All the time I was saying things like, 'Mona, have sense' – 'Mona, what is it?' – 'Mona, you *know* I won't hurt you.' That last time I sounded like a vampire soft-soaping his helpless victim-to-be.

I suppose, in a way, it was funny. If I'd seen the exact same situation in a film I would have laughed but, like the old banana skin routine, when you're directly involved it isn't funny at all.

Of course we couldn't go on with it indefinitely. I made a final desperate lunge for contact which I suppose must have looked very comical indeed if someone had been watching for I kept a sweetly affectionate smile on my face all the time I was doing it. She gave a sort of frenzied leap out of the way and then collapsed on the floor nursing her ankle. She started to cry. Her hair hung round her face and I suddenly noticed how fat and white her fingers were as they massaged the sprain. Her skirt had lifted above her knees and I could see the dark tan band at the top of her stocking and the pale flesh stretching away – but it didn't seem to matter now.

Quite suddenly I hated her. She was perverse and stupid and I never would understand how her mind worked. I hated her for not feeling the way I felt and not participating equally in my glorious plan. She was dull, common-place – worst of all like all bloody women, she had no imagination. I wouldn't explain now why I'd brought her here. I'd leave her little mind to do what it would with the situation. *I just wouldn't bloody well please her!*

She moaned loudly and I began to help her up. Looking up at me with hurt liquid eyes, she said, 'Oh, Frank, why did you

136

do it? I trusted you. I did.' And then the crowning indignity. 'I thought you were different.' Oh God, give me strength, I prayed, making for the door. *I thought you were different, too, but you're like every other bloody woman I have ever met . . .*

About a month ago on television there was a play about a couple of people, a man and a woman having one of those depressing English love affairs, completely joyless and routine, like putting the cat out each night. He was a drip but she was my ideal – warm, generous, experienced, sensual. The play revolved around them not being able to get a place where they could make love. They met in places like the Birds' and Reptiles Section of the British Museum and talked in whispers round the glass cases about had any of them any luck in the way of a flat yet or the flat of a friend? Naturally when they did get a room with a bed in it (the Museum Attendant's, by the way) they couldn't do it. I saw it a mile away. It must have been that play that started the idea off first in my head. Mona and I were the couple, their problem was ours, we were as desperate as they were (so *I* thought anyway). And then the idea, beautiful in its simplicity. All over the city hundreds of empty houses for sale, their keys to be had merely by walking into an estate agent's and asking for permission to view. An hour of love under a roof and safe, *safe!* – Heaven! I could think of nothing else. I saw us in a series of little domestic vignettes laughing together as we went through the property columns of the newspaper, choosing our next house – our next neighbourhood. I even saw me buying an inflatable air-bed. All shattered. But now I felt sick, sad, lonely. Would I never find a woman to match my dreams? Did such a woman or women *exist*?

I helped Mona down the path and the afternoon was dying already. Yelling children were coming home from school, a Corporation dust-cart rattled past with three men sitting thoughtfully on the tailboard and wheeling clouds of starlings were staining the darkening sky.

Driving back into the centre of the city we didn't speak or look at one another. We could have been on opposite sides of a glass partition. I let her get out at the bus-station. She said, ' 'Bye, Frank,' opened the door and was out on the pavement before I could think of anything to say. I was grateful. I saw her in the driving mirror for a second or two as I drove off. She was buying an evening *Belfast Telegraph* from a paper-boy. Then she disappeared ...

Round Smithfield Square I let the car take its course until a parking space opposite a second-hand clothes dealer's offered itself. I backed into it, got out, locked the doors, checked them and saw that she had left one of her gloves behind. It lay on the floor, small, white and pathetic, to remind me. She couldn't make the break clean, she had to leave something of herself behind, I thought. I knew it was unreasonable for she was always dropping something in the car, she couldn't help it – hairpins and clips by the dozen, single ear-rings, scarves, litter from her handbag, balled up Kleenex; but I pampered the feeling, let it grow to luxuriance. It swept away the first footholds of guilty conscience.

With an inch to my step I strode off purposefully through the crowds of workers rushing to catch an early bus home to the country. I was to meet Terry in Mooney's. It was all arranged. And the sooner I had a drink – many drinks – to wash the taste out of my mouth the better ...

TWO

THE illuminated dial of the big Guinness clock high above Castle Junction seemed to quiver gently before my eyes. I put it down to the soft fine rain that was falling all over the city, cooling and slaking. It was the rain ... nothing else.

'A Scotch mist,' I announced loudly and Terry giggled.

'You're drunk, Glass, so you are,' he said. We were standing in the doorway of a confectioner's shop waiting for Wilbur Todd who was buying cigarettes. We had come across him at the third pub in our crawl and he had seen us before we had seen him and now we couldn't get rid of him.

'Is he buyin' the bloody shop or what?' I growled. My feet were beginning to get sore with tramping. Terry giggled again. He was 'happy'. He was wearing a new camel-hair coat with a half-belt and a purple Paisley scarf and his hair had a moulded wet look like a tight black bathing-cap.

The shop door clicked and Todd came out. 'Well, chaps,' he roared, clapping our shoulders. 'Where's our next port of call? Eh? Any suggestions?'

I resented the easy way he had inserted himself into our company. And he was getting noisy too. That was the pattern of his drunkenness. I had seen his type before, loud-mouthed and fight-picking. He drew attention in every bar. He craved it, talking loudly to barmen, chaffing complete strangers and shouting his and our business at the top of his voice. He needed watching for I knew he would have us in a fight before the night was out if we weren't careful. Over his sports-jacket he was wearing a light-blue quilted anorak which drew glances. It was part of his 'outdoor man-of-sport' act – that and a short bristly haircut and the rugger club oaths. As a matter of fact, he had come up to town specially to buy him-self a new pair of expensive boots. He had left them in his car ...

Terry said, 'I know an interesting little place,' looking his wickedest. His cheeks seemed even more sunken than usual and his eyes had a feverish gleam in them. I hoped he wasn't going to say or do anything indiscreet in front of Todd.

'Good old Terry, lead us to it and maybe there'll be a bit of jiggedy-jig available. The old staff of life is in great shape. Ready to rise to the occasion. Eh? Ready to rise to the occasion, eh? Ha ha ha!'

Terry looked at me with a mischievous look and, when Todd turned away for a moment overcome at his own wit, he pressed a gloved finger and thumb to his nose.

'I'm sure there will be, Wilbur,' he said softly. Todd snick-ered loudly and we moved on.

There weren't many people about, just a few couples star-ing mournfully into the lighted store windows. The centre of the city was dead at this hour; all the nine to five-thirty life drained out of it to the suburbs and housing estates. All that remained were the jerking neon signs nervously covering up the emptiness. We crossed several streets until we were be-neath the leaning Albert Clock, then over cobbles, down al-most to the water's edge. A cross-Channel boat was in, its

139

funnel above the sheds and strings of lights like Christmas-
tree decorations looped from bow to stern. It was at the
Glasgow shed. People were standing about in clumps beside
suitcases and taxis were arriving. The atmosphere reached
out to me. I'm always affected the same way, at airports too.
Something makes me want to join the queue. I've only been
out of Ireland once and that was with First Kildargan Scout
Troop to Berwick-on-Tweed so you can see I haven't given
way to the feeling much . . .

*   *   *

Terry's bar was down a side street which smelt of grain and
animal foods – the cracks between the cobbles were choked
with the grey stuff. It seemed to be the only building that
wasn't a warehouse and from the outside it looked exactly
like a backstreet betting shop. There was a diagonal crack in
the frosted glass door and over our heads as we paused was
the usual indecipherable ribbon of print about so-and-so
being licensed to sell Spirits, Tobacco and Wine on or off the
premises, that was all, no sign outside, not even the owner's
name.

Terry led the way, with a wink to us over his shoulder. He
seemed to disappear straight into a red murk, which came
from maroon walls and ceiling and low-powered wall-lights.
There seemed to be a lot of people all sitting with their backs
to the walls and their drinks on low tables before them. I
noticed several sailors. It struck me as unusually crowded for
a Wednesday night. The three of us stood just inside the door
blinking short-sightedly. The only vacant seats were at the
bar. The whole row was empty. That struck me as strange
because a lot of men prefer to sit at a bar. The second odd
thing was the way we were stared at. It's normal to find
yourself being looked up and down when you first come into
a crowded pub – a natural reaction is for everyone to look
up when the door opens – you expect it, but when it goes
on for longer than usual, it bothers you. I felt as if my fly
were open or I had a rub of soot across my face. I was glad
to get on to a stool and turn my back on the eyes.

The barmaid came towards us from the cash register where
she had been talking to a little man in a Robin Hood hat. She
was fat and in her forties and I guessed by her approach that

140

she was wearing plimsolls several sizes too large on her bare feet.

'Well, Beatrice, darling, an' how's the oul' feet?' Terry greeted her.

Todd and I smiled in anticipation of an impending bout of friendly banter in which we wouldn't join but in which we would share nevertheless.

'Killin',' grunted Beatrice. Her face hung fat and immobile. Only her lips moved. 'I'm gettin' too oul' for this caper. A wumman like me should have her feet up at my time of day. But wi' himself upstairs there what can you do – the bloody *waster*!'

The last word shot out like a mouthful of foul-tasting medicine. I felt the spray on my face.

'Two Haigs and a pernod, love,' said Terry as she moved muttering over to the bottles like some vast fleshly science-fiction thing.

'Poor Beatrice,' he confided to us in a quiet tone, 'fourteen bambinos and a layabout for a husband. All he does all day is study form and place his bet and at night straddle her. Doesn't know contraceptives have been invented yet.'

'Ah, but if they are Catholics,' whispered Wilbur, and I'd never seen him so serious the whole night, 'they're not allowed to use them, you know. It's laid down.'

'You don't say, Wilbur,' said Terry and I knew he was having him on. 'Begod I never knew that.' He turned to me. 'Did you know that, Frankie?'

'No I did not,' I said and Todd looked pleased. When the drinks arrived he said loudly, 'This is my round. It's on me,' and slapped a pound note down to stick on the damp counter although Terry or I hadn't made any move in the direction of our pockets.

I watched Terry as he poured water from a jug into his glass. The milky explosion still fascinated me even after the half dozen or so times I'd seen it that evening. He'd let me try a sip earlier and I'd exclaimed aloud at the unexpected taste. It was made for him, nothing surer. I couldn't imagine him ever going back to gin and tonic after being introduced to such a decadent brew.

By this time I'd had a goodish look at most of the people in the place, using the long, discoloured mirror behind the bar.

141

We were still getting stared at and once or twice when my eyes encountered another pair in the mirror they would slide guiltily away. I still couldn't place the bar in a proper classification for it wasn't the typical tough public type with a predominant navvy, docker or tradesmen clientele, neither was it the upstairs lounge type with self-conscious spruced-up couples out for the night. It seemed a mixture of both, or rather, the customers were; teds, ratings and labourers in clean blue serge donkey jackets with leatherette shoulders sat beside quietly dressed middle-aged men and a lot of thinnish younger men who looked like clerks or shop assistants.

Two men got up and, after draining their glasses, made for the door. The one who led the way was short, broad-shouldered, coarse-faced and had an incongruous pencilled-in moustache far above his upper lip. It gave him the look of a vintage George Raft trigger man, an effect of which he was obviously unaware. His eyes were slightly glassy and as he rolled past our stools he gave the impression of rough embarrassment, which drink had failed to cover. Everyone in the place stared at him openly and several were grinning and nudging. Some secret was in the air.

I happened to glance at Terry and discovered the same conspiratorial smirk on his face. He had switched his attention to the man's companion who had stopped on his way out at one of the tables and was saying something to the couple of sharp-faced types behind it that was sending them into peals of high-pitched nervous laughter. Bending languidly over the table he was over six feet and thin as bamboo. He looked about our age, maybe younger, and he was wearing a leather flying jacket over a white cotton polo-neck sweater and on his legs were skin-tight washed-out jeans. Completing the effect, and it was obviously a highly studied one, were black high-heeled cowboy boots with silver stars. His hair was blond, so harshly glaring in the dim light that it looked like the hair in the negative of a photograph, a bright helmet enclosing a dark face. As he passed us he raised his dark glasses momentarily an inch with finger and thumb and grimaced at Terry who smiled, and said out of the corner of his mouth, 'Rather you than me, old thing.' The tall thin buck's cold eyes flickered as he replied, 'We can't all have your luck tonight, darling.' The tiny encounter lasted only seconds and was over

142

so quickly that I wasn't sure I had heard correctly. Glances and words had darted between them like flying splinters and the tall blond had barely shortened his stride.

I was still thinking about it when Terry said, 'Let's grab their seats,' and we moved, with glasses in hand, to the red imitation-leather banquette running the length of the wall. It was a relief to have a solid wall at one's back instead of eyes, eyes, eyes ... I drained my glass with a smack of the lips and set it down noisily on the wet formica hoping they would quickly follow suit and then we would move on to a brighter, less sinister bar, because the atmosphere of the place was beginning to tell on me. Everyone seemed to be waiting for something to happen and their impatience could almost be felt. I said, 'Look, why don't we move on? This place gives me the bloody creeps.'

Terry said, 'Sure it's nearly half-nine. We would only be in and out again. Relax, Frank, relax. Anyway you don't want to move, do you, Wilbur?' knowing full well that he didn't, oh no, for he had been staring at a couple of tarty-looking birds at a corner table for the last five minutes. They were the only women in the place. Todd reluctantly unfastened his hot gaze from the two 'pros' – that's what they looked like anyway – and said, 'I'm okay, chaps. I could sit here all night, I really could.'

'Good,' said Terry very cheerfully. 'And it's my round, so that's that settled.'

I shot him a look of hatred and, as Todd's eyes slid back to the corner table like two beads on a wire, he stooped and whispered, 'Stick around and see the fun. I thought you were the fella who had a "scientific curiosity".' I laughed into his face at his cheek, throwing back at me my phrase, and he straightened, pleased with himself.

While he was at the bar my mind quietly worked over what he had said. An idea grew out of the rakings, an idea which had presented itself to me before that evening but which I had dismissed as being just my imagination.

Terry set the drinks down with a flourish and said solemnly, 'May you live as long as you want to and may you want to as long as you live.'

Todd laughed over-loudly at that, hoping perhaps to attract the attention, even at that range, of the two in the corner who

143

had the typical cold hard lack of interest in their surroundings stamped on their faces that all such women have. Put into words the look says – *Run away, little boy, and play with your rattley*. It's their only protection in the most vulnerable of professions . . .

These great thoughts were rolling slow and oilily through my head and I knew there would be others equally as wise and Confucian to follow for the drink had just then unlocked the door of that inner chamber where life becomes clear, clean-cut and obvious. I was the cool one, the detached smiling one, looking down on my fellow creatures in almost fatherly wisdom.

Terry drew his head back so that it lay on the padded rest on the wall close beside mine and whispered, 'Your man's wastin' his time with those two bags,' with a tiny nod in Todd's direction.

I smiled blandly, too contented to ask for further explanation. What he'd just whispered seemed perfectly complete and reasonable in itself.

'Aye,' he went on, laughing, 'there's nothin' doin' there. Not tonight or any night.'

Slowly out of the warm luxuriant mists in my brain there grew an uncomfortable awakening interest.

'Why?' I whispered, 'do you know them?'

He laughed soundlessly. 'The Dolly Sisters? *Everybody* knows them. They've been comin' in here from the year of dot.'

'They don't look like sisters,' I said.

Terry's breath escaped with a hiss that I thought Todd would hear. 'Christ!' he said pityingly, 'but you've led the sheltered life.'

That idea that I'd dismissed earlier rose up and suddenly smacked me in the eye. I twisted my head around until I was staring from two inches into his black mocking pupils. 'This place—?'

'Of course, dopey. *You mean you didn't know?*' Dumbly I shook my head. 'Well now that you *do* know,' he whispered, 'sit back and watch the fun and games.' I jerked my head questioningly in the direction of Todd who was still squinting manfully through the smoke haze at the two in the corner. 'Green as grass. What do *you* think?'

He was right of course. Todd wouldn't have believed it even if we told him. After all, it had taken Terry to spell it out for me and *I* had known about such places; God knows, Terry had talked about them often enough and at such length that I usually had to tell him to give it a rest, calling him an obsessed old sex mechanic. Sitting there quietly with my glass in my hand I let all the pieces fall into place. The big question mark that had hung over everything – the customers and their eyes, and the two men who'd walked out and the words of the tall blond one and, above all, the 'feel' of the place – as I say, the question mark blew away like mist before the wind.

Taking Terry's advice, I sat back and prepared to watch the fun and games. And it was amazing, now that I was in on it, now that I knew what to look for, how much there was to see. I began to enjoy the game, from the touch-line, for unlike the customers, I wasn't hunting or being hunted. That tall, almost elegant type in the houndstooth check and suede desert boots further up, for instance, to my right was obviously a hunter. His prey sat beside him. He was a small fair-haired, cheap looking youth in a blazer with a club badge. I noticed the way the hunter held his gaze while he talked quietly, intensely, without gestures of any sort. At first the other tried to assert, if that's the word, what little personality he had. I could see him wave a pale thin hand nervously in the air, brush back the longish hair at the sides of his head convulsively with both hands, laugh aloud even, but gradually be stilled under the other's dominance. Finally turning up his glass the tall one stood up and marched out. His companion meekly trotted after him.

There was a titter at my elbow and, when I turned instinctively, a man of about forty with tight black curly hair and wearing a loose blue and white Fair Isle sweater stared back at me provocatively. I looked at him, stupid a moment from the directness of his gaze, and his two companions further up the seat leaned foward and grinned across at me too. For a moment I had a nightmarish vision of a chain reaction setting in along the row, of faces all dropping rhythmically forward in succession and smirking brazenly down at me.

I jerked my head round. Terry was killing himself, the bastard. 'I'll not let them touch you,' he giggled and then, before I could stop him, he leaned across me and said to the one who'd stared, 'Phil Boyle, I'm surprised at you ... frightening my friend here. I'll have you know he's a nice innocent young lad, so he is ... like myself ... you know, just up from the country.' The three to my right giggled and I grinned weakly into the bottom of my glass. Embarrassment rolled over me in fast hot waves. Terry's long pale inquisitor's face hung mockingly forward. He was getting drunk.

'Frank, darling, I want you to meet three *very* good friends of mine,' he said. 'Phil Boyle, Bernard Duckworth and Dermot Fox.' He winked. 'All bitter Papishes, the lot of them, but there's no segregation in Beatrice's.' The trio laughed, but not, I noticed, self-consciously, as normal Catholics would have done. 'This is Frank Glass, and don't you be lookin' like that, Bernie, you bad thing you, Frank and me's just good friends, aren't we, Frankie?'

I gave him a look that should have bored a neat scorched hole between his eyes but he clasped my hand to him and continued gaily, 'Isn't he a good-lookin' chap, eh? Look at those big brown eyes, eh? Bedroom eyes, *eh*?'

'Och, you're only embarrassin' him, Terry, so you are,' said the one furthest away. He had combed his thin mousy hair forward in one of those Roman haircuts and, like the one beside me, he too had on a brightly patterned sweater which looked silly on a man even when indoors. Bernie in the middle was the only fat one in the trio and his all-enveloping dirty showerproof had not the over-neat, over-washed appearance of his friends' clothes.

When all the cracks about me and my looks had died down Terry and the three of them started talking shop among themselves as if I had disappeared. Once or twice I found myself gasping at some of the things they were saying, and which must have travelled outside our immediate group. It was part of that same irresponsibility that Terry showed at times – capricious, fickle, giddy – nothing masculine or mannish in it. It struck me that Terry was not to be trusted – he wasn't dangerous, no, just not to be relied upon. Dermot, the thin one with the Roman hair-style, was having them in stitches with his telling of his adventures on the previous night. 'A ship in from Hamburg,' he was fluting, 'and the place was comin' down with big blond sailors. They wouldn't let me leave –

146

not that I had any intention of goin' – without singin'. It was awful, so it was. One of them with a whole lot of gold braid and, full as a lord too, lifted me up on to the bar. Strong as a bull he was. Oh I didn't know where to look, honestly. It was all a good laugh though. I didn't mind, and after a wee while the big tall one, he said he was an officer and, mind you, he spoke English as well as you or me – I tell you what he looked like, you know that German film star – what's-his-name? – Kurt Jurgens – him – the very one – well, he kept on buyin' me drinks till I had to tell him to stop it or I'd be footless ...'

Here, unaccountably he stopped, as if the story had come to a natural close, until Terry and the other two shrieked, 'Well, what happened next?' They didn't actually *shriek* but that's the sort of effect it had. All their actions were like that – over-exaggerated, out of proportion. Dermot looked bored. 'Ach, well, it was just one of them nights. I went out to the toilet—' The three of them smiled at that – 'and when I'd come back they'd all gone – to Delargy's.' There was a sigh of sympathy. I'd heard of the notorious Delargy's. It wasn't far from where we sat, the dirtiest dive in the Dock area and the haunt of most of Belfast's prostitute population.

'After that it was a dead loss, naturally. A whole bunch of teds from Peter's Hill came in and I thought sure that there would be a punch-up, I did indeed. Never saw such a rough-lookin' lot in all my life. Guess what one of them said to me?'

Three mouths silently formed a 'No?'

'He said, "Who's ridin' *you* tonight, hen?" so he did. A big ugly looking baste with red hair. That was enough for me, so it was, and home I went.'

The high spirits of the others seemed to drain away, and soon they were talking worriedly among themselves about someone named Desi who had been beaten up and robbed of his wallet. It seemed to have happened quite recently and not far from the pub we were in, and, as I listened, I realized that I was seeing Terry in a light I'd never seen him before. Here he was with his own kind. Before that night I'd always thought of *him* as being different, as the misfit in the society in which we moved back at home, but now it was me who was out of place. It was a strange feeling to have.

Terry said, with a seriousness that was out of character, '*I* wouldn't take a risk like that now. It's not worth it – especially here. Give me the good old Notting Hill and King's Road bars every time.'

The others nodded their heads sadly in agreement and lifted their glasses. They were all drinking lagers. Something came over me, seeing them like that, and I said, 'Come on, I'll buy you all a drink.' I felt a sort of affection for them. They were like a bunch of pathetic pigmies huddled around their camp-fires and telling each other stories in whispers of what the great race of giants outside their stockade could do to them if they decided to be cruel or wayward. They were engaged in the same sort of sex-war as women but with none of the female's advantages. That's what I thought anyway. Conveniently I had forgotten about the embarrassment they had inflicted so easily on me about ten minutes earlier ...

At the bar, which by this time had a fringe of drinkers (I still couldn't get over how crowded the place was on a week night) I tried to catch the harassed Beatrice's eye. She was puffing about pulling bottles of stout and beer and filling shorts as if her flat feet were getting hotter and hotter with the friction they generated. A lonely looking middle-aged man at my elbow shrank politely back to allow me to give my order and I returned his inviting smile. I was feeling wonderfully relaxed and tolerant now and I wondered what technique he would use.

He said, 'There surely must be easier ways to get a drink.' He had a pleasant cultured voice (I hate that word 'cultured', but it's the only one to describe his voice) and his clothes were quietly expensive.

'Yes,' I said non-committally.

'I'm a stranger here myself,' he went on, not companionably, but for my information, pulling out a gold cigarette case which he clicked open towards me. I shook my head, and, extracting one for himself, he continued, 'Yes, curiosity brought me along. A chap I know said I should try it some night – for laughs. See how the other half lives, you know.'

He laughed to show me he considered me to be on roughly the same social plane as himself, dissociating ourselves from all the people around us. He reminded me of Bradley, Terry's M.P. friend – not only the build and the clothes but the con-

148

fident manner. 'Are you a regular yourself?' he asked. It sounded so much like the laughable old *Do you come here often?* dance-hall routine that I couldn't keep from smiling. Misunderstanding, he smiled too and said boldly, 'What are you drinking?' For the first time I realized what a woman must feel like when she has been picked up too coolly, too arrogantly.

I said, 'Thanks all the same but I'm with friends.'

'Okay,' he said, in a matter-of-fact way that made me want to grab him by his fine polka-dotted silk tie and smack him one. It was the strangest feeling, not the way I wanted to do him, but the feeling that led to it. I felt as if he had degraded me just in that one word, 'Okay'. He didn't even make the slightest move to coax me (now I sound as if I wanted him to) but it's hard to explain. Anyway, I stood waiting for my drinks and he stood beside me, with his hard eyes moving restlessly, coldly over the other faces in the bar.

My order arrived and, gathering the three bottles to my chest with one arm and holding three glasses together with thumb and two fingers of the other hand, milkman fashion, I moved carefully away from the bar. I'd made up my mind. I was definitely on the side of the hunted . . .

They looked up when I arrived. Bernie, the plump one in the middle, said, 'Will you join the club, Frank?' and, caught up in the spirit, I mimicked, 'I don't know whether I could fit in or not, girls.'

Winking at the others, Phil said, 'Don't worry, we can fit all sizes in our club,' and I joined in the laughter. I saw Terry looking at me in an agreeably surprised way.

At that moment, Todd, whom I had forgotten about completely, turned a red petulant face in our direction. He must have given up the two at the corner table as a bad job. 'Is this mine?' he said boorishly with his hand already over the full glass I'd brought him from the bar. When I nodded, he grunted 'Cheers, queers,' and tossed it back.

For about a second there was silence and then Terry and his three friends burst out laughing. My mouth was still open when Todd said irritably, 'Did I say something funny or what?' His eyes jerked along our faces seeking an answer.

Terry said, 'We never heard that one before, did we, chaps?' The three shook their heads, and Dermot, the thin

149

one at the end, was holding his hand over his mouth. I realized that Todd had made the crack in all innocence.

'Let's push on,' I said, 'by the time we get home—'

'Ach, sit your ground,' said Todd, and I didn't like his tone.

He was getting nasty. I looked at Terry for support but his eyes had an unfocused look. Phil, Bernie and Dermot were watching with bright little rodent eyes. I felt as sober as they were, even on the whiskies I'd been throwing into me all night, but I wanted to get out before something happened, that was the difference, *they* were willing what now seemed inevitable.

'Who brought us to this fuckin' kip anyway?' demanded Todd. His voice was loud and slurred. 'Well, who was it?'

'I suppose it was me, old thingumabob,' said Terry and his waving glass flung a wet drop on to the table. 'Why, don't you like it?'

Todd's eyes seemed to contract. 'Stinks – the whole fucking place.' His voice was rising and heads were turning. 'Every-thing – *everyone* stinks.' Belligerently he glared around. But now I noticed no one was paying him any attention. After the initial moment of shocked interest they had all returned discreetly to their own affairs. I could see this angered him.

'Glass,' he said. So it was my turn, was it? Well, just let him have a go.

'Yes?'

'Glass, I hear you've applied for Matchett's job.'

'That's correct,' I replied, keeping my voice level. Oh, the rotten, lousy bastard!

Although I was looking straight ahead I could feel him studying me. He was trying to get a sneer on to his face but it came out as a twisted grimace. Full, he was, but that tiny warped thing he had upstairs for a brain wasn't fuddled enough for him to pass up a dig at someone. When he saw I wasn't going to react, he said slowly, in a way that showed he was using every ounce of concentration he had, 'I suppose you realize you haven't a pup's.'

'Oh?' I said, 'do you think so?' My voice was as cool as I could make it but my legs were beginning to tremble. I could feel the spasms under the cloth.

'Warwick'll walk it. Of course, he's the only bloody man

for the job anyway.' It was the nearest he had come so far to an out and out insult.

Mentally I measured him. Taller, heavier, probably in better shape too – all those exhibitionistic training runs in a track suit along the main Kildargan–Annagh road with the night traffic lighting up his face, hands and white basket-ball boots. Courage? That's what I would soon find out for I knew, barring a miracle, we would clash. I had a feeling he knew too ...

The last time I had fought was when I was about fifteen. It seemed a long time ago. Of course many men go through life and never fight once, fight seriously, I mean.

I felt I should say something but as sentence silently followed on sentence in my mind I rejected it as being more provocative than the last ...

'You know *your* trouble, Glass?' his head swayed like a befuddled cobra's. 'Do you? *Do you?*'

I looked at him, trying to bring him back to reason with the steady solemnity of my gaze, not realizing that he could only see – only *wanted* to see – through the haze a mocking, a superior face.

When he snarled, 'You think you *are* somebody. You *fancy* yourself,' I was smitten by the unfairness of it. By God, I didn't deserve this. 'Yes, Lord God Almighty Glass, going around him bein' fuckin' superior. And just who the hell are *you* to be so bloody high and mighty anyway? Eh? That's what I'd like to know, Mr. High-an'-Mighty Glass – Glass from the Red Row, ha ha ha! That bloody – *slum*! You're just one of the shit-house brigade too, Glass, an' don't you forget it. *You're* no different from any of the rest of them down there, you know. Why don't you go back home to your friends, Glass? Where you belong. Go home, do you hear me? Go home to your oul' fella. I hear tell he's on the buroo now. Is that true? Eh, Glass? On the dole, eh? Is it true he's—'

I said quietly, 'We'll go outside now, Todd. That's enough.'

He bounced in his seat. 'Any time you like, any time you like,' he said. 'God, I'm goin' to knock two colours of shite outa you, Glass. You've had this comin' for a very long time, indeed you have.'

Rising to my feet, I drained my glass as carefully and slowly

151

as I dared, my hands shaking as they were. Then I started moving through the crowd to the door. I felt as cold as ice, yet my brain had never raced so rapidly. The faces of the people I passed, the tables, the glasses, the chairs, walls, floor – were all sharp and intense, lit as though by an everlasting flash bulb.

The bite of the night air outside only increased the feeling I had of barely controlled violent energy. I really wanted to *kill* him at that moment, but without passion. I wanted to watch my fists, my arms, my feet – my whole body, beat him, beat him, *beat him*. Fear was the last thing in my head. If there had been a dozen Todds instead of one, anticipation and determination wouldn't have altered one iota. I had a mad notion which I believed devoutly at that moment that if I could land only one blow, no matter how many *I* received, the effect of it would be devastating ...

The door opened and closed at the back of me and I wondered why he was alone, for, without turning, I felt a single presence. Across the street the mouth of an entry broke the solidity of the facing buildings. I moved into its shadow and waited for him. My arms hung slackly. They felt as if they didn't belong to me, but would become tensed rods meting out retribution when the time came. It never struck me to adopt a defensive position. I waited carelessly, my overcoat open, for him to strike the first blow. Then, and only then, would my arms swell and harden. I think I expected some sort of miraculous physical transformation to take place – awaiting his blow the way a swimmer anticipates the unavoidable cold sting of first entry into water.

It was laughably naïve. When the blow did arrive, exploding on my face in a roaring orange-coloured detonation I was sure that I was damaged terribly, that a dreadful mistake had been made. From a sitting position on the cold wet cobbles I looked up at Todd standing over me. He must be made to realize what he had done, drunk or not. My fingers explored the mutilation, to find unbelievably that my face was the same, except for a wet trickle into one corner of my mouth.

Todd said, 'Get up and fight, you lousy bastard you!'

He was about three feet away, making sure that if I did

get up I would be forced *straight* up in the most awkward, vulnerable way, for I had landed against a wall. Instinctively I pressed my palm downwards and sprang up at him driving my head into his stomach. The air rushed out of him in a great 'Ooosh!' and he staggered backwards and sideways across the entry clutching his middle. I didn't even think of following up my advantage, I was too flabbergasted at the success of my butting, which I had only seen performed before in saloon brawls on the screen.

'Trust you to fight dirty, Glass,' he hissed. He was obviously in great pain, but funnily enough I felt no consolation. He stumbled into a lozenge of light and there were tears on his cheeks. He looked sick. All my previous feelings of revenge left me. All I wanted now was to make him understand that I hadn't meant to foul him deliberately, that it had just been an experiment.

Then his next blow landed like a thunderclap on my left ear. Instinctively, for the second time, I lashed out and I felt my fist sinking into the sponginess of his nose before the bones of his face jarred my knuckles. Blood spurted and ran downwards. I stared stupidly. Had I done *that*? He stood feeling his face just as I had done a moment before and then looked at the blood on his hands. A queer sobbing sound rose somewhere in him and he rushed at me, his arms flailing circles. I tried to move out of his way but he pinned me against the wall with part of his bulk. Blows rained down on my neck and shoulders but most of them, I realized, were missing and hitting the wall. He didn't seem to notice. He just kept up this inhuman roaring accompaniment to his battering fists. Mine too were working, hitting the blue nylon covered expanse of chest and stomach pressing on me. I felt sick and tired and dispirited because it was like striking one of those tautly-weighted punching sacks, and the reaction was not much different. I wondered how long we could keep it up. The strange thing was that I could feel no pain from his blows, just a slowly spreading numbness, no pain.

Then one of his fists caught me a ringing crack on the mouth. Thinking my teeth were broken, in a frenzy I hurled myself forward, upwards and through the protecting barrier of his whirling arms, determined to pay him back. My first blows thudded harmlessly on to his forearms but one struck

153

him square below the ear. It was a satisfying blow which cut off his roaring and sent him back reeling. For a split second I hesitated. I knew I should follow the blow home, everything screamed out for me to do it, but I wavered. Then the door of the pub opened and light spilled out. There were voices and I heard Terry shouting, 'Are you there, Frank! *Frank!*' It was the most welcome sound I think I've ever heard. At the same time I didn't, for a second, take my eyes off Todd, who was swaying a few paces away, one hand up to his jaw. It came to me that I was lucky the drink he had taken had dulled him otherwise he might have killed me. God! I felt really sick then and my legs jerked.

Terry came running over. He stopped when he saw us standing apart, motionless, and he stared first at me and then at Todd. 'For Christ's sake, what have you done to your faces?' He sounded as if he had sobered up in a hurry. 'Behavin' like a couple of weans, at your age! Well, what are you standin' like that for? Are you dummies or what? Come on, for the love of Jasus, and get away outa this.'

'What's wrong?' I said. 'What is it?'

'That wee shite-hawk of a husband of Beatrice's has phoned for the peelers, that's what's wrong. They'll be here any minute.' He started pushing me towards the entry mouth.

'Hold on,' I said, 'what about *him*?' Todd still stood there, stupid, absent-mindedly massaging the side of his face.

'Are you worried?' Terry said. 'Let the big bugger look after himself.'

'No,' I said. 'Go an' bring him with us.'

Terry looked at me, then he walked slowly back to Todd. He touched his arm. Todd jumped and, before Terry could duck, he had swung at him and the next thing Terry was sprawling on his backside on the cobbles.

'He hit me. He *hit* me,' I heard him whimpering as he scuttled like a crab away from the danger. 'Ach, Frank, did ye not see what he done?' He was weeping.

'Come on, for God's sake,' I said, fed up with the whole business, sick to the back bloody teeth of worrying about other people's sensibilities. 'Come on, damn you!' Yes, by all means, let the big bugger fend for himself . . .

Along narrow back streets, over wet greasy black square-setts, past warehouses and later, squeezed-in stinking houses with the bluish gleam of television in every window, I marched with Terry, still tearful, like a cur at my heels. He caught up with me under an old-fashioned gas-light at a corner.

'Frank, Frank, ach, Frankie, he's broke my jaw,' he whined.

'Well, hell slap it into you, is all I can say. You're to blame for everythin' that's happened tonight. A right clever lad you are an' no mistake. You'd no bloody business bringin' him, or me either, for that matter, to that – that—' Words failed me. The long trek through the York Street slum area hadn't cooled my temper any. Somewhere far back in the recesses of my brain I knew I was being unfair to him – a case of taking it out on him because he was the handiest at that moment. At the same time I was enjoying the righteous indignation act. My heart wasn't in it, of course, but I could have fooled an outsider. Terry certainly.

'Ach, Frank, that's not a bit fair,' he wept as he tried to catch up with my fast military stride which I was also enjoying. 'Pl-ease, Frank, wait for me, and let me explain.'

I kept my face firm and resolute the whole way to the car. 'Now get in and dry up, for Christ's sake.' I held open the door, half-pushed him in and slammed it on him. We drove up the wide winding Antrim Road, Cave Hill a shapeless black blur on our left and the chain of distant fairy lights that were the coastal resorts of Belfast Lough far down below us to the right across the water. Every time a street lamp flicked past, Terry's pale face grew out of the gloom and then receded. He hadn't made a sound since I'd bundled him into the car. I began to feel conscience-stricken.

'Do you think he'll be all right?' I said, hoping to work round to an apology of some description.

He said, '*I* don't know,' in a tone which said *I've been wronged, and nothing you can say or do can make it up to me, so there.*

'If he *is* caught,' I persevered, 'would he give our names, do you think?'

It was obvious he hadn't thought of that. He looked at me for the first time, jerked out of martyrdom. 'Ach, he wouldn't – would he?'

I began to think of the consequences if Todd had been

lifted by the men in blue-black. He might not have got away before the squad-car arrived. There was an odd look about him when we had left him, stunned, not quite sure what was happening. Headlines in the local paper lit up prematurely in my head. TWO ANNAGH TEACHERS FINED FOR ASSAULT. SHOCKING CASE, SAYS JUDGE. A BAD EXAMPLE TO THEIR CHARGES. And one of them, I tagged on, certainly not headmaster material. No! It was strange, but, *do you know,* I said to myself, *I really do think you'll be disappointed, Glass, if you don't get that oul' job.*

I said on an impulse, 'Look, Terry, I'm sorry about cutting up rough with you. It wasn't your fault – about tonight.'

To my horror he began to blubber. 'For pity's sake,' I said desperately, 'pull yourself together.' His sobbing filled the tiny warm car, harsh metallic sounds of unspeakable grief. I pulled over quickly on to the grass verge; we had just passed the blazingly-lit outer boundary of the city and darkened fields lay to the left and right of us.

'Easy now, oul' han', easy there.'

I spoke softly in the sudden silence as the engine died. A car approached, illuminated us briefly and rushed past. Its noise died and we heard a little mournful night wind feeling around the car. A few drops of rain fell as though by accident on the roof. At last he said, 'You're very lucky, Frank, do you know that?'

'Och now, Terry—'

'No,' he interrupted gently, bitterly, 'you are. You really are. You don't need anybody. You're very selfish, did you know that? That's why you're lucky. You *use* people, Frank ...' I sat listening, too tired to argue with him. I'd heard it all before. God, yes. Once I would have said, quietly, pleadingly, *Okay, I'm selfish, but I admit it, but you're every bit as selfish as me, but you can't or won't admit it. Why won't you, why can't you, what have you got to lose? Tell me.* But that was before I'd learned that you can't change people with words. *People.* Hell is the other fella, someone once said, and by God he spoke the truth. *People* had been responsible for this bloody awful day, so they had. *People* were always destroying me! A bloody menace the lot of them. Mona ... her tortured maidenly face swam before my eyes reproaching. Ach, damnation, why had I got involved with *that?*

156

And then tonight there was Todd. That crack about the old man. Only someone like him could have made it. The sting was still there. And a memory of a slow, shuffling line of quiet respectable men in washed dungarees, in the dole queue, none of them the cocky brigade of the popular press. Just serious men in clean denim. Those unsoiled trousers were the saddest part . . . and the old man taking up the end place, as I waited and watched from the car out on the street. Not looking ashamed; just stunned. He still didn't believe his working life was finished even when they slid his five pound eight across the counter at him . . .

Terry talking all the time, it flowing out of him '. . . you don't give a damn for anybody, you know that, you don't give a damn for me. Oh, Frank, I wish I was you, God, I do. You don't understand what it's like. That's where we're different. *We* have to have somebody. The sex part is nothin'. Believe me, *nothin'*. But it's the only way to meet someone. That's what all of us are searchin' for. And you never do. You're always disappointed. You saw that place tonight? Well it's like that *every* night. You go along hopin' that to-night this'll be it. But it always ends up the same way, up some entry with somebody usin' you . . .' That word again. I *used* him, you *used* him, everybody *used* him, everybody who was hetero, that is. I'm inside, and all you are outside. Self-pity, the biggest bastard of them all. '. . . loneliness is the worst part of it. You see there's nobody you can talk to about it. That's why I go to that place. I hate it, it's awful, but at least you can talk. Believe me, Frank, and I mean this, it's good to be able to talk to *you* too . . .'

Sitting there in the cooling car staring out into darkness, I thought, *why is it that everybody just wants to talk and never to listen to what the other person has to say.*

Then Terry said quietly, 'Why didn't you tell me you were in for old Baldy Matchett's job?' A hint of reproach coloured his voice. His maudlin mood seemed to have evaporated.

'I didn't think you'd be interested.'

He said, 'I'm interested in *everythin'* you do, Frank.' I looked at him suspiciously but his face was straight. 'You might have told *me*,' he pouted, 'I thought we were closer than that. Hearin' it tonight from that pig, Todd, like that, well, I was disappointed. Of course I knew about it already.'

'Oh?' I said, curious. 'Who told you?'

He smiled maddeningly. 'A wee bird. Never mind. Never mind.'

'Let's go,' I said angrily, switching on the ignition and the small green eye on the dashboard tinged our faces an unhealthy colour.

He put his hand on my arm. 'Don't get shirty. I can help you there.' The green eye winked out. 'Well, not *me* actually, but someone I know.'

I looked at him. What was this?

'He has a lot of influence. He knows a lot of people – the right people. He could pull strings, Frank. That's if you really want the job. I don't know.'

For the first time I let myself think seriously of what it could mean to me if I got it – the salary, the respect, the power – not because I believed for one moment Terry's friend, no matter who he was, was all *that* powerful, but because I felt now it would do me no harm to go in for a little therapeutic dreaming. Up to then I hadn't allowed myself the luxury of wishful thinking, but just then for a second or two I indulged myself. I saw myself driving up to the school in my new car wearing my new pearl-grey lightweight Aquascutum (it was summer) and the new caretaker (I had sacked Gorman as being a bad influence) was guiding me into my specially reserved parking place when Terry jerked me back to reality.

'Just say the word,' he said, 'and I'll arrange for you to see him. Some day next week? Will that suit?' He had his diary out.

'Hold on just a wee minute,' I said. 'Who is your friend?'

He paused before he spoke. 'Bradley.'

'*That bastard!* No bloody fear! Not if he knew the Prime Minister personally,' I spat.

'As a matter of fact, he does. They're very thick as it happens.' Then he became serious. 'Frank, what have you got against him? Why don't you like him?' He looked hurt and concerned at the same time. 'Why?' he pressed, 'Why?'

'I just can't stand him, that's all.'

I could see that he saw through my blustering façade. But I couldn't explain to him, or anyone, the mixture of my feelings on the subject of Bradley. I knew that my dislike was

158

compounded of too many childish, illogical elements which had nothing to do with him. For instance, I couldn't dissociate him from the auction at the Mill just because he was the one who had first told me of it, even though he hadn't been one of the crowd of fat cigar-smoking scrap-dealers in plastic waterproofs bidding for the contents that day. The Mill itself hadn't been bought. No one had gone above the reserve price. I knew it was unfair of me to blame him for that but I did, somewhere in the dark uncivilized reaches of my mind I did.

'No,' I said, 'I wouldn't go to Bradley if he were the last man alive, not if he were the last bloody man left on this earth, do you hear me? *Do you hear me?*'

AUTUMN

ONE

BRADLEY'S house was invisible from the road, but the high white wrought-iron gates, their pillars capped by gryphons and breaking the line of the boundary wall, plus the *tenanted* gatehouse, prepared you for something a cut above the ordinary. I was wondering just how grand it would be as I drove alone slowly up the lavishly winding drive. It was seven o'clock in the evening and the sun throbbed redly to my right, low among the young scattered trees which seemed to cover most of the land thereabouts. The weather was soft and settled and I had the car window down to the frame. I became more impressed the longer I drove for you don't expect a normal house waiting at the end of such extravagance. Even the wild life seemed immoderate. Twice I had to swerve around hedgehogs carelessly curled up in my path, and the trees seemed to be alive with squirrels and birds of every variety. It was so far from the road that no sound from cars and lorries penetrated. The name on the thick white headed sheet of notepaper I had received two days ago was perfect. *The Retreat.* 'Hope to see you at The Retreat on Friday evening at seven – Bradley.' Just Bradley. Like Windsor or Gulbenkian or Nehru ...

I was taken aback when the house did finally come into sight, not because it was smaller than I had expected, it was much larger, but because it was exactly like one of those old English houses you see in old English films on television on Sunday afternoon where everybody seems to spend their time drinking and making love on the terrace under striped umbrellas or systematically exterminating all the other guests, if it's that sort of picture. The immediate impression was of a detailed mass of dun-coloured brickwork painstakingly blurred with virginia creeper except where many small-paned mullioned windows reflected the sun. Six tall tottery chimney-stacks grew upwards from behind a pierced brick parapet which seemed made for dropping flower-pots from on to unsuspecting heads underneath. It was the unreal fictional quality of it that staggered me. And all the accessories – lawns, sunken garden, walks, tennis court and greenhouses like miniature Crystal Palaces – seemed to be perfectly in character.

Two honey-coloured retrievers, their soft feathery tails ruffled by the wind of their coming, threw themselves against my car door as I switched off. I felt their insistent pressure as I pushed outwards. They leaped up playfully, and I cupped a hand over each narrow pulsing head. 'Carson, Craigavon ... here, boy! *Here!*' The dogs wheeled and hurled themselves up the steps to where Bradley was standing. He patted each of their flanks and they streaked dutifully past him through the doorway into the house.

'You found the place all right, then?' he called out when I mounted the low step up to the terrace.

There were no striped umbrellas, just several scattered blue and white china tubs with plants growing in them. He was wearing dark-grey flannels and a cream-coloured linen jacket. From the breast pocket a corner of purple silk handkerchief overflowed carelessly. It matched his tie. He stood to one side to allow me to pass into the house and I smelt his after-shave – heavy, a bit cloying. It suited his dark, bulky presence. 'Push on ahead,' he said. 'There's a fire in the study.'

He sounded briskly professional, not the way I'd imagined he would be. The note he'd sent had the same ring, I remembered. I suddenly felt like a patient walking to a surgery after just having learned the doctor will expect the most concisely accurate account of symptoms and yet not knowing where to start. Good God Almighty, what if Terry hadn't explained to him? What if he'd left it *all* up to me? He was quite capable of it, not taking me seriously when I'd made him promise to make it absolutely clear in advance to Bradley why I *was* seeing him. In fact he had said he personally couldn't see any point in it at the time. I remembered that. I wanted to make it appear that the initiative had really come from Bradley and that I was just falling in with his plans, not really caring one way or the other. But now the truth had to be faced, and there was very little time for me to work out some way of softening the angular unpleasantness of a simple direct plea to this man I didn't even know to do me a very large favour. It was beyond me ...

I was now standing in the centre of a large circular hallway with a glass cupola high above my head. A wide staircase mounting from ground level at two points ran around half-way up the walls so that anyone coming out of the row of bedroom doors high above could lean over and look down on us in the hall. There was a hollowness in the air.

When Bradley spoke his voice echoed slightly. 'The door facing you. After you.'

The study, like everything else about the house, was too *right*. Walls of books in calf, deep leather chairs on either side of a log fire, an almost black purple Afghan carpet and brass lamps with glass shades that green you see in the big bottles in chemists' windows. I wondered spitefully how many of the books had their pages cut. After all if you begin by despising a man, it can sometimes make it easier for you to ask him for something.

Bradley said, 'Do sit down, Frank. And what is it now you drink? Gin or is it whiskey?'

'Scotch,' I said and my voice sounded rusty. It struck me that it was the first thing I'd said since I'd entered the house. From my chair I watched Bradley preparing the drinks at a marble-topped table in the corner. I'd never seen so many different varieties of bottles, outside a bar, arranged on the veined top. My tumbler when it reached me was almost full.

'I'm glad you decided to come to see me,' he said, sitting down opposite me in the armchair. 'I like meeting young people. I like them to come up to the house. In my job, you see, you don't get much opportunity of meeting the younger generation. I like to keep in touch with what's fresh and new and *alive* around me.' On the word 'alive' his dark heavy-lidded eyes slid smoothly all over me and then away before he smiled and said, 'You understand?'

I nodded and sipped minutely at my drink. There was enough in the glass to last me all night, if I was careful.

'Yes,' he went on, 'this place—' He flicked the air with a square white meaty hand – 'needs youth. Of course you're very young yourself so you may not understand this. What age *are* you, Frank?'

162

'Twenty-five,' I said.

I hate having to tell my age, not because I feel I'm too young or too old or anything silly like that but because after I've said it I feel I have surrendered something. I feel the same way about my name. I hate saying that too.

'You look younger, Frank. I wouldn't have put you at twenty-five. No.'

I looked down through the tawny swirl to the whorled bottom of my glass waiting for a shift to another topic. He made it but it was a continuation of the same theme.

'Terry Butler has told me a lot about you, you know.'

Terry *Butler*, I thought. Strange. It almost sounded as if they weren't on such close terms as Terry made out. I said, 'Oh?' and hated myself for being such an easy shell for him to prise.

He put more weight on the lever. 'Yes, you'd be surprised, I think, at some of the things I *do* know about you.'

His voice had become deeper, more sensual, and he had slid down into his chair so that his trousers had tightened. I tried to keep my eyes off the lump his genitals made under the grey flannel. Good God, this *soon*? I thought and took an unwise gulp at my drink. Tears prickled my eyes as I choked. Bradley sprang up in his chair and the lump smoothed out, as he inquired solicitously, 'Not enough water in it, eh? Here, let me fix it for you.' He took my glass and crossed to the table again. I thought to myself, you're moving in the right circles now, Franko my boy, where people 'fix' you drinks.

'Yes, Terry thinks a lot of you,' he continued, handing me back my glass which looked as if it had been diluted with more whiskey. 'He's very fond of you.' He made it sound obscene. 'Thinks the sun rises and sets on Master Frank Glass. But surely you knew?'

I said, 'No, I didn't.'

'*You're* fond of him too, aren't you?' Very slowly, suggestively.

For the second time I wondered if I *could* go through with this. A week ago when I had mentioned casually to Terry that I wouldn't mind going to Bradley's house now, that is if he was still interested, and he had announced excitedly that he would arrange it, I was sure of myself, sure that, no matter what happened, I wouldn't draw back. For the more I had

163

thought about it in the days and weeks following the night Terry first placed the seed in my mind that Bradley could help me if I 'played ball', the reward part had pushed what I would have to do to get it further and further towards insignificance. Now the see-saw was beginning to pivot.

'Drink up,' he said, pointing his glass at mine.

Dutifully I swallowed, feeling nothing until the balloon of practically neat Scotch reached my stomach and gently burst, releasing tendrils of warmth upwards. I realized I was drinking probably the best whiskey I would ever taste. Bradley had slipped down in his chair again revealing twin bands of hairy shin. Above his head a single glistening button in the black leather, navel-deep, stared at me. He twisted beneath it and his shirt opened. He was wearing a string vest. A tremor of disgust wriggled in me. 'Mr. Bradley—'

'Sam, *please*. My friends call me Sam and – I hope we're going to be friends, eh, Frank?'

I started again, conscious of his spreading smile. He must have been drinking before I arrived. Yet I hadn't smelt any on him. Then I thought of what he had in his glass – vodka neat.

'Terry has told me a lot about you too.'

His smile stopped where it was. 'Really, you don't say so?'

I lied of course. As a matter of fact, Terry had told me very little about him. So carefully did he avoid talking about him indeed, that I became suspicious, for it was unlike Terry not to chatter of his sexual exploits, even minor ones and I didn't need to be told that his relationship with Bradley was very major and, looking at the man sprawled before me, *very* sexual.

'What does dear Terry say about me?'

My original comment had been a spur of the moment job, just made to say something, anything. And I thought he would have let it lie, as I had when he had said the same thing to me, so I was forced into saying the first thing that came into my head. 'Oh, well, he says – ah – uh – you're a very – powerful man.' It sounded ridiculous.

There was a frosty edge to his voice when he answered 'Oh well, I hardly think *Terry's* good opinion will make me up all that much.'

The local phrase sounded strange coming from his lips. Up to then I'd never considered him as springing from the same sod as myself. I began to wonder about him and his background. He didn't seem to belong to the house somehow for a start. I noticed there were no portraits, in fact there seemed to be no directly personal links with a strong family past anywhere. His name too had a 'recent' ring to it, not like the out-and-out English, planter-Scots or vaguely foreign names one usually associates with big houses in this part of Ireland.

'Is your house very old?' I said.

He put the tips of his fingers together and pursed his lips. 'Not as old as it looks. Eighteen-thirtyish, I think. Yes, about that.'

It was obvious he wasn't going any further, so partly because I was curious and partly because I didn't like the way his big eyes inched over me when there were silences I said quickly, 'You must be very proud of it.'

He looked at me, weighing me up. Then, slowly, 'If you're thinking along the lines of a family tree and all the rest of it, Frank, son, forget it. My old fella was what is lovingly known in Irish social history as a gombeen man. He made the money to buy everything you see around you by grinding the faces of the poor down further into the muck. Not that I blame him, mind. If they were fool enough to let him, well, all the more power to his elbow. To tell you the truth, I'm bloody grateful to him, *now* that is, for he paved the way for me. This place is all his and he had it paid for before he was fifty. That's not bad, is it?'

He had got to his feet and was leaning on the marble mantelpiece. His glass slopped as he emphasized his points.

'He would sit in the back kitchen with his boots off, and the smell of his rotten dirty oul' feet reached every room in the house. It was a reminder to the rest of us that we owed everything we had to him, and not to be getting above ourselves. He didn't give one damn what anyone thought of him, man *or* God. He turned Protestant when he married my mother because it was profitable. And you can imagine how popular that made him. Of course that was out in some arsehole in the Fermanagh bogs somewhere. When he came here nobody knew a thing about him, except that he dug with the

165

right foot and had the lolly. And as you've learned by this time that's all that counts in this part of the world. And that's why I am where I am today, Frank, my boy, if you're interested. You can profit from my example or not.'

I thought of Matchett and what he had said about joining the Freemasons, the Golf Club, etcetera. *His* idea of the way to the top was the same.

The whiskey was beginning to make my eyes tired. I wished I could change places with Bradley, because the heat of the white and red ashes in the grate was smarting my ankles. I was relieved when he moved to the bottle-covered table for a refill for himself. When he returned, my chair was a surreptitious six inches back. He almost tripped over the edge of the sheepskin rug. I pulled back my feet so quickly he gave a short barking laugh.

'When are you going to relax?' he said. 'You've been as tight as a mainspring ever since you've got here.'

I felt that shock that comes when someone comments directly on something you hadn't thought they'd noticed.

'I wouldn't have thought, mind, you were a shy person,' he continued from the armchair opposite. His eyes gleamed below thick eyebrows that imperceptibly thinned above the bridge of his nose. I wished I could remember what eyebrows like that were supposed to tell you about a person. Somewhere I had heard or read the significance of it.

'You struck me that day in The Imperial as someone not easily put out. Someone like myself.' I felt as though I'd betrayed him. 'And I'm seldom wrong about people. I still think we're very much alike though. We both know what we like and we like to make sure that we get it. Isn't that right?' His voice was soft lulling massage. Then, *then* he said, 'And we both like Terry too, *don't* we?'

Up to then there might have been a slim possibility that I had been wrong but not now. It was going to be simply a matter of time before he made the first unmistakable gesture or touch. The sparring was past.

I took a long, slow drink and watched him nod appreciatively.

'Here's to a long and happy friendship,' he said and we clinked glass. 'We can do a lot for each other.' It came out slowly, suggestively – an afterthought – but it was what I

166

wanted to hear. A business arrangement. A fair exchange. On those terms some principles might be salvaged, and I wouldn't have to beg as I feared.

He leaned forward and his face was red with the reflected heat of the embers. A vein in his forehead pulsed like a tiny wriggling blue worm. He put his hand on my knee. I forced myself not to look down and found I had to look into his eyes instead. They told me that he was much drunker than I was. His lips had parted and he had a blurred look on his face which I suppose must have been lust but could have been any of two or three other emotions.

'Frank,' he began huskily, 'did anyone ever tell you that you're—'

He stopped because we both had heard a muffled cry that came from somewhere deep in the house. One unintelligible word had been called and, as we listened, it came again, pitched higher, but I couldn't make out. Bradley rose, his face expressionless, but I knew he was angry.

'Won't be a minute, Frank. Sit where you are, there's a good chap.'

He swayed once on his way to the door but recovered quickly. He went out and pulled the heavy door after him. Its force was spent however before it reached the catch, and, barely touching the jamb, slowly, silently, it swung back to a half-open position. My curiosity grew for I knew he had wanted to shut me in away from whoever or whatever was outside.

Across the carpet I tip-toed, at the door stopped, and put my head around. Bradley was out of sight, but above, on the staircase circling the drum of the hall, two bare feet showing between the banisters, stood a boy in pyjamas. He was looking down and listening respectfully to his father who was hidden to my right. It was Warren. I realized I had forgotten all about him and that, of course, he must have been in the house all along.

'What do you mean by it, sir?' Bradley was saying in a low intense voice, calculated to carry aloft and no further. 'Do you want me to go up to you and take a stick to you? Is that what you want? Well, sir, are you tongue-tied? *Answer!*'

The boy's lips I could see were quivering and his eyes full of misery. Ashamed of myself for watching his private grief,

167

I moved backwards intending to close the door gently behind me. I kept my eyes fixed on the small figure in the nursery printed pyjamas which were too young for him. I had the door almost closed when he suddenly looked down and saw me. Stepping back swiftly out of vision I shut the door. The mood of neutrality I had begun to build up disintegrated, and I knew that I wouldn't have time to reconstruct. I felt base at having seen the boy's humiliation, but worse, that he had seen me.

In school he was considered by teachers and pupils alike as 'difficult'. He was quiet, solitary and no one had ever managed to make him cry or show any strong emotion. He was the bane of Wilbur Todd's life, torn as *he* was between his instinctive desire to humble him and his respect for who's father's son he was.

I sat there in Sam Bradley's house by his fire drinking his whiskey, awaiting his return, and also thinking irrationally that his son must know why I was in the house and what was soon to happen. Those dark eyes inherited from his father had surely pierced my soul and each time they would look at me in the future, and there was an opportunity five days out of the seven, I would be reminded, and I didn't want to be reminded. No, I didn't want to be reminded . . .

Bradley came into the room, no sign of his recent temper on his smooth face. Delicately he closed the door with the splayed finger-tips of one hand, then, with his retrieved glass in the other, he moved towards the hearth.

He was different. The mellow mood had changed to one with an edge to it. He was back to the day-to-day Bradley – swift and mercilessly self-seeking. I realized for the first time his power over Terry, the fascination such strength would have for such a weak person. A man like this who was so *sure* of what he wanted and how to get it could not be denied. This was the strongest man Terry had ever met and therefore, his logic went, he *must* get what he wants. And so now *I* was to be the fatalistic pea-hen awaiting king cobra. A desire to squawk arose in me.

Boldly I said, 'How did you first meet Terry?'

Again that canny, speculating glance as before. Curiously, warily, 'Has he never told you?'

I thought I would be clever. What had I to lose now anyway? 'Oh, he's told me almost – everything, as I think you know, but strangely enough never how you met. Odd, isn't it?'

'Very,' he said and I thought I had overreached myself.

He swirled his glass, moving his big black head thoughtfully in time with the circling reflection. I became aware of the tiny fluttering tick of the square brass travelling clock on the mantelpiece. As if it were a signal to commence, other small night noises ventured forth – a whimper of wind outside the curtains, a floor creaking, a brief flare from an ember in the grate, an unidentifiable noise from deep in the house. I thought of the boy lying awake up in one of the darkened high rooms staring up to the ceiling where his night-light could never penetrate, and thinking of his father's guest . . .

'Dublin. Nineteen-sixty. The Shelbourne.' He had his head to one side and a faraway cynical look in his eye, remembering. A tremor of spiteful anticipation ran through me. 'In the bar to be exact. It was late and I thought I would just have one more before I turned in. He was sitting up at the bar on his own. As I remember it we must have been the last two customers anyway. The barman kept yawning and collecting ashtrays from the tables. Well, Terry asked me for a light and it was obvious he didn't smoke but I let that pass and one thing led to another and well that's how it started.' Pausing he looked at me. Then, he added slowly, 'He was very nervous. He hadn't much experience.'

I looked back at him with innocence, sensing full well his meaning. In a strange way I was beginning to enjoy this cat and mouse game; in this case, as the mouse, I was getting a longer run than usual for my money. Each time he carefully proffered his pass-words I showed no reaction. I wondered how long it would be before he tired of the game and got rough. It tickled me to realize that I had often played the same game with women with the rôles reversed, hoping naïvely that my own innuendos would inflame.

As well as all this I was thinking of the new light thrown on Terry. Nervous? Inexperienced? It didn't tally with the impression I'd been fed by the same boy himself. I found myself gloating that I now knew something about him that he didn't know I knew. A fine friend I'd turned out to be . . .

Bradley was laughing to himself. 'What is it?' I said.

169

He finished his private laugh before answering, 'We didn't find out until the morning how close we lived to each other. And by then it was too late.'

Yes, I thought, *it wouldn't be like you to take a risk like that, would it?* I joined in his laughter then too, seeing the funny side for the first time, for yes, even in Dublin, a hundred odd miles away, it's possible to pick up by mistake someone who comes from the same townland as yourself.

'Yes,' I said, 'I suppose you have to be careful about things like that.'

He rose slowly out of his chair and stretched himself. Laying one forearm along the bare mantelpiece he lounged against the fluted marble and gazed down at me benevolently. 'As a matter of fact, Frank, that would never worry me. There are ways of protecting yourself, you know. For a start, I would never make the first move.'

There was no barb in it but I felt pierced nevertheless. My face felt suddenly warm and I dropped my head.

As on that night in the dock bar, I was once again on the 'inside' listening to another of those little pieces of carefully-hoarded, well-tried and tested lore on what to do and what not to do. I wondered why on each occasion I had slipped into the inner circle so easily; was it because those of the fraternity were so keen to share their secrets, or was it because of something else? Something they recognized in me that I didn't know was there? I didn't want to think about that . . .

Bradley was pacing about the room now, abstractedly touching pieces of the furniture as he passed them. I felt uneasy sitting as I was shielded in on three sides by my high wing chair as he occasionally moved softly about behind me. His voice was low and lulling again.

'No, Frank, until we live in a more civilized age when a man can enjoy his pleasures freely and openly without fear of a dirty big cop pushing his nose in and asking questions, people like us will just have to go underground and have our good times in *private* . . .' One of the green shaded lights went off with a click. Two to go. '. . . of course, in other countries they take a more sensible attitude. I once spent a holiday in Cannes and the things I saw in broad daylight, well, Frank, if I told you I don't think you'd believe me . . .' Click, and darkness spread over another sector of the room.

170

I wanted to call out, 'What are you doing?' but I thought of ... Marie she had said her name was when I'd bought her a bitter lemon in the dance-hall and later in the back seat of the car, as my fingers assiduously worked their way through the defence works of hooks and buttons and straps and layers of tightly stretched silk until they touched her warm moist shrine and she surrendered with a sigh, she kept on repeating *What are you doing?* even after the question was pointless ...

'... on the beaches, in bars, in the *streets*, and nobody taking any notice except the British, of course. A nation of peeping Toms, as you know. Ah, some of the times, Frank, some of the times! I remember once ...' Click, and just a faint glow on my legs and face from the fire, while he stalked dangerously somewhere in the darkness behind me, '—someone like you, only swarthier, more Latin, you know? And full of fire, Frank.'

He laughed above my head and I knew he was leaning over me. The heavy scent of lotion overlaying his personal smell filled my nostrils.

He whispered, 'It can be difficult for people like you and me living in a black puritan hole like this, Frank. The South and the Sun is the place. Yessss ...'

Exhaled breath fanned my face and I told myself – *Relax, RELAX, you knew it would happen like this, and after all YOU made the first move, didn't you now, didn't you?*

His hands began to crawl in parallel courses down over my shoulders under my jacket over the thin cotton of my shirt until they entered under my belt and then converged steadily, remorselessly. I could hear his breath coming more heavily now and although I tried to remain calm under the edging fingers my heart began to thump more strongly.

'Frank, Frank, *Frankie*,' he was whispering, the words coming out in gasps. 'Relax now, take it easy. I know how you feel but ... Relax – ssss ...'

I hated him for keeping on about it. My God, what did he want? *I was relaxed!* If I could laugh in some way, not out loud, it would all be much easier on me – this – but I couldn't, hard and all as I tried. The humour was there all right – our ridiculous positions, the pantomime of switching off the lights, the things he was whispering now in my ear straight out of True Confessions for Servant Girls – but the situation was all wrong. His fingers reached my skin, and halting their march, marked time. Lower down I began to feel the unexpected. Amazement and a sort of disgust that my body had betrayed me, turned in me. The cold control I had been so sure of had given way. My God, I thought, I'm meeting him half-way!

His fingers moved, sliding down the last few inches and as they touched me finally, irrevocably, I knew there was no use worrying now for there was no going back. Spoiled, *handled* goods. Melodramatic phrases like neon messages flashed in my head.

One of his hands stopped its coaxing and slipped out. Neatly swinging round the side of the chair, he dropped to his knees facing me and the right side of his glistening face flashed into the firelight. He was sweating. The freed hand slid in and started expertly unbuttoning. I suddenly realized I would have to say something soon and that worried me more than anything else. I thought also of what I would do if he expected me to begin touching *him*.

Heat from the fire smote my bare stomach. It was so unexpected I sucked in air. Bradley's voice rose. 'It takes *you* a long time to warm up.'

My body began to shake inertly under his attentions. A strange feeling of unreality tightened around me. It was almost as if I were looking down, instead of being involved, in a tableau. Who was this kneeling man rocked with such passion, who was I and why were both of us in this darkened, ceiling-less room? I realized that my reasons for coming had lost any importance they had. One simple desire and one only had chased them, it seemed, for good. All I wanted now was for *this*, whatever it was, to end in as orderly a manner as possible. I was prepared to submit for an hour, to bring it about if he wished it, so that, when it was over, I would be able to rise and, freely without recriminations, walk out of this house and into the night air. The night air had assumed cooling, opiate qualities out of all proportion to its reality.

What had started off as a gentle lingering touch, I realized suddenly, had become pummelling. He forced me to gasp, 'Easy on!' once and I twisted quickly to the side.

'What's wrong with you?' he muttered.

'Nothing,' I replied weakly and closed my teeth in a hurry

172

as another twinge shot through me. I would have to stop this. Couldn't he see he was only wasting his time anyway?

Resting from his exertions, Bradley said, 'You're a strange one. What's wrong with you?' and stared up. His eyes shone in the firelight and his face was an unfamiliar one, with its new-found shadows and lighted planes.

I coughed embarrassedly and said, 'It never happened to me before.' I didn't add to it and he studied me in silence.

'Well then,' he said slowly, 'it doesn't seem to work, does it, dearie?' and rose to his feet. A moment later I heard a clink of bottle and glass. I felt like a fool sitting there not knowing whether to pull up my trousers or not and feeling the full contrast of my absurd bareness with his fully dressed form upright in the darkness. He could probably see the twin degrading bumps of my white knees shining in the gloom.

'Here,' he said, and a full golden glass descended out of the air to hover beside my cheek. 'And button-up for Jasus' sake. We don't want you to catch your death.'

That and the 'dearie' pushed me into trembling humiliation which, thank God, must have gone unnoticed in the dark. For a moment I really wished I'd been able to meet him half-way or even out-pace his passion, and any challenge he might have offered back there. Lights sprang on again under his moving touch and I waited, wondering how he would go about getting rid of me after I'd finished my whiskey. I was curious about it in a dispassionate way. He said, 'I suppose you would have been fine if it had been Terry instead of me.'

The words fell carelessly, flatly, but my mind leaped. I found it hard to believe that *he* could be victim to such a simple emotion as jealousy of a younger man, or rather, bitterness at being considered old and unattractive. A second later he righted the balance.

'Good God Almighty!' he said, feigning surprise, 'is that the time?'

We both looked at the little brass travelling clock with the handle. It was twenty past nine. I helped him out, not that he needed my help, by rising and saying, 'Yes, I must be pushing on.' Then I realized my shirt was hanging out over the front of my trousers and he turned away as I stuffed it in. It was an awkward reminder of something both of us were pretending now hadn't happened.

He opened the door for me and, walking across the wide open amphitheatre of hall and down the carpeted corridor beyond with him at my heels, I wondered if I could force myself to ask now point-blank what I had really come to ask. Not once had it come out straight between us. I had about thirty seconds left in which to beg my favour, and I saw it like that still, despite the services rendered – well half-rendered anyway...

The silence between us was becoming noticeable. I cleared my throat but it was he who said, 'Frank, you'll have to come up again some time,' when we were on the steps. I found myself looking up at him standing on the top step, one of his shoes resting on the scraper, his hands bunching out the thin fabric of his coat pockets.

He sighed, 'What a beautiful evening. I wish to God I had a job like yours to enjoy this time of year. You don't know how lucky you are.'

In some distant meadow bottom a corncrake rasped joylessly and a new moon slid up and over the tallest chimney.

Again he breathed in noisily. 'Will you just smell that new-mown grass? Eh? Isn't it powerful?'

Silently I agreed with him and any faint hopes I had of cornering him ebbed away finally into the night air. 'It's lovely weather, right enough,' I said quietly.

'*Well*,' he said conclusively, 'I'll love you and leave you.' I searched his face for some sign of private amusement but all subtlety was masked by the wide professional smile. 'Safe home then, and—' a slight pause, checking me as I was turning, '—drop in any time you're passing, now, that's an open invitation, mind.' There was no doubt in either of our minds that he meant exactly the opposite of what he had just said.

'Good night,' I said, walking away.

*   *   *

In the car driving home something occurred. I felt a sudden delayed tightening and stirring between my legs. In the words of our local delicate turn of phrase I was 'touching cloth'. I had to laugh, partly because of relief that my condition of an hour ago was now proven to be temporary after all, but also because of something else. I was just on the edge of realizing that it might be safer to see the night's encounter in as humorous a light as possible – for my own conscience sake.

174

WINTER

OUR car, in accordance with undertaking etiquette, was immediately behind the slowly travelling motor-hearse, or at the head of the winding procession of the other four Daimlers and all the private cars, if you prefer to look at it that way. However it wasn't something I thought much about. Through the windscreen to the left of our driver's head, I kept my eyes fixed, for something to do, on the brass plate below the hinged window on the back of the vehicle in front. The etched capitals read, Josiah Boyle. Weddings and Funerals. Scotch Street, Annagh. Walter and I were the only passengers in our car. We both had a desire to sprawl in our corners of the broad leather seat and hang on our tasselled pulls, but like every other natural instinctive action since the death, we repressed it. A harsh heat spread upwards from the floor and my heavy overcoat with the black diamond stitched on the sleeve felt like a ton weight of stifling, prickling, choking material. I no more thought of opening a window than of breaking into song. Outside the wind still scourged the already stripped trees and hedges and the country roads under our broad well-shod wheels were bone hard and dry.

'Will the taxis bring us back home afterwards?' asked Walter. He looked as if he had been in a fight. His eyes stared at me piteously from red puffy pouches and his face looked bruised. His hair hadn't had its normal daily Brylcreem bath either and was dead and ugly.

'They'll bring us back home,' I said, feeling sorry for him. 'Look, leave everything to me. I haven't let you down so far, now, have I?'

'No, that's true enough,' he said, nodding his head like a tired old man. 'I would have been no use to Mammy if we hadn't you, Frank,' and he began to sob. I reached him my

175

brand new handkerchief which, like the overcoat, had also been bought specially for the funeral.

What's wrong with me? I thought, watching the white ball of crumpled linen becoming a wash-rag in his grasp. *What make of a cold, inhuman, unfeeling sort of a bastard really are you?* I hadn't cried once; not once had tears come to my eyes since my father had died. A couple of times I'd even *pretended* to be overcome but my mother and Jennifer and Walter were bawling so hard themselves that they hadn't noticed my fabrication. My eyes were two cinders. Truthfully, I was obsessed more with the fact that people might notice my absence of external grief than any personal worries. Why do people weep when someone dies anyway? Certainly it's not for the one in the box, because that would be stupid seeing as all the pain is over. I think it's for themselves they're crying; for *their* loss.

Ever since Friday afternoon when Ernie Matchett came into class in the middle of a geography lesson and told me that my father had just died, I'd kept my mind turned away from memories of the old man and our life together. Even a half-hour later in the hushed parlour with the blinds pulled down – how fast someone must have moved into gear after the last breath had been taken – and I looked down at the frozen face (there was already a growing whitish-ginger stubble on the cheeks and the cheeks were slaty like the eye-hollows), I held my thoughts stiffly suspended. I was surprised how easy it was. It could be done by concentrating unflaggingly on eating, drinking, setting fires, carrying coal and water, taxi-ing relatives, sending telegrams, preparing meals, dressing myself and helping Walter and Jennifer to dress themselves. It was the first time in years I had helped my sister with her clothes and hair-ribbons and shoes. While I moved her little inert body about, buttoning and tying, she had kept up an intermittent sobbing which was an imitation of my mother's grief. The tears came, I noticed, with all of them, Walter included, when they lost concentration for a moment and thought of the past. I could see it in their eyes. It's hard to talk like that without sounding a cold fishy creature, but there were many many times when I would have gladly exchanged my own emotional deep-freeze for their tears and shared grief ...

176

'Frank?'

'Yes?'

He gave a final scrub to his face and stared dumbly at me out of still more inflamed eyes. 'Frank, where's he – where's he being buried?'

It was unbelievable. But then it struck home to me just how lost and bewildered he really was, just how unreal the last two days had been to him, since, like myself, he was called home suddenly from work to find himself fatherless.

'Rushy Hill,' I said as gently as I could. 'Rushy Hill Cemetery.'

I refrained from going into details – ministers, grave-diggers, a new plot of land in the big graveyard overlooking Annagh (I had discovered my father's side hadn't a family plot in *any* graveyard) and all the other pettifogging details before you can open a hole in the ground and lower a body into it to let it lie in peace . . .

Our motorcade spilled over the crest of the hill leading down into Annagh. The streets were empty – not a sinner, except for a young fellow moodily weighing himself on a chemist's slot machine. His girl stood waiting, listlessly swinging a handbag and her umbrella. All the pent-up bore-dom of Sunday – people indoors, knees up to the fire, reading the good old *News of the World* or masturbating in the lavatory with the pin-up from the same paper spread on the damp seat. (*What's keepin' you in there? Are you all right? Ach, go away, and give us peace! Is there no privacy anywhere?*) Idle hands finding mischief . . . The boys after church smashing panes in old Molly Lavelle's greenhouse, or sublim-ating it all in long, long walks. When I think of how my feet used to ache after those bloody hikes. Never again . . .

In the field beside the Parochial House there was a hurling match in progress, and the players in green, yellow and white quarters leaped and swung their sticks exaggeratedly as if to mock any passing Prods. with their foreign but legalized bravado. I felt resentment as we crawled past. Ridiculously I half expected them to stop their game until we were decently out of sight, but the only recognition was a few old men among the spectators momentarily baring their heads. *Bloody micks*, I found myself automatically thinking and that made me think really for the first time of the old fella, for that was one of his favourite catch phrases. *Bloody micks! YOU never had to work beside them. You wait until they out-breed you, an' then your tune will change. Livin' off the Family Allowances and the National Assistance. ACH!* Hatred bred out of ignorance. I felt it wasn't the way to remember him – not that . . .

Rushy Hill is a flat, windswept few acres of burial ground high above Annagh town. To get to it you have to drive through what was once a war-time army base over cracked and cratered concrete strips of temporary roadway that still stand fifteen years after the last Tommy, G.I. and Belgique pulled out. The Nissen huts are still there too with the same families living in them since the day they moved in immediately the troops moved out. Tin-Town, as it's known in these parts, is the bitter end. It has even a worse reputation than The Dardanelles because the Council won't even *claim* it and the families living in their tarred, corrugated tunnels fester despairingly and don't even bother any longer to inquire if their names have jerked up the waiting list for a new council house.

Women with arms folded below sagging breasts with children clinging to their skirts watched us sullenly as our procession wound through. Once a funeral car knocked down a small child (God knows how at that pace) and someone who was there told me that the women poured out like bees and the half-bricks and milk bottles began to bounce off the cars. The police had to be called in to break it up. What a place to have to live in. The Red Row is like bloody Pall Mall in comparison.

Walter was looking out of the window and I was looking out of mine – like a couple of visiting diplomats. The eyes from the doorways stared back resentfully as our stiff-backed driver took our car through at a fast walking-pace. Then he accelerated as we passed the last shack (its windows and doors were a bright luminous purple) and up above to the right we saw the crop of white headstones growing at regular intervals out of the smooth fall of hillside. A brown trodden scar blemished the pattern. We both saw it together and turned away simultaneously.

From his corner Walter mumbled quickly, 'Is Uncle Alex stayin' at our house tonight?'

I looked at him, sort of sadly, I suppose. We would never be able to *talk* to each other, never. We just made noises with our mouths, like two cave dwellers.

'No, he's gettin' a train back to Derry. He has to start his work in the mornin'.'

I saw him think about saying something and then change his mind. I was sure it was to ask me if *he* should go back in the morning too. Then something made him think that it wouldn't be 'right' to mention such a thing now, so he checked himself. I felt despair once more, because, sincerely, I wouldn't have chewed him up if he had spoken; the reverse, in fact, for I had tenderness towards him which I wanted to show to him but never got the chance.

Sitting there in the smoothly pulling car, I asked myself again the question which was so familiar to me. Could it be something in *me* that held people back? I thought of Uncle Alex from Derry and all the other relatives who had entered our lives over the last two days. The cars behind were full of them – uncles, cousins, and nephews whom I hadn't seen for years. (*The last time I saw you, Frank, you weren't THAT height . . . Oh, he's like his mother's side, no doubt about that . . . Good God, lad, but I wouldn't have known you!*) Each time I encountered one of them on his own in the house or outside strolling bored in the garden I was sure the barrier that dropped between us wasn't entirely that one caused by awkwardness of re-discovering kinship and the harder I'd tried to 'pass' myself in their talk of sport, politics and wages, the more I felt shut out. I was liked all right. They saw me as a nice, pleasant sort of a lad, not a bit stuck-up either despite being a teacher, and they kept identifying my looks with one side of the family or the other but still *I wasn't one of them*. So I was back to that one again, was I? I laughed out loud, a short bitter snort, and Walter turned hurt eyes to me. I looked at his profile when he turned back to the window again. A slight streak of blood beneath his ear showed where the razor had slipped. I cringed inside as I thought of him skirting the outbreak of pimples around his mouth. I tried to see his looks objectively, returning the blemishes to their proper place, and I wondered if he could be termed good-looking.

A few weeks ago my mother had taken me aside solemnly,

mysteriously, and thrust one of his shirts into my hands. 'There!' she said and burst into tears. I looked stupidly at the lipstick on the collar and wondered what the hell she was getting so upset about. After all, she had been used to scrubbing marks like that off *my* shirts for years. 'What am I goin' to do? I daren't tell his father, Frank.' I told her not to be daft, there was no harm in *that*, but she wasn't to be consoled. 'He's been comin' in with his shirts like that for over a month now. I never told you. And he's been sneakin' into the house some nights even later in the mornin' than you.' I certainly didn't know about that, I had to admit. It must have been those nights when I'd turned in early. Still what was all the fuss about? I looked at her, waiting for her to explain but she couldn't go any further. And I remember I felt anger that she couldn't, not then, not ever, put into words for me what she really felt. It was the anger a parent has for a slow child who continues to disappoint by his lack of progress. Her big fear was of him putting some wee piece of goods up the spout. Oh, the disgrace! *The disgrace!* And now she would never have to worry again about the old man finding out things like that and breaking somebody's back. She must have seen my father as some sort of chastising Old Testament chap. I saw the danger in that line of thought and swerved away from it.

A few minutes later the hearse reached the gates of Rushy Hill. Walter and I climbed stiffly out of our car and the icy throttling wind buffeted us. Right down the line of parked and arriving cars doors began to open and then slam shut with a sound like muffled pistol shots. At the sound a dozen or so seagulls rose in the air above the graveyard, their long limp legs trailing like kite strings. They hung overhead, resenting our disturbance. Bad weather on the way, as the old saying goes, about gulls being so far inland. But just then the sun came out and began to strike gleaming streaks off the polished Daimlers and the line of cars coiling unendingly below us right to the foot of the hill. I could imagine the talk on the way home in the cars – *Were you ever at as big a funeral? Did you ever see as many cars? Not as big as Johnny Brown's. No you're right there, that was the biggest funeral ever I was at too* – and so on, the endless working over and over of the obvious.

A discreet hand touched my elbow and I turned, colliding

180

with the pale-faced man in the top-hat who had sat beside the hearse driver. Smiling sadly, he waited until my whispered apologies were finished and then motioned his gloved hand towards the coffin which had already been slid half-way in readiness out of the glass end of the hearse.

'Will you and your brother, Mr. Glass, take the last wee lift?' he murmured.

Walter and I put our shoulders under the coffin and clasped each other under its varnished bottom. Two uncles slipped under the back end and the hearse driver, carrying the wreaths, held open the gate and we commenced to walk up the hill crunching the limestone chips under our black shoes. Walter was weeping and I felt his shudders travelling along his outstretched arm to my shoulder. His quietly desperate outbursts were touched off each time by some obvious physical reminder. My own eyes felt hard and tight and were beginning to ache out of deprivation, I suppose. The going started getting harder and we had to shorten our steps to prevent a slip.

Behind us I could picture the slow bobbing procession of hard hats and, under them, the red chapped country faces of relatives, neighbours and workmates of my father. I had been to a dozen funerals like this in the past, always bored, but a little of the other mourners' unquestioning acceptance of the ritual and the need for them to be present reaching me.

The minister was waiting for us on a mound above the black slit trench. He was Dallas, the old Presbyterian minister from Kildargan, and I'd felt ashamed when I'd gone to ask him to play his part for us. We'd never belonged to any church and I resented having to beg, meanly, I felt, for a service to which we weren't entitled. He was dressed in a shiny old-fashioned frock-coat and an umbrella was rammed, point an inch deep, in the soft ground beside him. As we neared the soil-sprinkled area of grass around the open grave his carefully brushed white hair lifted slowly in the wind and he clapped the Bible in his hand peevishly down on top of it. He looked at me sternly, as if I were responsible, as we lowered the coffin carefully with the help of the hearse-driver and his mate on to the waiting spread purple cloth on the grass.

181

The short stark service began. I began to look around at all
the faces, marvelling at the complexity of a life which
brought all these men unquestionably out on to a bare hillside on a December day like this. It was as if I had descended
from another planet and was watching something new and
strange and much too complicated to grasp. It was the old
familiar sensation again. I wanted to shout aloud and jar
them out of their passive acceptance of all this and everything
else in their lives which *I* could never practise in their calm
content way. I envied their smoothly rolling lives and I
wanted to be one of them. When I was younger I remember I
used to be paralysed with shyness when anyone ever stopped
me to ask for direction on the roadside. Lying, I would say,
'I'm a stranger here myself.' That lie had turned to the truth.
I was afflicted with the idea that I was a stranger and my
search for some place, any place, where I *wasn't* the stranger
narrowed and narrowed until such a territory became
bounded by the bones of my own skull and even in there had
I found it? Had I? What was it that made me feel different?
Was it them or something in me? Were these people around
me, these men holding their hats to the windward side of
their faces, and who had talked about nothing except racing-
pigeons, football, motor-bikes and cars (my father's side were
all 'mechanical') over the last day or so, were these *my*
people? Could I trace all my attitudes, feelings, and physical
appearance back to them? I wanted to say 'yes', but I
couldn't. That was the trouble. I was unsure. *I wanted to be
certain. I wanted not to have to think about it – like them.*
For the first time, ironically, I felt tears might be possible,
more from self-pity than anything else, but possible, yes ...

Beside me Walter's face looked even more grotesque, for
the knifing wind had mottled it blue. I saw one or two men
watching him curiously, evaluating his grief. They would
talk about it like the way they would talk about the number
of cars present. To my right two of my father's brothers
squeezed handkerchiefs to their eyes and the service wound
on. My eyes moved over the faces, halting momentarily at
each one I knew. Curry of the shop in an incongruous tweed
overcoat and matching cap (how had he denied himself his
weekly moment of glory in that echoing tin temple of his?),
all the menfolk of the Row, in a clump, with Tom Snoddy ris-

ing among them, straight-backed, bare-headed and beautiful
in the oldest but best overcoat in the company. He smiled at
me, when he saw me looking at him, and my heart went out
to him for I knew he had come because of me despite the
cold. Dr. McRory, burnished about the face and reinforced, I
felt sure, from the hip-flask he kept in the glove compartment
of his car wedged tight among all the blotters and hand-outs
from drug firms. I had travelled with him the afternoon my
father had died to his surgery where he signed the death cer-
tificate in my presence and I had read 'coronary failure'
under 'Cause of Death'. Somehow I had always associated
that with fat businessmen with gluttonous tastes and never
with whippets of men like my father. Someone was having
a joke to himself somewhere ...

My glance slid to Wilbur Todd, his face as high in colour as
the doctor's – I noticed that the faces in the crowd were either
purple or deathly white – and wearing an overcoat that
looked like his father's. He was watching the minister dully,
without interest, as he read aloud in a high carrying mono-
tone.

Somewhere among the faces there should have been Terry's
thin, suffering one. If he had been there he would have had
the best 'mourning' face in the crowd because of his flair for
funerals, but he wasn't there. I missed his old mug. It made
me feel even more alone. I never would have thought you
could get a passage to Australia as fast as that. His last post-
card had been posted in Aden. Aden! *Just been ashore. What
a wonderful place. Sun, palm trees and lovely young native
boys. Kildargan was never like this. Will write soon about
ALL my adventures. Love, Terry.* He'd got back his old cheek.
A big contrast to the mood he'd been in the night he'd come
down home to tell me he was going to Sydney. I looked at
him with my mouth open. 'Sydney! *Australia?* What the hell
are you talkin' about?' I felt bloody angry as well because it
was two in the morning and he'd wakened me by throwing a
handful of gravel up on to our skylight window. I didn't
want Walter to get the wrong idea about us. I'd never seen
him in such a state. We went out to the car, got in, closed
the doors and he blurted out this fantastic story. It seemed
that our friend Bradley had tipped him off about a big scandal
that was on the point of breaking in Annagh. Several men

183

were about to be arrested for offences of an indecent nature. When Terry told me their names I couldn't believe him for I knew most of them by sight and always regarded them as ordinary respectable working men – some of them with families. I asked Terry if he was mixed up in it. Why would he be so hysterical otherwise? Mad, he was. *Who was I insulting? Who did I think he was? What sort of a friend was I?* All that brand of old guff, etcetera, etcetera. But when he cooled finally I did squeeze out of him that a long time ago he *had* had a fleeting, sordid encounter one night in a pub lavatory with one of the men involved and now he was terrified that his own name would be mentioned when the pressure started. But when he'd gone to Uncle Sam Bradley, our M.P. friend had washed his hands of him. That seemed to be what had hit poor old Terry hardest.

'Frank,' he cried, his eyes filled with tears, 'he said I couldn't be trusted! I talked too much. And och, Frank, you know I never told a thing about him, you know that.'

I felt conscience stricken for I had been to blame there. His only course then, as he saw it, lay in a sudden passage to Australia. I didn't ask for further details but I wondered how on God's earth he had ever constructed any sort of yarn at all for his old lady. Still, he had managed it somehow and was on the high seas. He certainly wasn't a figure to feel sorry for now; he'd come out of it all magnificently, but that night in the car, I remember, I'd looked at him with cruel objectivity, seeing him probably for the first time for what he must become. He would either be a victim to his craving or else become set in his ways like an old maid, pottering about auctions with a life built around tea and library books. He was gone anyway, and although I'd never looked on him as a real 'friend' in the close sense, there was no one at all now. This year that was coming to an end had certainly made up for the previous ones when time had only been *marked* in the calendar. I had the feeling that I'd done more changing, growing, than in the past three or four. It was as if growth came in jerks – shooting forward, and then slow consolidation and then another rush. Painful too. Yes, painful. I had moved forward too fast this time. I ached . . .

Near a tall, quartzy obelisk with deeply cut capitals across its face stood Warwick. He had his head bowed slightly, and

184

the birth-mark on his face was so sharply defined that it seemed to stand out from the flesh. I looked at it, thinking how strange it was that only recently had I become conscious it was a disfigurement. It was as though he had kept it unnoticeable by making you hate him so much that you never gave his face much of a thought. For, yes, it was true, I no longer hated him, that's if I ever did. But sure I was of one thing, the feelings I had had towards him had changed on that day of the big final Interview for the job. That was another strange thing. It was hard to realize now that there had even been a job and that I'd cared so much at the time about it. Warwick *still* cared. It was obvious from every line of him that he was a man preoccupied, and I knew what was the recurring thought that never left him any peace and had changed him from the infallible despot in school he once was to the maundering figure that some of the children had now begun to cheek openly. His smooth façade had received that first fatal hair line crack the day of the Interview ...

Three men on a hard bench in a small, cold waiting-room in the County Courthouse with the door separating us from the sitting County Education Committee and their deliberations. Warwick, myself and *him*, third on the short list, *Times Educational Supplement* in his hands and he was *reading* it, he hadn't it up before his face to distract attention from the internal spasms and dryings which Warwick and I were sure were so noticeable to the others. His suit wasn't as new, dry-cleaned or well-pressed as ours, and no one, not even Matchett knew much about him – outside the fact that he was a graduate of Trinity College, Dublin (a degree didn't really count against Warwick's 'Ex-Servicemen will receive preference, all things being equal' trump card) and that he had taught for eight years in some place in Bucks. Plump, bald and not much else, really. At the end of the row.

The three of us waiting for the door to open. We had all been in, in our turn, to stand like somebody out of Dickens on a small platform thing to be gazed at by the Committee who were arranged around the big dusty room. The Secretary read out the list of qualifications you had written on the application form and made each one of them sound like a lie. Then he'd said warningly, 'Does anyone want to ask Mr.

So-and-So a question?' and glared around to see if anyone was foolhardy enough to take him at his word.

I saw Bradley. He was sitting next to a woman in a wide-brimmed pink and blue hat and they were smiling and whispering together a lot, obviously not about me, for they didn't stop their carry-on, even when the Secretary asked his routine question.

I knew all the bored faces in the room. I'd shaken all of the hands that went with the faces when I'd canvassed each one of them in each of their bloody big inaccessible houses in the County of Antrim, for you had to canvass, oh God, yes, even though it said on the form 'Canvassing will immediately disqualify'.

We'd all been in, Warwick first, Your Other Man – and then me. Warwick had been in about a minute longer and it was obvious from his face that he felt it was all over bar the shouting and that he could take over from poor old Ernie Matchett any time. He was smiling to himself when the door opened and the Secretary said, 'Mr. Fitzherbert, will you come in please?'

The door closed behind The Dark Horse and I got to my feet. I was going to say, 'Ah well, back to porridge', as a rough attempt at consolation to Warwick for we both knew that when you were called back the second time that it meant you had got the job, when I saw the look of despair on his face. And that was when I had first begun to feel sorry for him.

Looking at him now, almost a month later, as the cold wind ruffled the edges of his sleeked cap of oiled hair I could see traces of that same look of frozen shock on his face. In a way he had made it easier for me to forget my own disappointment, which at the time seemed a mere whim beside *his* monumental despair. Even Matchett had been touched by it. He stood beside him now, his glasses two shiny discs in the sun as if he had come to look after Warwick first and pay his respects after. Our principal had been steadily climbing back upwards in my esteem. His humanity to Warwick had been an extra reason for my rekindling respect.

The minister was reaching the climax of the burial service and the eyes of the onlookers brightened momentarily as they watched the handful of dry soil held in readiness.

186

There were three compelling parts of the ritual which never lost their disturbing thrill for them – the coffin being lowered, the clergyman sprinkling soil and the first shovelful falling, sighing on to the padded top.

'Dust to dust, ashes to ashes.'

The fine grains dropped like threads from between the Rev. Dallas' fingers. Those closest to the grave craned even closer and all eyes returned from the sky, the distant hills, the surrounding headstones to fasten on the man of God. Another fit of sobbing seized Walter and my soft-hearted uncles rubbed their eyes.

'Let us pray,' exhorted the Rev. Dallas and the heads dropped to stare at the short trampled grass. 'O Merciful Father, Who art the Divine Creator of all things and the taker away of that same life, we beseech Thee this day to receive our departed brother. We commend his spirit to Thy eternal all-embracing and infinitely merciful love and, Lord, let Thee comfort his sorrowing family in this their hour of grief and Lord, would that their sorrow be . . .'

I was shaken by a feeling of unreality, listening to the words. Could he be referring to *my father*? For the first time since he had died I felt inside me the warning nudge. I began to shiver with a kind of little fear at what I might still feel. I began to understand Walter's desperate grief and for the first time also I realized that thinking of the future might be every bit as dangerous as thinking of the past. My own future deprivation began to eat like an acid in me.

He would never be sitting at home again, he would never come in from his work to his tea again, he would never be about the house or in the garden at the back to be called if you wanted him. He wouldn't answer – ever – for he was in that hole there, lined in with one layer of satin and one of oak.

A nausea started to rise in me. I was sure my face must be so screamingly white that everyone seeing it must be jolted into anxiety for my well-being. My mouth felt as if it was wide open, stretched sinew-tight, strained to gulp in air, as much air as there was overhead and all around. Self-pity lent a hand so that I wanted to beg, *Why has this happened to me? Why should I have to bear this? Why should this be sprung on me in a load that should have descended slowly one small piece at a time?* I felt like smashing and splintering the marble slabs around me. *I refuse to accept it! I REFUSE! I won't have a tune played on me! I've kept myself intact and encased too long for me to FEEL like this now.*

There was a contest being decided inside my head. One way and then the other. My self-control winning and then – the memories pressing, pressing ... like soft, implacable sponges ...

All the softly coloured memories before the age of twelve, the dangerous nostalgic memories, all the incorruptibly romantic ones. It seemed an impossibility that just yesterday I'd said to myself that it might even be *for the best* that he had died at his age the way he did, for I knew he feared getting too old in the same way that I did, both of us doubting secretly if we would be able to cope with that sad desperation and, what made it so much worse, its inevitability. That was yesterday. *Now*, today, as the grave-diggers spat for the first time with suitably diminished force into their cupped hands, I marvelled at such selflessness. Now – it was me – and *my* loss that consumed ...

The first shovelful fell quietly slowly downwards, and burst starring outwards below on the purple quilt. Then the second and the third and on and on rhythmically and the sound of the soil striking, changing and softening to a whisper as the trench filled up, up towards our feet. The two men, they looked like father and son, worked facing each other crouched at the knees, the metal scoops at the end of the long smooth shafts moving a controlled foot or so. The soil was piled behind a sheet of corrugated tin to keep it from falling too suddenly into the grave. Men started moving off quietly talking in ones and twos down the hill towards the cars. Others came up to the grave to watch impassively as the bumpy soil rose. The young grave-digger was beginning to sweat and redden. His shovel slipped once and his father shot him a look from under his eyebrows. I could see the layer of cut sods on which they had piled the soil. They looked blanched already as if the weight of dark soil that had rested on them throughout the night had sealed off their juices. When they would be fitted into place over the scarred ground they would slowly join and heal again like living skin. Then we would come and place flowers on an area which we would only

188

know by its wooden marker to conceal the body of our father, a small thin sad man in life and now ...

Walter touched me gently.

'Frank,' he said.

I looked at him. Then I lightly placed my fingers on his upper arm and we moved away. The time had come to look ahead and it was my task to point the way.

*   *   *

Going home in the now fast travelling car we passed a young fellow walking aimlessly by himself along the side of the road. He was wearing a cheap brown overcoat and dark tapered trousers. His hair was cut flat like a crew-cut on the top with long sides but he looked clean and respectable. I turned round in my seat and watched him through the back window as he receded. His face seemed even more bored through the darkened glass. I thought suddenly with a quick savage ache that it could have been me, five, six years ago. *It was me*. I twisted in my seat but he had disappeared. My eyes strained even though I knew it was stupid. Then quickly, sadly and quietly I felt myself crying. The tears slid down my face. 'Here, Frank,' said Walter softly, 'use mine,' and he handed me his wet handkerchief. He looked relieved. He thought that I was at last weeping for the loss of my father, but I wasn't. I was crying for the loss of someone else, me, as I had been once, three, four years ... a year ago.

On the following pages are other recent paperbacks
published by Quartet Books.
If you would like a complete catalogue of
Quartet's publications please
write to us at 27 Goodge Street, London W1P 1FD

THE LUCK OF GINGER COFFEY
Brian Moore

The Luck Of Ginger Coffey is a brilliant example of Brian Moore's shrewd observation. Ginger Coffey is a thoroughly likeable failure; his new life in a new land (from Ireland to Canada) is hardly off the ground before it starts to crumble around him. At his lowest ebb, Ginger suddenly decides to fight back against his fate, and armed only with the luck of the Irish and a lot of bravado, he starts running uphill in hope, into a hilarious series of misadventures, disasters – and victories. *The Luck of Ginger Coffey* is a superbly entertaining novel.

Fiction 35p

VANITY OF DULUOZ
Jack Kerouac

'A dazzling sunburst of white-hot prose' – *Tribune*

The Duluoz saga is known to thousands through such classics as *Desolation Angels* and *on the Road*: *Vanity Of Duluoz* relates the beginning of the whole story from the day Jack Duluoz/Kerouac won an athletic scholarship to university up to his wild time in New York City just as the underground scene there was starting to simmer. In it Kerouac rushes headlong into a frontal assault on life, 'a total abandonment to feeling' (*Guardian*), producing a book that is every bit as brilliant as his modern classic *On the Road*.

Fiction 40p